Endorsements

This sweet romance is a beautiful debut by author Beth Pugh. Filled with heartfelt moments, an unexpected proposal, and lots of love, this story reminds us that sometimes what we want isn't nearly as important as what we need. Pugh has woven a unique and memorable happily-ever-after that is sure to have romance readers adding her to their bookshelves permanently.

~Susan L. Tuttle

Author of the Along Came Love series

With twists, turns, and surprises all along the way, *The Valentine Proposal* is wholesome, uplifting, and completely delightful. Beth Pugh has written a wonderful story about acceptance, forgiveness, second chances, and love. At both times entertaining and inspiring, this is a book about our plans and God's plans and the way He works things out for our good. A fantastic read. You'll actually want to hug this book when you're done.

~Amy Willoughby-Burle

Author, Teacher, Encourager of Dreams

A charming, Southern-flavored story about a decade-old marriage pact that turns into an engagement of convenience before finally maturing into love. Wonderful characters and vivid prose will delight readers who love inspirational romance!

~Meghann Whistler

Author of *The Billionaire's Secret*

What a charming debut! This heartwarming story features an intriguing premise, a relatable heroine, and a sweet romance. I appreciated the beautifully expressed theme—that the second chance God blesses us with may not unfold the way we expect, but in a manner we need the most. *The Valentine Proposal* is sure to delight!

~Rachel Scott McDaniel

Award-winning author of *The Mobster's Daughter*

The Valentine Proposal

BETH PUGH

IRON STREAM FICTION

Birmingham, Alabama

The Valentine Proposal

Iron Stream Fiction
An imprint of Iron Stream Media
100 Missionary Ridge
Birmingham, AL 35242
IronStreamMedia.com

Library of Congress Control Number: 2021949928

Scripture quotations from The Authorized (King James) Version. Public domain.

ISBN: 978-1-64526-346-3 (paperback)
ISBN: 978-1-64526-347-0 (ebook)

1 2 3 4 5—25 24 23 22
MANUFACTURED IN THE UNITED STATES OF AMERICA

DEDICATION

To God the Father: the giver of joy, comfort in sorrow,
and peace among the chaos.

ACKNOWLEDGMENTS

Writing takes a village and, for me, that village is led by God the Father. During a time when darkness surrounded me, God lit the path with stories He placed in my heart. His eternal hope spoke to me through the words He gave and I cannot thank Him enough for turning my mourning into dancing. I give Him all praise and glory for wherever this story ends up and whoever is touched along the way.

Special thanks to my amazing agent, Julie Gwinn, for believing in a newbie writer like myself. I will be eternally grateful for all you do. Your dedication to this story made my dream a reality. From the bottom of my heart, thank you.

To my critique partner, Meghann Whistler, I am so glad and beyond grateful God put us on this writing journey together. Your insight is invaluable, my friend. Danielle Grandinetti, thank you for reading this book in its infancy and helping smooth the roughness away. I loved walking through our debuts together. To Susan Tuttle, you didn't have to answer my out-of-the-blue message, but I am grateful you did. Thank you for befriending a stranger. You, too, Stephanie Jaye Taylor. Your sweet texts and happy mail never fail to uplift and inspire. Ladies, I so appreciate your friendship and encouragement.

Huge thanks to my editors, Jessica Nelson and Nancy J. Farrier. Jessica, you pushed me to be the best writer I could be from day one. This book would not be what it is without your knowledge and wisdom. To that end, I wouldn't be the writer I am without you. Thank you for all you have taught me. Nancy, you are a blessing to your writers. I appreciate your patience, kindness, and guidance through this process.

The tender care you put into this story made it more than I ever thought it could be. Thank you so much.

To my friends, coworkers and family that encouraged me, thank you. I love you and appreciate you putting up with my ramblings. Bobbi Anne, Erica, Breanna, Jill, and Bea: Thank you all for taking the time to read (and reread) this story, the prayers, the feedback, and everything in between. I cannot tell you how much your support means to me. To my adopted sisters, Nicole and Kat, you girls cheer loudly and love louder. I am blessed to have you in my life. Travis, you are the revision master. Thank you for being my sounding board. Love each one of you so big!

Lastly, to my boys—my husband and son—I will forever thank God for both of you. Izaiah, you are my reason to chase dreams. God made you to do hard things and I don't want you to ever forget that. Or that I love you bunches, because I do, from now until the end of time. Ryan, you are my real-life happily ever after, complete with starry nights and Sunday morning coffee. Thank you for your unending support and belief in my dreams. I will always love you like children love pennies.

Chapter One

Mason Montgomery sat at a back-row table and nursed his diet soda, because he was a responsible adult. A tax-paying, churchgoing, calorie-counting grown-up who knew what he wanted and how to get it. That was the man he'd become between the last time he'd left the high-school gymnasium and this reunion, the first he'd attended, celebrating ten years since graduation.

He was a man who'd learned to work smarter, not harder, understanding time was of the essence—fleeting and in demand. It was why he'd scheduled a meeting with Ol' Man Rowe a few hours before the reunion, killing two birds with one stone.

After the appointment, Mason wished he'd opted to wait. The first bird flew the coop with Mr. Rowe's swift rejection. The second left little hope for a happier ending while Mason wallowed in misfortune.

"Mase, is that you, man?"

Mason stood from the table and shook hands with the approaching figure, seeing past the suit-wearing professional to the guy he was blessed to call a buddy. Shoving aside his pity party, Mason worked on turning his frown upside down. He owed his friend that much.

"Sure is. How have you been, Clay?"

"Decent." Clay Hart blew out a breath as he released Mason's hand. The slightest shadow slid down his face, but a smile replaced it so fast, Mason second-guessed seeing it.

"Good to see the Windy City hasn't blown you away yet." Mason chuckled and returned to his seat, gesturing for Clay to join him.

"It came close, for sure." Clay sat, propping his ankle on his knee and resting his hand just above his loafer. "This internship is tough, but in the best possible way."

"I'll bet," said Mason. "Is Sammie Rae in town, too? She's living in Chicago with you, right?"

"Yeah, Sis is sharing my apartment. She's already back there. Caught a nonstop flight from Lexington a few days ago. Mom couldn't convince her to stay another day in Kentucky. The city suits her. Me, not so much. I'm glad the reunion gave me an extended holiday in the mountains. It was a stroke of genius to schedule it for the Friday after Christmas. Most everyone I know still comes home for the holidays. Mom would kill me if I didn't." Clay released his leg and scooted his chair a little closer to the table.

"Same for me, man." An image of his mother flittered through Mason's mind, her smile brighter than the tree itself when he'd told her he was staying in Pine Valley indefinitely. For Mason, the Kentucky roads didn't just take him home. They were home.

"What about you?" Clay reached for his pop bottle. "How are things going, Mr. Big Shot Photographer?"

"To be honest, not so great. Did you know Ol' Man Rowe is looking to sell Forget Me Not Photography?"

"Nah, Mase, I didn't. You thinking about buying it?"

"More than thinking about it." Mason examined his hands, paying close attention to his left ring finger. "I made an offer today, but Mr. Rowe turned me down. Said he wanted a local family man to turn the business over to. I am neither. Apparently, I've been gone too long to be considered a Pine Valley native, and my bachelor status doesn't fit the bill. I don't get it, man."

Clay, his brow furrowed, drummed a beat on the table. "I mean, the studio's been going for thirty years so I can understand wanting to leave it in reliable hands, but does it really matter if those hands are attached to a married man or not?"

"You wouldn't think so, but it is what it is." Mason blew out a deep sigh. "I'll figure something out." After another long exhale, Mason remembered his manners. "Tell me what's new with you."

Clay wasted no time diving into the details of the new law firm he'd signed with. The legal mumbo-jumbo dazed Mason like his former teachers' lesson plans but he nodded along as he drank his soda and watched the back door for his classmates. Mid-sip, a familiar face stepped into his line of sight, making him swallow hard to keep from spewing pop everywhere.

Lily Anne Dawson. *Chief*. Editor-in-chief, to be exact, leader of the *Pine Valley Gazette*, the school paper that had pushed the two of them together all four years of high school. Chief for short, and for the frenzy the name worked Lily Anne into. There was no prettier sight than a wide-eyed, red-cheeked Lily Anne.

Watching her, Clay's voice faded away, replaced by a rushing of blood between Mason's ears. She was exactly as he remembered her: slightly crooked nose and knock-your-socks-off smile. Poised, graceful, and elegant in a little black dress beneath a fitted fire-engine-red blazer. A few stray curls framed her face while the rest of the unruly locks were secured by some sort of twist.

Mason let his gaze linger, adding the picture to the mental album he used so much it had never collected dust. She wasn't "the one who got away," but the unexplored "might have been" since he'd never worked up the courage to make a move. Instead, he preferred sideline stares, watching from afar while she carried on, none the wiser.

Mason straightened his chair as she floated across the shiny gym floor. Maybe tonight he'd get a fresh start. Maybe he'd ask her to dance. Maybe he'd work up the nerve to tell her h—

"What do you think?"

Mason blurted the singular thought he was capable of forming in that moment, not even caring enough to turn back to the table. "She's beautiful."

"Huh? Who? Ohhhh, gotcha." Clay had crossed his arms over his chest, a smug grin firmly in place when Mason turned back to face him. "Guess some things never change."

"Shut it and tell me what you were asking before this drink finds its way over your head." Even though the threat was hollow, Mason narrowed his eyes at Clay from across the table. The last thing he needed was commentary on his high-school crush that refused to die. Try as he might to keep his feelings for Lily Anne under wraps, Mason's attraction to the blonde beauty was no secret to the man seated across from him. When Lily Anne received an anonymous rose with a knock-knock joke for a message sophomore year, Clay had put two and two together and got four, recognizing the joke from a book Mason had toted around.

"Well, now that I have your attention." Clay chuckled. "I was wondering if I need a new bio pic since I took on the internship."

"It's your preference but an update is never a bad idea. I'll knock it out for you before you head back. I'm in town indefinitely."

"Interesting. Lily Anne is home again, too, and single." Clay leaned across the table and waggled his brows.

Mason gave him the evil eye before scanning Lily Anne's hands. Being only two tables away, he spotted the glint of a stainless-steel band on her fourth finger. He felt the air rush out of him until he realized it was on her *right* hand and looked identical to the purity ring attached to his key fob. There'd been chance after chance to renege on his vow of celibacy. All those women abroad—gorgeous, mouthwatering women eager for his attention and appreciative of his looks—had been tempting. But he'd never crossed that line, regardless of what might have been said, or printed, that stated otherwise. He'd reserved true intimacy for marriage, and after seeing evidence that Lily Anne had done the same, he'd never been happier with his choice.

Tonight might be his second chance. Before he talked himself out of his seat and into Lily Anne's space, the DJ interrupted.

"Y'all are not going to believe what I found. It's the most redneck time capsule I've ever seen. Anyone remember what's in here?" The DJ stood from behind the turntable and looked around the gym. The graduates of Pine Valley High did not disappoint as shouts flew from across the room. *Prom Queen's garter. Band conductor's wand. Senior Edition of the* Gazette.

The last guess glued Mason's feet to the floor as the guy behind the turntable started holding up each item. When a copy of the aforementioned gazette waved in the air, the room got hot. Too hot for comfort. Mason shifted under the heat wave, begging to find a nonexistent breeze in a room without windows. He clutched the front of his shirt and fanned himself, but it did little to cool his rising temperature. He knew what was in that periodical. A promise he'd made to Lily Anne, as well as to himself, a decade ago. It didn't matter, though. Did it? Surely not. Except, Mason knew better.

Their agreement mattered more now than ever.

With trembling hands, Mason drained his drink. Fizz from the carbonation tickled his nose as he gulped, welcoming the frosty soda. The relief ended much too quickly, for as soon as the cool liquid slid down his throat, his mouth was dry again. Desperate, he tipped the melting ice into his mouth while his mind raced with possibilities.

Maybe this really is my second chance.

This was the kind of killing-two-birds-with-one-stone Mason was down for. If Mason made good on their agreement, he'd be the protégé Ol' Man Rowe wanted: a married man living in Pine Valley. *Ludicrous?* Maybe, but Mason needed that studio to move his career back home. If fulfilling a ten-year-old promise gave him the business of his dreams *and* a chance with the girl worth waiting a decade for, even better.

"This segment seems interesting. I think it deserves a read." The DJ cleared his throat and started reading. When the title echoed above the crowd, Mason recognized it as the excerpt he'd been hoping for. He mouthed the words he knew by heart in time with the DJ, his knee bouncing a frenzied rhythm to the familiar line.

"*If in ten years we are both unattached we will get hitched on Valentine's Day. Signed, Lily Anne & Mason.* Awww, how sweet. Mason, you here?"

Mason didn't answer but sat slack-jawed, trying to process. How many times had he recited those exact words? The unofficial valentine proposal had become a chant to push him through the lonely hotel nights or the unbearable frame-by-frame early-morning edits. It was the mantra he recited when home seemed but a memory instead of a dot on the map waiting for him. The promise was more than a spur-of-the-moment quip. To him, it always had been. What was it to Lily Anne? *Only one way to find out.*

"Mason?"

The DJ repeated his name, but Mason stayed still. Not for fear of embarrassment or indecision, but because he needed to find a ring. With a deep breath in and out through his nose, Mason willed the trembling in his hands to stop as he scanned the room. In seconds, his gaze landed on Clay's empty pop bottle.

"You done with that?" asked Mason.

"Yeah, why?"

6

Mason didn't answer. Instead, he grabbed the bottle, unscrewed the lid, and pulled the plastic ring off as fast as he could.

Clay took hold of the bottle with the caution of a snake handler and sat it down easy. "Mase, I know that look and nothing good ever comes from it. Whatever's rolling around in that thick brain of yours, don't do it."

"Come on, Clay. You're heard the DJ. I've got a proposal to get to." Mason stood up as eyes from all across the gym centered on him. The back of his shirt pulled taut as more sweat beaded beneath the material. With each step toward Lily Anne's table, the room quieted until Mason's own breath was all that broke the silence in his ears. He inhaled deeply and prayed for a miracle, saying "amen" just as Lily Anne jumped from her chair. As if on cue, Clay pointed at the two of them and clapped. When Lily Anne's eyes met his, Mason knew he was a goner.

Too late to turn back now. It's show time!

"Hey, Chief." Mason dropped to one knee.

Chapter Two

"**W**ill you marry me?"

"C-come again?" Lily Anne's voice sounded small and squeaky, an accurate representation of how she felt. Hushed whispers of her classmates circled around the gymnasium, transforming to low-level screams within her ears, making it impossible to concentrate on the question at hand. Not that she wanted to.

Concentrate, that is.

Currently, sinkholes were more interesting to focus on, specifically the possibility of one opening beneath her feet. Did that kind of thing happen in real life? In Pine Valley, Kentucky? To her?

Doubtful.

A throat cleared in front of her, pulling her back to the man kneeling on the newly buffed foul line. Mason Montgomery grinned wider, as if he hadn't a care in the world, like this behavior—asking for her hand in marriage after not speaking to her for a decade—was par for the course.

"You've not changed a bit, Chief, making a man repeat himself while in the middle of a proposal." Mason paused, showing his flair for the dramatic.

Lily Anne ducked her head as a rush of heat passed over her cheeks. Though Mason had grown silent, his nickname for her still rang in her ears. When he'd called her Chief in high school, the name had rankled her nerves. But, tonight, as it replayed over in her head, Lily Anne heard an affectionate endearment rather than a teasing sneer.

With a deep breath, she raised her head back up, her eyes immediately finding Mason's. If the gorgeous combination of browns and greens staring back at her wasn't enough to make her stomach somersault, the mischief fueling his stare surely was. Beneath the whimsy, though, another emotion peeked out. She recognized it immediately. *Fear.* Without a mirror, she knew the same feeling shone back at him as her stare flip-flopped between his face and the makeshift ring he held.

What was he holding up? A piece of a pop bottle? For a ring? Lily Anne never thought of herself as high-maintenance, but this was a whole new level of simple.

With great care, he inched the "ring" to the edge of her finger before repeating the question and blowing her plan for a quick night of solo mingling. The reunion was supposed to be so simple. Sneak in, sip some punch, smile nonchalantly, shake hands when necessary, and go home to a warm bath with bubbles a foot high. Maybe join a dating site or two if she worked up the nerve. Up until this point, the reunion had followed the expected trajectory, a path that zig-zagged into chaos when that blasted memory box was brought out. She made a mental note to thank Emma Lou properly for reminding the class about it, since it had led to Mason kneeling at her feet.

Mason Montgomery. Handsome. Talented. *Annoying.* She'd put up with the scrappy photographer's shenanigans in high school because it had been in the paper's best interest, as well as her own. His photographs were the most delicious arm candy to her carefully crafted words. But there was no article to be written tonight. No deadline to meet. Absolutely no reason to indulge in the prank.

But Lily Anne couldn't break the moment. If she were honest with herself, she didn't want to, even if his insanity induced sweaty palms and itchy skin. Mason's magnetic personality was as strong as ever, and in his presence, even with all eyes on them, she felt lighter. It was that feeling that had taken their relationship from coworkers to friends all those year ago. Tonight, he was still that friend.

A friend cashing in on a decade-old promise of marriage?

Not exactly the kind of friend Lily Anne expected to find at the reunion. She blinked hard, half expecting Mason to be gone when she opened her eyes. But he wasn't. He remained, eyes fixed on her, his chest rising nearly in sync with hers. They were both breathing faster than normal. She'd never told Mason why she'd gone along with the proposal because she'd assumed he'd been joking like she had been. *Mostly joking*. A small part of her, though, agreed to counter the rising fear of loneliness, a fate her mother had been sentenced to after divorce.

A warm hand captured her left palm, the action centering her thoughts on the question suspended between her and the joker of a boy now turned man. Mason chuckled lightly before repeating the question.

"I'll say it again a little slower, so it sinks in. Lil, will you marry me?" The repeated proposal ignited another collective gasp from the crowd and a shaky breath from Lily Anne. She wanted to ask if he was kidding, but the sweat-drenched brow and spike in his voice proved otherwise.

"Mason, I … I don't know what to say."

"Say yes, Chief, and let's make good on our agreement. It *is* recorded in black and white, after all, and I know how important your *word* is to you." He gentled his verbal jab with a wink.

The validity of his statement knocked her back on her heels. For Lily Anne, words were more than letters strung together to pass the time at the coffee shop. Words were the strongest tie that binds, a light among the darkness, and certainly meant to be exchanged with the utmost care. Her word was as good as gospel, but a marriage proposal written over ten years ago? That was a bit much, even for one as beholden to the written word as herself.

Yet, it wasn't. Not really, with Mason in front of her asking for her hand and Dr. Branham's warning playing in her ears.

I'm not trying to scare you, but if you're looking to start a family, sooner rather than later would be best.

Lily Anne couldn't go back in time, but with Mason offering marriage, she could start at the present without having to search high and low for a date. The love department had not treated her kindly. No string of broken hearts left in her wake, and no men banging on her apartment door. Her apartment above her mother's garage. Not that there'd be time to answer them if there were. Busting butt at the family bakery and begging for scraps at the newspaper office took up all her time. *And what do I have to show for it?* Nothing. A failure who spent Saturday night alone. Panic ridden. Unlovable. Barely-making-ends-meet journalist. Whereas Mason was the opposite. Life of the party. Handsome. Top-of-his-field celebrity.

When Lily Anne chanced a glance up from the floor, earth-gaping holes faded from her mind as a family picture developed. Simultaneously, key words from her internet research on infertility popped up like thought bubbles. Ovulation disorders. Hormone levels. Dying eggs. All suspects the gynecologist believed might be causing her irregular menstrual cycle. If ovulation was the problem like Dr. Branham feared, Lily Anne needed to get started on a family as fast as possible.

To do that, she needed a husband, and Mason miraculously stepped up to the plate.

Concern for the future tipped the scale in Mason's favor. Accepting his proposal was an easy choice. Better yet, it was a safe choice, since he'd skipped the wooing portion of the relationship and went straight to forever. The pressure of getting-the-guy, which Lily Anne had always struggled with, melted like cotton candy in the rain. Failure wasn't an option.

Regardless, marriage meant forever, and the thought of being stuck in an unhappy relationship made Lily Anne's skin crawl beneath her blazer. So much time had passed. Lily Anne had changed, and from the looks of it, Mason had as well, from class clown to an award-winning photographer. From aggravating to amazing. Did the two of them realistically have a chance at making it work?

It's worth a shot.

Lily Anne schooled her features and drew in a long inhale. Before she had time to rethink her decision, she whispered, "Okay."

"Okay?" Mason cocked his head to the side as he repeated the word, one corner of his mouth turning slightly up.

"I mean, yes." She rolled her eyes. "Yes, Mason. I'll marry you."

The smidgen of a smile he'd smothered minutes before burst across his face as he gently slid the ring onto her finger. Applause sounded as Mason rose to his feet and opened his arms to her. Lily Anne stepped into them, wondering how absurd the two of them looked. Mason was now her fiancé, for goodness' sake, and she was giving him a church hug. Oddly enough, he didn't seem to mind as he tucked the top of her head beneath his chin.

The sweet gesture sparked an unfamiliar sensation, starting in her chest and spiraling outward to the tips of her fingers and toes. Excitement? Foolishness? *Redemption?* Lily Anne was still sorting through the myriad of options when she stepped away from Mason and into their new reality. The depth of the transpired events hit her full force as she finally pinpointed the odd emotion filling her frame.

Calm. The calm before the storm.

Chapter Three

Less than seventy-two hours in Pine Valley and Mason found himself in a state of regression. He didn't live on the fly anymore. He'd grown out of that, but one high-school reunion set him back a whole decade as his past, where impulsivity governed his life, resurfaced, resulting in an impromptu proposal and impending marriage.

"Marriage." Mason voiced the craziness out loud, the word tasting foreign on his tongue.

The proposal had surprised him as much as it had the rest of the room, but he meant it, and not merely because it gave him a shot at getting in good with Ol' Man Rowe. That weighed heavily on the decision, but so did Lily Anne's shy smile and sweet personality.

Mason sat down in the corner chair of the foyer, trying to get his head on straight. Silenced filled the lobby of The B&B Inn, except for the occasional hint of footsteps above his head. The light *pitter-pat* made a good thinking soundtrack.

If he were honest, the valentine proposal between him and Lily Anne had been tucked away in the back of his mind since the day he signed it. A couple of times a year, he'd dust off the memory and entertain the what-ifs surrounding the hypothetical arrangement. Still, thinking about it and acting on it were two different animals altogether. No, not merely different animals. Different species entirely, on different continents, on the opposite ends of the earth. But when the DJ read their pact aloud, his heart leaped within his chest. Mason didn't think, he simply acted, and the result? Nothing less than a miracle.

She said yes. *Good gravy, the girl said yes.*

Why? He had no idea. Lily Anne was more than a mystery. She was a Rubik's cube and he was colorblind. Judging from their interaction the night of the reunion and their stilted phone conversations that had followed since, she was still as introverted as ever.

In high school, Lily Anne had locked herself up so snug, his best efforts to draw her out often ended null and void. They'd had meaningful moments, but too few and far between, making him wonder if the relationship he remembered was all in his head. Perhaps their connection was one-sided, alive for him but dead for her. No matter, he was a strong believer in resurrection, especially when it came to his fiancée.

Mason laughed a little to himself as the phone in his pocket buzzed. When he fished out the device, his brother's face lit up the screen.

"Hey, Mikie. Whatcha up to?"

"I think that's my line, Deuce. Ready for your engagement party Friday?"

Mason huffed. "As if I have a choice."

"Hey, now. Big brother knows best."

Mason turned his gaze to the ceiling, remembering all the times he'd heard that line after their father's stroke. With their dad in rehab, Mikie had been tasked with caring for the house and *the little brother* after school. Of course, Mikie, being the overachiever that he was, took it to the extreme. Mason had never had to lift a finger to do anything, and he hated the feeling of helplessness that had filled him in response.

Mason gripped the phone tighter. "You know that's not true anymore, right?"

"Sure, it is."

"Nope." Mason sighed, loud enough he was sure Mikie heard it. "Ace, I really don't think an engagement party is a good idea when Lily Anne and I haven't even had a chance to talk about the wedding."

"Which is why you have to let me do this. An engagement party will prove how excited you are. You want her to know you're happy, right?"

"Of course, but Lily Anne doesn't like surprises an—"

Mikie's baritone laugh rumbled through the phone speaker. "Says the man who proposed on a whim at a class reunion. I think it's safe to say the party is peanuts compared to that."

"Touché." Mason nodded to himself. "Since you won't take no for an answer, I'll be there. Thanks for throwing it together on such short notice."

"Thank Mary Ellen when you see her. All I did was book the community center and get supplies."

"Still, we—I—appreciate it, especially with how you feel about the engagement. I know you think I'm joking, but I'm not. I'm serious."

"You don't know the meaning of the word, Deuce." Mikie chuckled again.

Mason bolted upright in the seat. "I do."

Why did talking to Mikie make him revert back to that helpless kid he'd been growing up? The kid cloaked in the shadow of a perfect big brother, only visible to the family when causing a scene or making them laugh.

"Oh, yeah? Have you made any plans beyond your big display?"

Mason pinched the bridge of his nose. "That's what today is for. I'm meeting Lily Anne after her shift at the bakery."

"Maybe there's hope for you yet." A keyboard clicked to life and then there was a rustling sound through the speaker. Mikie exhaled loudly. "Be real with me, bro. Are you *actually* going to get married?"

"That's the plan."

"Okay." Mikie elongated the last syllable. "If this really isn't some kind of twisted joke, why don't you put your money where your mouth is?"

Mason raked a hand through his hair. "Money where my mouth is? What do you mean?"

"What I mean, Mase, is that I know Ma already dubbed you the new groundskeeper for The B&B Inn, and if memory serves me right, you hate landscaping. Whatcha say to a little wager?"

A crinkling sound rang through Mason's ears, followed by a muffled, "Boys. Stop that. Chase, you're old enough to know better. Screwdrivers are not swords. What? That's not an excuse. I don't care if Caden started it." Another rustling roared. "Sorry about that," Mikie continued. "What was I saying?"

Mason rubbed his fingertips over his temple, making small circles he'd read were supposed to be calming. "You wanted to bet. On my marriage."

"Oh, that. Yup, it seems like a safe wager. If you get cold feet, you'll be taking care of Ma's yard *and* mine every three weeks, no exceptions. But, if you end up making it down the aisle, I'll take over Ma's as a wedding present."

"That's not worth it." Mason squeezed the phone between his ear and shoulder as he popped his knuckles. "What's some yard work between brothers? Besides, it's time I pay my dues to Ma."

Mason stared into space, thinking of all the times he'd wanted to help but wasn't needed. Big brother took care of it all, leaving him no room to contribute.

"No, you'll hire someone to do it for you." Mikie's tone dared a denial. "If I lose, you can save your money and take care of both Ma and your new bride, as long as you prove to be a man of your word. If you back out, you deserve to suffer. Maybe the itchy eyes and bug bites will remind you to look before you leap. It's time to quit playing around."

"Do you think I don't know that?" Mason gritted his teeth, reminding himself his brother meant well. Someday Mikie would see him as a responsible adult instead of the kid he had to take care of. Mason prayed for someday to come soon. "Look, I appreciate your words of wisdom. But I got this. I'm not going to let Ma or Lily Anne down."

"I hope not, Deuce, but there's no way you can pull this off by Valentine's Day by yourself. That's, what? Six weeks away? Seven maybe? Do you have any idea how hard it is to plan a wedding? Let me help you."

"You don't have to do that." Mason picked at the lint on his jeans. Did he need help? Probably. From his brother? Nope. "Y'all got enough on your plate as it is, with the boys and the store."

"You and I both know I can run the store in my sleep. Besides, we've got a babysitter on standby in my sweet mother-in-law."

"Right, but I can take care of it."

Mikie belly laughed. "You say that now but when you're knee-deep in rose petals and ribbon you'll be singing a different tune."

Mason thought about the no-win proposition. Not taking Mikie up on his offer all but confirmed his brother's suspicion of insincerity. Letting him pitch in, though, marched Mason right back through that old familiar feeling of helplessness. Neither option seemed pleasant, but Mason chose the lesser of two evils.

"Fine." Mason swallowed hard and rushed on. "To the help *and* to the bet, but not because I want out of lawn duty or because I can't handle the wedding. I learned a long time ago life is full of hard things, like allergies and engagements, and I'm more than capable of tackling both. I understand my responsibilities."

"I don't doubt that, but it never hurts to have a helping hand." A jingle rolled through the speaker. "Hey, I've got a customer at the counter. I'll see you Friday."

"Yes, you will." Mason nodded for emphasis, even though his brother couldn't see him. "Really, though. Thanks again for the party. Oh, and Mikie?"

"Yeah?"

"Be sure to check your email. I forwarded you a sales ad from John Deere. Gotta go."

Mason ended the call, laughing at his own joke. As he jumped up and headed for the door, he reminded himself being an only child was for the birds. At least that's what Ma liked to say and she didn't lie.

Chapter Four

The squeal of a timer commanded Lily Anne's attention, jerking her back to the kitchen and out of the mental fog filling her head. Between the afternoon rush, the upcoming meeting with the *Vine*'s editor about her new life-hack column, and her impending date with Mason, she hung by a thread. When a peppermint mocha splashed across the front of her buttercup t-shirt, soiling the Country Confections logo and her mood, her calm demeanor snapped.

As hot tears threatened to roll, she flung the mocha into the trash, not even caring that she had to start over. When the drink was redone and the customer gone, she stomped into the storage room, whimpering each time her foot hit the floor. She counted to ten. Twice. After the second go-around, her breathing had leveled and her eyes were dry. *Much better.* With her emotions under control, she rushed back to the front.

A blur of a body raced past the window and Lily Anne waved, thankful her replacement was on time. While she waited for Mandy to clock in, her thoughts centered on marriage and Mason. After not seeing her for ten years, he couldn't love her. There was no way.

No man could.

Her father's rejection assured as much. What had driven him away might remain a mystery, but his absence proved she wasn't capable of keeping a man's affection. She was too anxious, too big of a failure, too much of a mess to make any man fall in love with her, let alone stay in love with her. That truth made accepting Mason's proposal all the easier. Other women might need a movie-type romance or a sunset ending to their love story, but she didn't. The surety

Mason offered was more than enough. After their morning meeting, he would know that.

"When will Miss Danny Jo be back?" Mandy stepped up to the sink, jamming the stopper in as she spoke.

"Today is a spa day. Then she's heading to Ohio to visit Aunt Betsy. Mom says she's staying a week, but I told her to take as long as she wants."

As Mandy turned on the faucet, she side-eyed Lily Anne. "I give her eight days, at most."

"Why's that?" Lily Anne pushed a fist against her hip.

"Because I've been here long enough to know what a workaholic your mama is." Mandy threw the dishrag at her and grinned.

"But she needs the rest." Lily Anne smiled, making it extra bright and shiny to support her case. "Besides, I'm good." It was true. She was good, among other things. *Busy?* Extremely. *Tired?* Totally. *Stressed?* To the max. *Still good, thank the Lord!*

With a wave, Lily Anne trudged to the time clock. "Mandy I'm gone. It's all yours, doll!"

"All right. Have fun on your daaaate." Mandy made kissy noises for good measure and they both giggled.

Lily Anne ran straight for the bathroom, pausing in front of the mirror. She wrinkled her nose at the less than impressive reflection. *Why didn't I bring a change of clothes? Or pluck my brows last night? Or straighten my hair?* With a huff, she gathered the yellow frizzed curls into a messy bun atop her head. At least with her hair up, only a few strands puffed out. A quick twirl around her pointer finger and a touch of hairspray reset the flyaway pieces to resemble a soft curl instead of limp spaghetti. After reapplying a coat of lip balm and a couple swipes of mascara, she called it quits. *Mason's seen me look worse, right?*

The freshly applied make-up buoyed her spirits but did little to calm her. Lily Anne's nerves jittered like lightning bugs in June as she slapped her hand against her forehead and let it linger. *I said yes? What was I thinking? Is it too late to find a sinkhole?*

From the lobby, a jingle sounded, the ring breaking through the bathroom wall. Lily Anne sucked in as much air as possible, hoping to stifle the panic. *In. 1-Mississippi. 2-Mississippi. 3-Mississippi. And out. I can do this. I can 100%, without a doubt, confidently and courageously walk out there and make my case.* The sight of a manila folder on the storage shelf behind her reflection bolstered her courage.

Knowledge equaled power, and tucked between that sandwich of cardstock was enough force to recapture the leverage Mason's curveball proposal had stolen. Today was a new inning and she was swinging for the fences. With rejuvenated steps, she strolled to a back table while her husband-to-be chatted with Mandy.

Mason's rich voice floated through the silence as Lily Anne sunk into a seat, making the most of the few minutes she had alone by taking another big breath. *Hold. 1-Mississippi. 2-Mississippi. 3-Mississippi. And out.*

Mandy laughed at something Mason said and while he was distracted, Lily Anne took the time to covertly look him over. Teenage Mason had been cute with a bedhead coif in desperate need of a trim and superhero attire lacking maturity. That image was a far cry from the man who now stood before her.

The smooth face of yesteryear had been swapped out for a nicely groomed mustache and shortest of beards. A long-sleeved dress polo replaced the comic-inspired t-shirt and he no longer rocked the skinny jeans, but straight-leg dark denim with boots meeting the hem. He must've finally found a decent barber, too, as the once overgrown locks were exceptionally styled, not too long, not too short, messy, but not messy. Practically perfect. Coupled with his leather jacket, Mason played the part of a sharp-dressed man perfectly.

Chill, Lil. It's still Mason. That reminder conjured memories from high school. Mason's motorcycle during the homecoming parade with her hair windblown and frazzled. The two of them stretched out on the bleachers, begging the sun to warm them after the end-of-the-year water fight. Her teenage cheek smeared with pancake batter and Mason's gentle touch as he wiped it away *sans* his usual wisecrack or chuckling stare.

Lily Anne rubbed her face as heat filled her cheeks. Did Mason remember that day too? Had he noticed the gasp she'd tried to hide? How she'd flinched when his fingers brushed the bridge of her nose. Her broken nose.

Lily Anne covered her mouth with both hands. *The broken nose!* How had she forgotten? The particular bone-breaking incident had escaped her during the proposal hoopla, but as the memory came back to her, she shuddered. Of course, she had no proof Mason was the cause of her injury. In fact, he'd flat out denied being responsible for the prank that had sent her spiraling toward the student center floor after the fire alarm suddenly sounded, initiating the start of senior skip day. A worn orange seat attached to one of the cafeteria tables had kept her face from kissing the tile. Too bad the impact from the hard plastic had broken her nose in the process, not badly enough to bring the blood or even a bruise, but enough to leave a bumpy, crooked bridge. Oh, and an ache to rival a root canal.

Lily Anne tightened her grip on the folder, clinging to it like a lifeline. In the grand scheme of things, what was a broken nose compared to a barren life? She needed a husband, and Mason was ready and willing to take a chance on her. What if she did the same and let bygones be bygones?

Mason's long legs made short work of the space between them. She stood as he neared, drumming her fingers at her side and contemplating what to do. *A handshake?* Too formal. *A hug?* Too friendish. *A kiss?* Too forward, at least for her. Thankfully, Mason decided for her, quickly snagging both palms and tugging her to him as he planted a quick peck on her cheek.

"Hey, Mason." Her voice dropped to a barely audible decibel. She mentally scolded herself for the slip of composure. *Strike one!*

"Hey, Lily Anne. How was your shift?"

"Not bad. Sorry I couldn't get out of work today, but with Mom out of town there was no one to replace me. I know the bakery isn't the best place to talk, but the afternoon is usually pretty quiet, especially on a Monday. I really appreciate you meeting me here to discuss our agreement."

"Engagement, Chief, not agreement." Mason glanced at her left hand with his correction. His smile slipped at the sight of her bare finger. *Strike two!*

"The ring! Oh, Mason! It's not what you think." Lily Anne reached for his hand on the table and squeezed gently. "The ring is pretty loose and I was afraid it'd slip off while washing dishes today."

"And it's tacky." He rolled his eyes.

"Maybe a little, but that's not why I'm not wearing it."

They both laughed. Mason blinked back his disappointment, revealing eyes the color of a forest floor in fall. Mossy greens and warm tans with flecks of burnt orange sprinkled in. *Oh, how she loved those colors.*

"That's okay, Chief. Consider it a placeholder until we go shopping, which I'd like to do as soon as you're free. We can make a day of it. Do lunch, shopping, maybe a movie. Whatever works for you."

Lily Anne tilted her head in confusion as Mason rambled. This was a side she'd never seen before. Gone was the class clown who lived to laugh and in his place was a shaken, dare she say, flustered doppelganger full of consideration and sensitivity. It was nice, and freaky. Not knowing how much time she had before the real Mason returned, she released his hand and hastily retrieved the newly drafted documents needing his approval.

"Sure, we'll plan it. But first things first." Lily Anne pressed her back flush against the chair as she rotated the papers for him to read. "Can you sign this for me?"

"Maybe." Mason's brows raised as he pulled the packet closer to him, scanning the top sheet with laser focus. "What is this?"

"It's an expansion of our original vow, a formal Valentine Proposal if you will. As you so sweetly pointed out at the reunion, the written word is extremely important to me, so I've outlined our engagement week by week until the ceremony itself. Nothing specific, mind you, and all is subject to change due to availability issues or personal preferences." Lily Anne folded her hands in front of her after finishing the pitch and waited for him to respond. *Had someone turned the thermostat up?* Must have, since her palms were wet. She clenched her hands tighter together.

After a few more seconds of silence, Mason busted a gut, laughing so loudly Mandy turned to check on them. Lily Anne touched her temple, hiding her eyes from Mandy's stare. Thank goodness only the three of them were in the bakery.

"You're not serious?" Mason answered himself before she was able to. "Of course, you are. Still the proverbial planner, I see."

"If it ain't broke, don't fix it. Besides, having a guideline to follow can't hurt." Lily Anne squared her shoulders. Mason wasn't attacking her, but it was difficult to keep from shrinking under his teasing.

"No, I guess not. Let's go over it together, shall we?"

Lily Anne twisted her wrist to check the time. It'd taken months to pin down a meeting with Howard, editor over the

Lifestyles section of *The Valley Vine*, and being late wasn't an option. "Sure, but I can't stay too long."

"Ah, duty calls." Mason smiled, but it didn't meet his eyes.

"I'm s—"

"That's okay. Give me the rundown." Mason looked at the papers with curious eyes. The absence of his classic smirk took Lily Anne by surprise, causing her to lean closer in search of his usual humor. She found only a tender smile and willing gaze.

Mason bent across the table, too, making the crowns of their heads almost touch. His cologne kicked up around them, a hint of citrus and salt, reminding her of dancing ocean waves, a stark contrast from the smell of snow that rushed in when Mandy opened the back door beside them.

A sudden gust of cold air ruffled the pages Lily Anne held. She tapped the top sheet and sat back, putting space between them. "So, this proposal states either of us can walk away at any time, right up until the vows are exchanged. Not to speak ill of arranged marriages, but I'd like to be happy, and for you to be, as well. If it becomes apparent a joyous union isn't viable, it's best to make a clean break." Lily Anne heated from her clavicle to the tips of her ears as she spoke, but forced herself to continue.

"To, um, facilitate a lasting and caring relationship the agreement necessitates at least two dates a week, dine together four out of seven nights, and spend family time alternately when possible on the weekend, including church services. Doing so will provide adequate research to flesh out potential problems and allow us to make an informed, thought-out decision about our union."

Mason scratched his chin and nodded. "Sounds doable, as long as we agree to divvy up the planning. I plan a date, you plan a date, and either of us can interject a spur-of-the-moment outing as long as the datee has no objections. Will that work?"

"That might be tough with my schedule, but I'm open to giving it a shot."

"Lily Anne, if this—us—is going to work, be honest." Leaning across the table once more, Mason's hazel stare held her captive. "It's not your schedule that's the problem. It's your need for order. You can't stand living life without a plan and that worries you. Right?"

She stared at the napkin she'd absentmindedly shredded as the air grew thick in her lungs, panic threatening. *Not now. Please not now.* As smoothly as possible, she breathed deeply and held it. *1-Mississippi. 2-Mississippi. 3-Mississippi. And—*

"Chief, what do you call a spontaneous man named Lee?" Mason's warm hand settled atop hers as she searched his face for clues to the out-of-nowhere question. The breath she'd been holding eased out, an afterthought to the riddle. Offering a half-shrug, she acknowledged she'd been stumped.

"Spontaneous-Lee. Get it?" Mason grinned, a dazzling, contagious smile, sparking her own.

Lily Anne tried to remain still, but her laughter won out, setting her shoulders to shaking. "That's awful. Don't quit your day job, Mase. Your pictures are way better than your jokes."

Mason clutched his chest but smirked just the same. "That hurts. I'll have you know I've become quite proficient in comedy relief since high school."

After the moment passed, his gaze found hers, honest and vulnerable. "Be real with me. Is that the problem?"

Lily Anne bit her lip. She wanted to say yes *and* no. If she were honest with herself, the problem ran so much deeper, to the bottom of her heart that had accepted a life without love long ago. She should tell Mason to forget the whole thing before he wasted his time and she became too invested, but when he tightened his hand around hers, she couldn't. At his touch, the answer dislodged from her throat. The easy answer he expected, not the hard one where she admitted she was unlovable.

"Yes. We're so diffe—"

Mason shook his head. "You don't have to explain. I've been careless, maybe even reckless at times, but I was a kid. I'm not now, Lil. Can you give the new me a chance?"

Lily Anne worked her bottom lip back and forth between her teeth, not buying time to decide an answer, but working up the courage to defend the decision she'd already made.

"I can't erase the past or the memory of you I once knew, but I promise to keep an open mind."

"Thank you, Chief. I know it won't be easy, but I'm up for the challenge. I'm all in. Are you?" Mason asked, taking her hand again, tracing circles gently with his thumb. The intimate gesture took her by surprise, causing her to look up and meet Mason's gaze. She searched the hazel hue for all it was worth, searching her heart with the same intensity while she did. What she found in both was hope.

"I'm in." Lily Anne confidently signed the proposal and watched Mason do the same. "I hate to rush, but there's a meeting at the *Vine* I can't miss." She stood and immediately started counting the tile. Then, the cracks between them. Anything was prettier to look at than the disappointment she anticipated on Mason's face. Bailing on him couldn't be helped, but it made her stomach clench. "I know we have a lot to talk about, so my next day off is all yours. Okay?"

Mason slid out of the booth. "Sure, Chief. No worries."

The proper ending to their date proved to be as much of a mystery as the greeting had been. Without making eye contact, Lily Anne slipped her arms around Mason's waist and hugged lightly before rushing to the door. She waved and he gave a two-finger salute like he'd done at the end of every newspaper meeting. The nostalgia released a swarm of feel-good fuzzies so intense she giggled.

Mason's expression softened like he was remembering, too, but then he blinked and the moment was gone. As he stepped forward, his face morphed from childhood friend to man-on-a-mission. The new expression stopped Lily Anne in her tracks, wondering what he was up to.

"Lily Anne, before you go, I need to ask you something. I know covering for Danny Jo makes time an issue for you right now, but can you squeeze in one date? This Friday night?"

"W-w-wow, Mason. You don't waste time, huh?" Lily Anne tapped her fingers across her thigh. "Um, sure, I'd love to. What did you have in mind?"

Mason shoved his hands into the front pockets of his jeans sheepishly. Lily Anne remembered that look. It was a tell she knew like the back of her hand, a silent confession that screamed *I did something you're not gonna like*. As he opened his mouth, she braced for the bomb about to drop.

"Our engagement party."

Chapter Five

Mason slammed the passenger-side door as Lily Anne stepped away from the car, glancing at the community center. Slamming the nerves circling his insides wasn't an option, but the door made a nice substitute. He half expected her to chastise him, if not for making them late to their engagement party, then for his childish behavior.

Nearly four days had passed since their meeting at Country Confections, but the reminder of Lily Anne's professional demeanor still lingered fresh in his consciousness. Tardiness had to rub her the wrong way. To his surprise, though, she didn't even look up from retying her scarf a few feet in front of him.

Figures. Did Mason want to be reprimanded by his fiancée? No. Did he want to be noticed by her? Yes, a thousand times over. How she remained oblivious when he was beyond enamored, he'd never know. Worse, his frustration did little to weaken the pull she had on him. While she smoothed her dress, he was powerless to do anything except admire her.

Mason scanned Lily Anne from head-to-toe, basking in her quiet beauty. Poised and perfect, she waited a few steps ahead of the parked car, unaware of his appreciative stare. All her curls were pulled into some sort of prissy twist, but the flyaway wisps framing her face kept the look soft and dainty. So did the pearl earrings adorning the elven ears he'd always admired but never commented on. Her crimson ugly-sweater dress hit mid-thigh, short to be fun and flirty, but paired with leggings and black suede boots to maintain her modest appearance. She looked every bit the beauty she had always been, and knowing that Mason had miraculously secured a future with her made all his momentary anger melt away.

In no mood for a repeat of senior year, Mason hurried to her side and extended his arm as soon as Lily Anne glanced back. If he didn't catch her now, she'd be walking in front with him following behind like a lost puppy. Been there, done that.

"Shall we, m'lady?" Mason tried to sound British or Victorian or whatever the heroes spoke in those Regency romance novels he'd seen on her bookcase.

Lily Anne rewarded his effort with a mock curtsey. "We shall, kind sir."

She slipped her arm through his and the two rushed on, up the steps and through the front door. As they did, Mason worked his tie loose enough to unbutton his collar. January might have been cold, but between his leather jacket and the lovely Lily Anne on his arm, the chill lost its effect.

His brother was the first to greet them. "You're early, Deuce. I didn't expect ya 'til at least half past. She's already a good influence on you." Mikie smirked in his usual know-it-all way, but Mason ignored the bait. Without releasing Lily Anne, he returned his brother's embrace with a half-hearted hug.

"That she is, Ace." Mason lifted his chin to let his brother know now was not the time for teasing. When Mikie chuckled, Mason knew his message had been received but ignored.

"Mikie, thank you for doing this." Lily Anne tilted her head as Mikie leaned in for a peck on the cheek. "You and Mary Ellen outdid yourselves. Where is she so I can thank her?"

Mikie pointed to the door on the right that led to the kitchen. "Her and Ma are busy in the kitchen, but I know they're dyin' to see ya."

Lily Anne darted her gaze between him and the door, finally focusing on the door. "If you two will excuse me, I think I'll join them."

"Of course, Chief." Mason released her arm. "I'll wait here for you."

"Thank you." Lily Anne walked away in search of the party's hosts, leaving the men alone.

Mason placed a hand on his brother's shoulder. "You ready to fulfill your best-man duties?"

"Sure thing, *if* you make it to the altar." Mikie raised a brow, while Mason shook his head slowly. Convincing Lily Anne he was for real was going to be impossible if his own brother didn't believe him.

"Engaged, huh?" said a voice from behind him. When Mason spun around, Mr. Rowe met him with a teasing grin. "Congratulations, Mason. Wish you'd told me the other day when we met."

Mason stiffened at the reminder of the previous rejection, but relaxed in the same breath as he realized the golden opportunity before him. "I hadn't asked yet, sir. When we talked, there was nothing to tell."

"Ah, I see. Didn't want to jinx it." Mr. Rowe wagged a finger between them. "Anyhow, I'm glad to see you settling down. Roots are good for young men."

"That's exactly what I'm going for, and there's no one I'd rather have by my side than Lily Anne." Mason held his tongue to keep from laying it on too thick, but it was hard. Not because of the good impression he wanted to make on Mr. Rowe, but because of just how true the words were. Thinking of porch-sitting with Lily Anne someday made sense, even though it shouldn't. They'd been apart for years, a decade even, but his heart didn't care. It still beat out a rhythm to her name.

"Young love is precious, that's for sure." Mr. Rowe stood up straighter, his hand trembling slightly as he tucked it in his pocket. His green eyes lighted as they landed on a long gray braid across the room, lingering for a moment before turning back to Mason. "Say, Mase, I know you're going to be busy with the wedding, but let's get together again and revisit our last discussion. If you're still interested."

"Yes, sir." Mason reminded himself to breathe. "I am very interested."

"Good. You call me and we'll set it up." Mr. Rowe smiled brightly. "Oh, I see the missus waving me down. Gotta go, son."

"I understand. Thanks for coming tonight."

Mr. Rowe lifted his chin toward the food table. "I wouldn't have missed it, especially when Mikie said your mother was catering. She makes some mean meatballs."

"That she does," said Mason.

"Enjoy the party."

"You, too." Mason nodded as Mr. Rowe weaved his way through the crowded room, a little shell-shocked from their conversation. Shock soon melted into elation as he fist-bumped the air. Mason was still reveling in the victory when a warm hand entwined with his, catching him off guard.

Without thinking, he twisted and took hold of the person by the shoulder, bringing him face to face with Lily Anne. She tensed, but when she didn't move, he began softly rubbing the arm he'd claimed captive. A tiny gasp passed through her parted lips, calling to him like a siren. After a quick release of her shoulder, his free hand crept upward until it landed on her soft cheek. Lily Anne's eyes tripled in size, but she didn't shy away. As the seconds ticked on, her face relaxed, eyes fluttering shut and chin lifting slightly, sending an invitation Mason was more than ready to answer. Slowly, he leaned in, closing his own eyes when the warmth of her breath tickled his lips.

"Y'all ready to play some games with the happy couple?" Mary Ellen's voice whirred around them, breaking the spell.

The moment faded like rising fog. Not wanting to show his disappointment, he gently squeezed the arm he was still holding before taking her hand in his. No doubt his cheeks were pink, but he didn't care. What he did care about was how nervous Lily Anne looked. With her quickened breathing and wide eyes, Mason needed to defuse the situation, and fast.

Mason dropped Lily Anne's hand and situated his feet in a fighting stance. "Step right up, folks. We're ready to wipe the floor with the lot of you."

Making a show of searching for an opponent, he danced around, throwing punches in the air every few seconds. The room focused on him, just like he'd hoped, leaving Lily Anne to compose herself with as much privacy as a party allowed.

Putting an end to the display, Mary Ellen stepped in front of him. "Mason's raring to go, but he might change his tune after he hears about our first game." As she spoke, Mikie pulled out six chairs from the tables and made two rows of three facing each other. Ma scurried out of the kitchen with a rolling cart and three large metal bowls.

Mary Ellen scanned the crowd. She turned to Mason and grinned ear to ear. "Normally, I'd never wish cold feet on a couple, but in this case, I'm going to make an exception. In fact, the colder, the better. To win this game, ladies and gents need to go toe-diving for some dimestore rings beneath the ice water. Whichever team collects the most jewelry in a minute, wins."

"Now, I'm not one to gossip." Mary Ellen took a breath as the room filled with laughter. "But if y'all wanna win, this might be your best shot. I heard through the grapevine that our soon-to-be groom has a thing about feet. He may or may not sleep in socks year round because he can't stand them getting cold."

Mason's cheeks flamed as Mary Ellen ratted him out. As he scrambled to the first seat, dragging Lily Anne along with him, laughing fits busted out from all over the room. In an instant, his boots and socks were shucked.

"Is she telling the truth? Do you really sleep in socks, Mason?" Lily Anne's voice remained even but as soon as the words were out, her hand flew over her mouth, covering a grin.

"Maybe. That make me any less handsome, Chief?" He waggled his eyebrows at her but averted his gaze at the first sign of her blush.

From his peripherals, he watched her shake her head. He wanted to laugh but knew better. Contrary to popular belief, he didn't bait her for entertainment. Was it comical to knock her off her game? Oh, yeah, but that wasn't his motivation. It went deeper than that. With her defenses down, Lily Anne beamed and the light she projected woke up places inside him that had never existed until she came along.

Mary Ellen waved her arms above her head to get the crowd's attention. "All right, guys. Let's count them down. Three. Two. One. Go!"

Without hesitation, Lily Anne plunged her foot into the bowl. It was the same kind the church used for foot-washing so there was plenty enough room for Mason to join her. He closed his eyes tight, sucked in a breath, and pushed his foot beneath the water, cursing the cold as he did. While he searched for the trinkets, Mason concentrated on warm thoughts. Sandy beaches, a crackling fire pit, fresh-out-of-the-oven biscuits. When his toe slid through a small hoop, he exhaled loudly. *Finally!*

Lily Anne laughed at him as she dropped a pair of rings on the ground. "Your face is priceless! If I didn't wanna win, I'd bow out right now to snap a picture for blackmail later."

Mason smiled wide. Rarely did she let her accent come through, but when she did, he swooned at the music it made. The twang in her voice plucked his heart's strings.

Why she thought it was more professional to disguise her roots, he'd never know.

"Don't think I missed you avoiding my question, Lil. Does the sock thing make me any less handsome?" Mason didn't expect a reply, but when she narrowed her eyes and opened her mouth, his ears perked up.

Mary Ellen interrupted, calling time before Lily got a word out. "That's it. Feet out. Mikie's coming around to count."

Mason surveyed their loot, comparing it to the other two teams. No surprise, they'd lost, big time. He'd expected as much.

"It doesn't matter," Lily Anne whispered, so softly Mason wondered if she'd actually spoken.

"What, Chief?"

"I said, it doesn't matter, i-if you wear socks or not. You'd still be handsome." Lily Anne remained soft-spoken, low enough for only him to hear. She flushed but held his gaze, her eyes turning the color of caramel as she stared back at him, intense and deep. His jaw dropped as her admission sank in. It was bold and real and made his blood pump harder.

Without another word, she grabbed the towel at her side and dried off her feet, first the right and then the left. When she had finished, she slipped her shoes back on and headed to a round table for the next game, but not before handing the second towel to him. Mason mumbled a thank-you as he rubbed his feet dry, buying himself time to adjust to Lily Anne's compliment. Sure, plenty of women had commented on his hazel eyes and messy hair, but none of those women had agreed to marry him.

Mason shoved his feet into his boots and laced them tight. By the time he caught up to Lily Anne, the rippling pulse beneath his skin had smoothed to a normal rhythm, but he knew a dazed smile continued to split his face.

"Y'all know I'm a cherry-lover, and for this game I'm looking for a few people who share my taste in fruit." A few hands went up. Charlie and Alexis, Emma Lou, Shelby Jane, Ruby Jean, Eliza Lee, and Clay, still in town on vacation. Mason didn't get Clay hanging with the group, Emma being his ex and all. It took some nerve to sit across from her and her family, but Clay remained chill with one arm draped across the back of Emma's chair.

"Before y'all get too excited, it's not a contest to eat the most cherries. It's a test of skill. Now, I'm not the bragging kind but I am sort of famous for my hands-free Starburst-unwrapping ability." Mary Ellen flashed a coy smile at Mikie, sending the room into fits of laughter again. "But I can't tie a cherry stem to save my life, at least not with my tongue, which is what y'all are going to be doing. The team with the most knots wins. I hope you do better than I can. Y'all got three minutes, starting now!"

Mason sucked a cherry into his mouth, chowing down instantly. It had to be easier without the fruity part weighing it down. Right? After he swallowed and went to work tongue-tying the first cherry, he spared a glance at Lily Anne. When he realized she'd already placed three pretty knots on a paper towel next to the bowl, his mouth went dry.

Mason tried to ignore her as she plopped the next cherry in her mouth, but being a red-blooded male made it near impossible. Her full lips taunted him and knowing how close he'd been to them minutes earlier made it so much worse. Trying to focus, Mason reangled the cherry stem with his tongue as Lily Anne's eyes met his, sending his thoughts straight back to the almost-kiss.

To distract himself, he waggled his brows. In seconds, her face matched the color of the cherries. Mason grinned, making sure his gaze never left hers, but when she pulled out another tied stem from her mouth and squinted, the tables turned. With a pointed stare, she plucked not one but two cherries defiantly from the bowl and dropped them dramatically in her mouth. The smile she flashed after said it all. *Challenge accepted.*

Now, it was Mason's turn in the hot seat. With a loud exhale, he turned away, trying to hide the flames licking up his neck and across his face. *Where was that ice water?* A combination of pride and shame filled him as he removed the first knot with a minute left in the game. He barely tied another one before Mary Ellen called time and Mikie made his trip around the room again in search of the victor.

This time, Mason's hand went up with Lily Anne's. Knowing she'd singlehandedly pulled out the win, he wriggled free and bowed to her. She blushed at being the center of attention but managed to cover it with a fine impression of a beauty-pageant wave before heading to the table where the last game was set up.

Mason followed with quick steps, staying right on her heels. "I'm impressed," he whispered as they took their places.

Lily Anne promptly elbowed him before stopping dead in her tracks. She stared at the front entrance of the community center, slack-jawed and skin white as a sheet. When a voice cracked over the ruckus of the party, he knew why.

"Lily Anne Dawson!" Danny Jo stood with fists on her hips. Before he or Lily Anne could say a word, she rushed on. "Surprised to see me home so soon? Yeah, I am too, but when I called the bakery this morning and Mandy answered, I got a little worried. Until she told me she agreed to cover for you because of your *engagement* party."

Mason's stomach clenched as the scene played out, realization settling like a rock in the river. Lily Anne hadn't called her mother to tell her about the engagement? Mason scrubbed a hand down his face. There was no fixing this, at least not tonight, not with Lily Anne freaking out beside him and Danny Jo seething in front of them. Appeasing the angry mother glaring at them was a lost cause, but maybe he could save his fiancée.

An idea popped into Mason's head—crazy and reckless—the kind of thing he'd been known for in high school. It went against his every conviction to prove himself to Lily Anne, but with panic frozen on her face, it was worth a try. Mason closed his eyes and prayed. *Lord, please don't let this backfire.*

His eyes popped open. Lily Anne's feet were still cemented in place, Danny Jo hadn't moved a muscle, and the crowd had grown awkwardly quiet. Gently, Mason wrapped an arm around Lily Anne's waist and pulled her to his side. The movement startled her, but she quickly recovered, snapping her pale face to his.

"Whatcha say we get outta here, Chief?"

Lily Anne agreed with a terse nod and the two of them bolted toward the door. In under a minute, Mason was driving away from the community center with no real destination in mind while Lily Anne fiddled with the heat.

When the vents kicked on she collapsed against the seat. "You do realize we just abandoned our own engagement party, right?" Lily Anne slapped her hands on her thighs like his nephew did when Mikie refused to give him a cookie.

Inside, Mason chuckled. Outwardly, he knew better, so he kept his eyes on the road ahead of them. "I do."

"And you're still smiling?"

"Of course. You're beside me, Chief."

"Unbelievable." Lily Anne leaned her head against the seat. "Sweet, but unbelievable. My mom was furious, you know?"

"I kinda picked up on that. It'll blow over." Taking a chance, Mason reached across for her hand. She accepted and laced her fingers with his, shocking him almost as much as Danny Jo had at the party.

"Maybe, but it'll take more than fifteen minutes for that. Can you drop me off at Emma Lou's house? I texted her and she said I could sleep on her couch for the night. She's already on her way there. So is Eliza Lee. Apparently, she needs the skinny on what just went down."

Mason blinked as he tried to make sense of the impromptu slumber party. "Girls," he mumbled under his breath before answering Lily Anne. "Yeah, I can take you to Emma's. She still live beside Davey's old place?"

"Yup."

With the route decided upon, silence filled the cab until the jeep rolled to a stop in front of Emma Lou's house.

"Mason?"

"Yeah?"

"Thank you. You really saved me tonight." Lily Anne's small voice knocked the wind right out of him as she leaned over and threw her arms around his neck. As he returned the hug, an aftershock vibrated straight through his heart. She thought he saved her?

Mason didn't play the part of hero. There was always someone more qualified, older, better equipped—like Mikie—so Mason took the scraps and resigned himself to the role of court jester. But, at that moment, he longed to be a knight. *Her* knight, to swap the robes of mirth for a suit of armor, to slay the dragon, to guide a white horse into the sunset with Lily Anne as his bride.

But seeing as how they'd been engaged all of a week, he had no idea how to tell her that. Instead, he shrugged. "What are future husbands for?"

Mason held his breath, waiting for her to answer, but before she could, Emma Lou knocked on the passenger-side window, then walked toward the house, motioning for her to follow. Lily Anne reached for the door at the same time he spoke.

"Lil, I'm sorry tonight ended the way it did. I'll talk to Danny Jo with you, if you want me to."

"No." Lily Anne smoothed down her dress, watching her hands intently. "If I know my mother like I think I do, she'll cool down in a few days. She's riled up because I didn't call her after the reunion, but she was on vacation and I really didn't want to explain things over the phone. I knew she'd have a ton of questions. Honestly, *I* have a ton of questions. Like your career, Mason. How will that work? What's the plan for after the wedding? Where are we going to live?"

Leaning closer, Mason took her hand. "My career is mobile. All I need is my camera and a computer. As for the plan? We're getting married on Valentine's Day, like we agreed, and we'll live right here in Pine Valley."

"You make it sound so simple." Lily Anne raised the shoulder closest to him in a half-shrug. "But it's not. We can't hold our breath and hope for the best."

"We'll figure everything out. I promise, but right now, let's focus on getting to know one another again and take it date by date. Sound good?"

She nodded, looking less than convinced. Slowly the light in her eyes returned, giving Mason reason to believe her trust in him had done the same. Before it wavered again, Mason charged on. "Speaking of dates, I was hoping you had some free time to spend with me on Monday. I'd like to take you shopping."

Lily Anne tilted her head. "Why? Most men hate shopping?"

"I won't lie. I do, usually, but we need to go shopping. For a ring." The steadiness in his voice shocked Mason, especially since his knee had begun to bounce uncontrollably. A ring meant no going back. Without a doubt, Lily Anne understood that, too.

Her eyes widened as she licked her lips and rubbed them together. Mason mimicked the motion, his eyes never moving from her mouth. Lily Anne Dawson was in his front seat, looking just as kissable as she did when they were teenagers. He leaned further across the center console, holding his breath and waiting for her to meet him halfway. But she didn't.

Instead, Lily Anne nodded again. "R-right. Just, uh, text me when to be ready."

Mason leaned back in his seat. "Can do, Chief. And thank you, for tonight." He smiled wide before he could rein it in. No doubt, he looked like a lunatic, but he didn't care. When Lily Anne's expression transformed to match his, Mason didn't think she minded his insane appearance, either.

"Thank you, too. Goodnight, Mason. Go rest up for our shopping excursion."

"I sure will, Chief. G'night."

With that, Lily Anne opened her door.

Mason grabbed for the handle beside him. "Wait, let me walk you up."

"Thanks for the offer, Mase, but Emma Lou is spying. You stay put."

Snapping his head toward Emma's house, Mason saw a blind in the front window pushed to the side and nodded. "As you wish, m'lady."

Lily Anne rushed toward the house. At the door, she turned around and waved. Mason started to mirror the motion, but at the last second he changed his mind and blew a kiss instead, earning him a headshake. He laughed out loud as he slowly backed down the drive, thanking God for his bride-to-be and replaying the absurdity of the party.

This might be a night to tell his grandchildren about.

Chapter Six

"**M**hmmm." Lily Anne danced in her seat, mumbling around a big bite of pastry perfection while staring at her new engagement ring. The pearl set in white gold with polished black coral on either side was a sight to behold and she'd never grow tired of looking at.

"Lily Anne Dawson! You better slow your roll or you'll make yourself sick." *That voice.* She twisted in her seat just as two arms caged her in. Her brother's arms. "Better yet, why don't I finish this for you, so we don't take any chances, huh?" Without warning, he yanked her plate away and dropped into the chair across from her.

Lily Anne folded her arms across her chest. Her set lips unglued, releasing her jaw as the freckle-faced man with the carrot-top locks picked up the cinnamon roll and crammed the remaining dough in his mouth.

She sent him a death glare. "Logan White, how dare you!"

"Still not good with sharing, I see," said Logan. "Must be that only-child syndrome you hear so much about." His green eyes shone bright, like they always did when he was making trouble. Though four years separated them in age, Lily Anne had never felt the difference, not with Logan's maturity level.

"Must be." Lily Anne laughed loudly. Logan did, too, his gruff bellows garnishing the attention of the few patrons inside Country Confections.

Logan shifted his eyes from her to the counter where Mandy stood. "You working hard today, Lily Anne?"

"Taking my lunch break, actually."

"Right." Logan averted his eyes toward the pastry case before doing a double take and letting his stare settle on her. "Since when do you wear make-up to work?"

"I don't, usually, but I'm expecting comp—"

"There you are, Chief. I was beginning to think you'd left for the *Vine* already. Oh! Am I interrupting?" Mason stopped short and eyed the table curiously. His gaze raked over Logan as he started walking toward them again.

"Not at all. Logan was just saying hi. I think?" Lily Anne let her eyes wander over her brother, realizing how strange it was for him to be in Pine Valley. After Logan's stint in Triple A baseball, he kept his distance from people, Lily Anne included. He rarely came to see her and, over the years, her visits to him had grown sporadic. Their talks had, too. Between the bakery and the newspaper, Lily Anne didn't have time to do much. How long had it been since she'd called him? Two months? Three? She didn't even know. The realization shamed her, but she battled it as best she could by keeping the conversation going. "Why is a homebody like you an hour away from your nice neighborhood of Hickory Hills?"

Logan glanced at his watch and then back at Lily Anne and Mason. "Saying hi, like you said, and getting a coffee before I make my way back over the mountain. I've got a few more minutes before I have to head out."

"Well, then, let me introduce you. Mason, this is Logan. Logan, Mason."

"Nice to meet ya." Logan held out his hand and Mason accepted. "Mason? That name sounds so familiar. Didn't you go to school with some guy named Mason?"

"Y-yes, I did." Lily Anne's heart pounded as she quickly covered her left hand with her right. Thank goodness for Logan's teasing to distract him from the ring she'd been admiring moments ago. Too bad there was nothing to weaken Logan's elephant-like memory. Why couldn't he have fried a few brain cells back in college, like the ones concerning her fiancé? Judging from the look on his face, though, maybe he had. At least, the puzzle wasn't entirely put together yet. There was time to act, if she was fast. She needed to get Mason away from Logan before he realized *why* her fiancé's name sounded so familiar.

Lord, have mercy.

If Logan found out Mason was *the* Mason that Lily Anne blamed for her broken nose all those years ago, there's no telling what he'd do. Despite the fact there was no blood that tied the two of them, just a marriage between Logan's mother and Lily Anne's father, he had driven over two hours to bring her an ice pack after the accident. He claimed it was his brotherly duty. It was the first time he'd dropped the "step" in front of their relationship, right before Logan ran off in search of Mason, bent on giving him a broken nose to match hers. Lily Anne was so moved by the gesture, she didn't dare try to stop him. Luckily Logan never found him.

Back then, Mason was just some boy in class who'd never had to meet Logan. Lily Anne worked hard to keep her life in Pine Valley with her mother entirely separate from the visits with her dad in Hickory Hills. The hour drive between the two towns made it pretty simple to do. No one ever knew she had a stepbrother.

But now that Mason was the man she planned to marry, everything was different. How could she explain that to Logan without his ginger temper taking over and her fiancé ending up on the ground? She had to protect Mason from Logan at all cost.

Mason narrowed his eyes at Logan like he was a key to a lost lock. "My reputation precedes me. I can't say the same about you th—"

"Mason, can you grab me an iced mocha and another cinnamon roll?" Lily Anne convinced herself a second helping of carbs and more coffee fit into the parameters of all cost. "We, uh, can share since it's my second helping. Just tell Mandy to put it on my tab, m'kay?"

"Sure. Watch my stuff for me?" Mason set his cell on the table and Lily Anne nodded as she covered the phone with her hand.

Her thoughts scattered like a bag of spilled marbles on the old oak floor. She needed to break the news of her engagement to Logan gently, when she could explain the situation without the possibility of Mason getting a bump on his nose to match hers. What if, even after she told Logan everything, he insisted on payback for the broken nose? What if Mason hit him back? What if she wasn't enough to bring the boys together? She certainly hadn't been enough for her parents. Why would it be any different for Logan and Mason? Lily took a deep breath to ward off the impending panic. *1-Mississippi. 2-Mississippi. 3-Mississippi. And ou—*

A tutting noise broke her meditation.

"Are you blushing?" Logan worked a day's worth of stubble between his thumb and forefinger before pointing at her. "Yeah, yeah, you are!"

"Bite your tongue. I am not." Even as the words slipped out, a second wave of heat charged her cheeks.

"You totally are. Why, I don't think I've seen you blush since I caught you behind the bleachers with Davey Barnes."

"This again? You know why I was there with him!" Lily Anne's voice rose, loud enough to land all eyes on her. Ashamed, she ducked her head and lowered her voice before continuing. "And you wouldn't have caught me if you hadn't been waiting for Shelby Jane Andrews."

Logan's body went rigid at the sound of Shelby's name and the whimsy in his eyes faltered. But then, he laughed, returning to the mischief-maker she knew so well.

"I know why we were both there. *Extracurriculars.*" Logan's brows tip-toed a few times beneath the unkempt bangs threatening to obscure his sight.

"Technically, yes, but unlike *you*, mine was not of the social kind. It was for the paper. Davey was slated to be on the mound for the first game of the district finals and he wanted to talk strategy."

"Strategy, huh? Is that what you kids were calling it?"

Lily Anne threw her hands up in defeat. Meticulously, she pushed a mouthful of air out through pursed lips, hoping to release her frustration. When she was calm, she went on.

"I had all the league's stats, including Kyle Meadows. Remember him? Davey hadn't won against him all season. I'd covered every game between them as well as several more of Kyle's starts throughout the season. Davey wanted to know his weakness before taking the mound. It might have been a breach of journalistic integrity to share Kyle's tells with Davey, but the championship was on the line. You'd have done the same thing." Lily Anne sat up straighter knowing she had the upper hand.

"In a heartbeat, Lil. That was a big game. Even my college team was excited for it. I'm messing with you, kiddo."

"Yeah, I know. It's your favorite pastime."

Logan didn't argue, but stood, rounded the table, and draped an arm over her shoulder in a lazy hug.

With a quick cut of his eyes, Logan found Mason at the counter. "This isn't over, but I'm giving you a pass for now. Soon, I'm gonna get to the bottom of that blush. Maybe next week? Over fried chicken?"

"Fine." Lily Anne pursed her lips as she nodded. "But since you're the nosey one, you're buying."

"Done. I'll call you later." Logan hugged her softly once more and then he was out the door.

Lily Anne blew out a breath to calm her nerves. When her hands started quivering, she was sure a full-on panic attack was minutes away until she realized only one hand was trembling, specifically the one covering Mason's forgotten phone. *To answer or not to answer. That is the question.* She bit the bullet, slid the flashing light on the screen, and lifted it to her ear.

"Hello?"

"Hello. This is Margie Campbell from *As the Belle Told*. I was hoping you might have a moment to chat?" The lady on the line was either too distracted to notice Lily Anne's distinctly female voice or she'd never spoken to Mason before.

"Um, let me get Mason for you."

"Oh! So, the rumors are true then? Am I speaking with Lily Anne Dawson?"

"Yes, this is she, but how did you know my name?"

"A little birdie told us our favorite photographer was suddenly engaged, and now, hearing your sweet voice, I'm much more inclined to believe it."

Lily Anne crossed her legs at the ankles and leaned back in her chair. "I can neither confirm nor deny that for you, Mrs. Campbell, but I'd be happy to tell Mason you called."

"What a pity! That same little birdie mentioned you were an aspiring journalist and I knew the fates had aligned for us. *As the Belle Told* was hoping for an exclusive on the engagement, and who better to write such a feature than the bride-to-be herself? And to make it even better, we'll keep it under wraps until it hits the newsstands. What a wonderful surprise for the groom, don't you think?"

"Wait, what?" Lily Anne felt her eyes bug out. "You want me to write an article? For *As the Belle Told?*"

"That was the idea, dear. Our next issue hits the stands on Valentine's Day. It'd be just perfect! Oh, but I do understand if you're the shy sort. I just thought, well, it might be a springboard for you in the print world and the perfect wedding gift for Mason! But if you're not interested, maybe I can set up a phone interview with the two of you? Just have him call me back." Mrs. Campbell's voice practically sang in the speaker, sweet and cheerful, but with a certain calm only businesswomen know how to master. Eager without being enthusiastic. Persuasive without sounding desperate.

"Okay, sure." *Am I dreaming?* No way the South's most popular magazine was asking her, a lowly life-hack columnist without so much as a byline to her name, to write for them. The black hole had opened in Kentucky after all, and it had sent her to an alternate dimension where wishes were granted with no genie required. *Shut the front door!*

Lily Anne pressed the phone closer to her ear. "Mrs. Campbell? Mrs. Campbell, are you still there?"

"Yes, dear?"

"I, um, I see your point and completely agree." What felt like a stampede of buffalo went wild in Lily Anne's stomach while her heart rate climbed to an astronomical level. She had to be chill, though. Sure, a break like this could make her whole career, but she needed to adopt the same composure as Mrs. Campbell. Calm. Collected. Professional. Lily Anne cleared her throat and squared her shoulders. "It'd be a wonderful surprise for Mason. I'm more than happy to give you that exclusive."

"You are?" asked Mrs. Campbell, in a tone a bit higher-pitched than before. The break in demeanor made Lily Anne pause. *To write or not to write? That is the question.* Lily Anne shut her eyes. In the dark, a scene emerged. A magazine cover, with her name on it. She smiled and placed her trembling hands in her lap, the answer on her tongue.

"I am." The words came out shaky, matching Lily Anne's insides. She'd made her decision, but the choice left her unsettled.

"Splendid! I gotta run, but do give Mason my best wishes and most sincere congratulations on your engagement. Oh, and have him send me your contact info." Mrs. Campbell's voice, on the other hand, was back to normal, sure and even as a balance beam.

"Yes, ma'am, and thank you." Lily Anne managed to speak at a normal volume but inside she was screaming as she wiggled in her seat.

"Thank you, dear. Bye, now."

"Goodbye." There was a click on the other end before Lily Anne finished her farewell, but it didn't matter. Mrs. Campbell had heard the most important part, her agreement to an exclusive.

A laugh escaped Lily Anne as she lowered the phone back to the table. She thought Mason's proposal was destined to be the wackiest moment of her life. How wrong she'd been! Since saying yes to him, her life had been reduced to nothing but a series of unbelievable events, each one leaving her more disheveled than the previous. If this was any indication to how their marriage might be, she was in for a wild ride.

"Here you go." Mason eyed her with furrowed brows and a frown. "Did your *friend* leave?"

"Friend?" Lily Anne tipped her head in his direction. *Friend? Who?* The conversation with Mrs. Campbell left her dazed. She did a quick mental rewind, nearly coming up blank until a familiar, freckle-faced nuisance of a man materialized. "Oh, Logan. Uh, yeah, he left already."

"Right, I have been gone a bit. Sorry. Mandy had to run out to the storage building for another sleeve of lids."

"No biggie." Lily Anne dismissed the apology and accepted the drink he slid across the table before snatching the plate between them. With carpenter-like precision, she made a center cut down the pastry and began tearing her portion into smaller bites. After the first forkful of ooey-gooey-goodness, she remembered her manners.

"Mase, your phone rang and you'll never believe who was on the other end."

"Lemme guess. Margie Campbell, right?" Mason speared a piece of the roll from her side and smirked.

"Yeah, how'd you know?"

"She's called me a dozen times since Christmas. Wanting an interview, or a cover photo, or last week's gossip. That woman won't take no for an answer."

"You told her no?"

Mason swallowed and took a sip of coffee. "Every time, but she's persistent. I'm sorry you had to deal with that."

"Don't be." Lily Anne shrugged as she tried to reconcile the nice lady she'd talked with minutes prior to Mason's aversion toward her. "She was sweet."

"I'd expect nothing less. That's how she reels you in. Deep down, I think she's a genuinely good-hearted person, but the rest of her staff is questionable." Mason rolled up the sleeves on his button-down, looking like a man ready to play hardball.

"W-what do you mean?" Lily Anne's eyes lingered on his forearms a few seconds more before meeting his steely gaze. Yes, Mason had *definitely* grown up, and she didn't mind one bit, even if her cheeks were on fire. She took a long sip from the iced mocha, hoping to temper the heat before Mason saw. It must have worked, because he went on without missing a beat.

"Last summer an article ran accusing me of, how did it read? Oh, yes, 'Playboy tendencies.' Apparently, an intern trying to make a name for herself did a follow-up after Mrs. Campbell interviewed me and her findings, false as they were, made it into the feature." Mason sliced into his side of the cinnamon roll, a little too hard, if the sound of scratching metal on the ceramic plate was any indication.

Lily Anne winced and relaxed the grip on her fork. "Mason, I'm so sorry. I had no idea. What, um, grounds were there to report a thing like that anyway?" With a quick stab, Lily Anne portioned her own bite and shoveled the pastry into her mouth, giving herself something to focus on other than the topic at hand.

"It seems an ex-girlfriend of mine, Rachel, had been contacted for a quote, just something cute to go along with the piece they were doing about my career. Mrs. Campbell didn't realize we were no longer together and gave the contact to her intern. Rachel took the breakup harder than I thought and must have been out for revenge, best I can figure. She told the magazine she had nothing to offer, except a warning for the next girl to watch out for my 'love them and leave them' ways." A deep sigh rushed out and Mason covered his mouth with a napkin. He wiped his lips, wadded the paper up, and tossed the ball on his side of the table. "The *Belle* printed the quote verbatim."

"That's awful." Lily Anne's voice rose to a squeaky how-rude octave as Mason's hazel eyes, more green than brown, locked on hers, reflecting such deep pain that Lily Anne's stomach dropped. She swallowed, hard, as he went on.

"And entirely untrue. I was nothing but a perfect gentleman when Rachel and I were together. In fact, I turned down her invites for nightcaps, not the other way around." Mason spoke with precision, clear in tone and intent.

"Mason, you don't have to explain." Trying for nonchalance, Lily Anne took a bite of cinnamon roll before tucking her fingers beneath her thighs to keep from wringing her hands. She wanted to hear about Mason's experience in the bedroom about as much as she wanted to wear wool without a camisole, but she didn't want him to know that.

Mason scooted his chair around the table until they were on the same side, their knees slightly touching. "I want to explain. What Rachel said, what *As the Belle Told* printed, was a lie. I'm no choirboy but I'm not the man they made me out to be, either." Gently, he tugged her hand free and settled his palm beneath hers, spinning circles with his thumb along her skin the same way he'd done after they had signed their agreement.

"Mason, it's okay if I'm not your first." Lily Anne fought the fiery blush racing across the bridge of her nose to the tips of ears, trying not to seem like the awkward virgin she knew herself to be, and braced herself for the can of worms she had cracked open.

Before she lost her nerve, she held up her right hand and went on. "I know I'm probably the only twenty-eight-year-old wearing her purity ring and I'm at peace with that."

"That's the wrong hand, Lil." Mason smiled and squeezed the hand he was still in possession of.

"Yes, I know. I switched it because everyone kept asking when the big day was. I got tired of explaining. But I couldn't bring myself to throw it in the jewelry box. I want to see it, to remind me of the promise I made to myself, to God, to my future husband. To *you*."

Mason seized the hand she'd just showed him and held it, too. In seconds, the swirls began on that palm as well. He was so kind, so understanding, so patient. And *so* not talking. Worse, he was staring at her. Lily Anne met his stare with one of her own, but the longer they sat with eyes locked, the more she realized how wrong she was. It wasn't a stare. Mason's look ran warmer than any stare could. It was almost loving. *Loving?* She had to be seeing things. Lily Anne sucked in a breath as Mason started to speak.

"Lily Anne, I know I talk a big game. I laugh when I should be quiet. I zig when I should zag. And I ask for marriage when I should probably settle for a date." He laughed, small and sweet.

"But what that purity ring represents?" Mason thumbed the back of her band. "It's worth waiting for, and I have. Waited, I mean, like I promised the same night you did in youth group forever ago. You're not the only one who still has it. I don't wear mine anymore cause my fingers got fat, but I still carry my ring with me. See?" Mason let go of her hands and dug in his pocket, producing a set of keys in seconds.

Lily Anne leaned forward and gasped when she spied the ring. Between a plastic wildcat—their high-school mascot—and a random loyalty card hung a stainless-steel band matching her own. A calm engulfed her and before she knew it, she was hanging around Mason's neck like a set of pearls.

"I thought I was the only one." Her words rushed against his shoulder, muffling the statement. She tried to pull away to repeat herself, but Mason held her against him.

"Oh, ye of little faith." He rubbed her back gently and laughed. The scent of sand and salt floated around her. Of course, he'd smell like a day at the beach in the middle of January. The man was a constant contradiction, able to unnerve her like no one else but soothe her soul just the same with those hazel eyes of his. Before doing something stupid like asking what surf shop he bought his cologne from, she unclasped her hands and sat back.

With a shy smile that didn't suit him, Mason combed his fingers through his hair. "Right. So, now that *that's* settled, what did Mrs. Campbell say?"

Lily Anne bit her lip. Knowing Mason's history with the magazine, how could she tell him that *As the Belle Told* had offered to make her dreams come true? Worse, how could she turn the job down when the feature might jumpstart her stagnant journalism career? She couldn't. Could she?

"Oh, Mrs. Campbell wanted to, uh, congratulate you, on the engagement."

"Of course, she did. I'm sorry."

Lily Anne squirmed in her seat. "Stop saying you're sorry. It's fine."

If only that were true. No way did Lily Anne want to back out of the article and kill her chance at a national byline in the process, but what other choice did she have? It was the only option.

Or was it? Grasping at straws, she ventured a final question.

"I know there's some bad blood between you and the magazine, but would you ever consider working with Mrs. Campbell again?"

Mason laid his fork across the plate. "If you asked me that when it first happened, I would have said no. Now though, with as many times as I've spoken to her, there's a chance I could bury the hatchet. I get the feeling she's clueless as to what went down. Rachel told me about the quote in a pretty hostile text before the article was published. In it she let the name of the intern slip. As it turns out, that person was let go not long after the article ran."

Mason shrugged his shoulders. "If Mrs. Campbell agreed to print an apology, I'd work with her again. Unfortunately, *As the Belle Told* isn't known for such practices. They run fewer than five retractions a year, which is why I haven't broached the subject yet. I don't like burning bridges if I can help it, even with editors who can't take no for an answer."

His answer revived the hope within her. If she played her cards right, there was a chance she could still get her dream and clear Mason's name in the process. She'd make it a stipulation of the contract and get Mason the retraction he deserved.

The only downside was keeping it from Mason while she worked out the kinks. He'd been burned by Mrs. Campbell before. If—and when—he found out Lily Anne had accepted the assignment behind his back, he'd be upset, to say the least. But when he saw that retraction, he'd understand. Mason knew better than anyone how much Lily Anne longed to have a shot at real journalism, not just life-hacks and copy editing. He would never ask her to turn it down. At least, she hoped not.

A chime between them sounded, bringing Lily Anne back to the table where Mason glared at his phone screen.

"Lily Anne, I don't know what you said to Mrs. Campbell, but you must've made quite the impression on her. She wants your email."

"You can give it to her. I mean, if you don't mind. Maybe she can help with wedding planning?"

Mason's brow furrowed. "Maybe. But after everything I told you, are you sure that's a good idea?"

"Yeah, I'm sure. I'll be careful, Mase." Feeling his need for reassurance, Lily Anne leaned in and pecked his cheek. She hated keeping the whole truth from him, but it would only be for a short while. "She knows people who can get things done on short notice and with our time crunch, I might need her contacts."

"Okay, Chief. I hope you know what you're getting yourself into."

"Me, too."

Chapter Seven

The phone in Mason's hand dinged, interrupting the banter between Mikie and Chase as the two of them hunted through the inn's hall closet looking for a deck of cards. In theory, merging family game night and date night seemed to be a stroke of genius. Doing so would give Lily Anne a chance to get to know everyone better and see Mason in an intimate setting. However, with his brother and nephew arguing behind him, reality did not live up to the ideal in his mind. More than ready for an excuse to sneak away from the madness, Mason hit the lock button to reveal the new message.

I'M HERE.

Mason's pulse jumped. OK. BE RIGHT THERE.

Not waiting for Lily Anne to reply, Mason set out to meet her at the end of the sidewalk, wiping his palms down his jeans as he walked to the front door. Sweaty palms were not on the agenda. For good measure, he tucked both hands into his pockets as he started down the steps. With two left to clear, the door behind him shut again.

Chase caught up with him as Mason's boot touched the concrete walkway in front of The B&B Inn. "Hey, Uncle Mason! Can I come, too?" A gust of wind kicked up, whirling light snow all around them.

"I'll be right back. I'm just walking Lily Anne from her car to the inn. I have to be a gentleman or Ma will skin me." Mason gave a quick look-see over his shoulder. He caught Chase mid-pout and changed his answer. "If you hurry, you can come. Lil's got to be freezing by now."

Mason popped the collar of his coat, the white flakes standing out against the black leather. Then he flipped the hood on Chase's coat and zipped it all the way up despite his nephew's protests.

"Uncle Mason, I play ball outside every morning before the bus runs. I'm used to this. And Lily Anne? She's still in her car. See?" Chase proudly pointed to the back of Lily Anne's vehicle where exhaust rolled out of the muffler.

"Get a move on, anyway." Mason ran his knuckles over the top of the boy's head in noogie fashion, realizing immediately he didn't have to reach as far down as he did the last time he was home. Mikie warned him the boys were growing fast, but hearing and seeing it were two different things. Thirteen years old and Mason had missed most of it. Not wanting to think about all the time he could never get back, he focused on the moment.

"So, I told Ma to open the dark room for you whenever you want."

Chase stopped suddenly mouth agape. "For real?"

"For real." Mason nodded once and then motioned for Chase to keep walking.

"Yes!" After a high jump and fist pump, Chase started walk again. "Thanks, Uncle Mason. You sure you don't care?"

"Not at all. Why would I?"

Chase made a you-really-asking-that kind of face before answering. "Because it's like your secret headquarters or something. You should show it to Lily Anne tonight. I bet it's a great make-out spot." His nephew elbowed him sharply and grinned, clearly proud of himself for sounding like one of the guys.

"Don't even think about it, Chase. I can't believe I have to say this, but under no circumstances are you allowed to bring a member of the opposite sex into my dark room. The last thing I need is for your father to think I gave you the idea for a date den." Mason sped up his steps.

"Date den?" Chase doubled over, laughing hysterically. "That's funny, Uncle Mason, and a great idea. Too bad I'm only allowed on group dates to the movies with one of the moms in the row directly behind us. They won't even let us sneak in candy. Kissing? Forget that!"

"Good, some things are worth waiting for. High-school stuff, college stuff, marriage stuff."

"Marriage stuff?" The sweet voice that was beginning to narrate his dreams chimed in as Lily Anne appeared in front of him.

Mason ignored the question and tugged her close, intending to get a side hug, but Lily Anne surprised him by wrapping one arm around his waist. With a nuzzle, she settled in beneath his arm and started walking. It surprised him, but he was never one to look a gift horse in the mouth. Besides, she smelled too good to let her go, like peach cobbler bubbling in the oven on a crisp fall day. Never had a woman smelled so sweet, and the longer he held her, the closer his pulse ticked to broil.

"Hi, Lily Anne. We were *just* talking about you. Weren't we, Uncle Mason?"

Mason snorted. "Were we? Because I thought we were talking about the dark room. Maybe you weren't paying attention."

Chase knocked the hood off his head so Mason could see the mile-wide smirk he shamelessly directed toward them. "Yes, I was. I heard every word you said about the dark room and making out and marriage stuff being worth the wait."

Mason had to give it to the kid. Chase was good at being bad. In fact, if he wasn't the one being teased, he'd have applauded the boy for his efforts, probably egged him on. Instead, Mason was about two seconds away from shaking the silly right out of him.

"He's right, it is worth the wait," said Lily Anne, smiling sweetly.

Mason expected her to avert her gaze like the other day in the bakery when the topic of "marriage stuff" came up, but she met his eyes instead. Warmth filled him as her stare spoke to his heart, making a promise that they would figure out the marriage stuff together.

"Chase! Get in here and help me set up the card table," Mikie yelled from the front door of the inn. "Same goes for you lovebirds, too."

Mason removed his arm from around Lily Anne's shoulders and motioned for her to lead the way. She obliged, skipping up the inn's front steps with Mason on her heels. Side-by-side, they slid into the living room where the coffee table had been pushed against the back wall. A plastic table stood in its stead with three fold-out chairs tucked to one side and the couch under the other. Chase sat in a seat at the end nearest the dining room, Mikie in the chair on the opposite end, and Ma in between them, leaving the sofa available for the two of them. Mason sat down on the sofa corner and patted the middle cushion beside him.

His mother spoke first. "It's so good to see, Lily Anne. How are you?"

"You, too, Mrs. Montgomery. Between the paper and the shop, I'm worn out." Lily Anne smoothed down the front of her skirt. Then, she folded her hands in her lap and crossed her legs at the ankles.

"I'd say. And now with the wedding on top of that! I don't know how you're doing it all." With talk of the wedding, Ma lit up like a lighthouse. Her excitement would have been cute if it didn't make him blush.

Lily Anne glanced at Mason. "Well, we've not done too much planning yet, except for picking out the rings." Her voice, shy but sure, surprised Mason, but when her warm palm snuck over his, a feather would have knocked him over.

"Don't worry a thing about it." His mother sliced the air in front of her with a chopping motion. "It'll all come together, wait and see. There's plenty of time to get the church and pick out the cake and write the vows and plan the reception and—and—Shew, listen to me ramble. I'm sorry. I know I'm talking your ears off, but I ain't seen you or Danny Jo in forever. I need to get to the shop more often. Our guests would go nuts over those cherry cheese Danishes."

Mikie chuckled. "If they didn't, you would, Ma."

"Yeah, and what's your point?" With a mock scowl, Ma crossed her arms over her chest.

"Nothing," said Mikie. "Just calling them like I see them."

"Well, stop calling and start shuffling, Michael Montgomery. You're the dealer this hand."

"Ha, ha!" Chase teased, giving Mason a high-five.

Mikie gave Mason a death stare as he dealt but remained quiet. Apparently, Lily Anne's presence brought out the polite side of his brother. Scooping up the cards, Mason smoothed his expression. His nonexistent card-playing skills required a strong poker face.

Ignoring her children's antics, Mrs. Montgomery turned to Lily Anne. "Is Mark excited about the engagement?"

Mason's eyes immediately connected with Lily Anne's. The usual almond shape elongated as the lids widened. The copper light dulled while she shrank further into herself and away from the table, away from the cards, and away from him. Lily Anne never talked about her dad. He knew from chitchat around town that Danny Jo and Mark had divorced years ago, before his family had moved to Pine Valley, but that was the extent of his knowledge.

The tip of her tongue darted out to moisten parted lips and she swallowed, seemingly stalling the answer. She'd start counting soon, he knew, from sneaking peeks when she wasn't looking in high school. He wasn't sure what had prompted her anxiety late senior year, but he'd noticed the change.

Her breathing increased, making the rise and fall of her chest quicken, while Mason searched for the words to say to bring her back to him. She was spiraling. A few more seconds and she'd be so far down the rabbit hole he'd never reach her. He had to act fast, but while he thought through his options the room filled with a high pitch buzz followed by a quick pop of electricity. Then, darkness.

Lily Anne gasped and grew still beside him while whoever was to their left pushed out from the card table. *Was that Mikie? Or Ma?* Didn't really matter. It was a body, one ready to take control of the situation. With the sudden hush of the room, Mason noted a scratching sound and howling at the window.

"Guess that snowstorm decided to blow in after all," Mason said. "It probably weighed down a power line or something."

"It must've come down in a hurry. It was barely flurrying when we came in." Lily Anne's voice was soft and had the room not been so quiet, her words would have been indiscernible. A light on the backside of the parlor flickered, and then another on the opposite side, and another, until a candle stood in each corner of the room.

When his mother had finished, she slid back into her seat. In the dancing candlelight, Mason noticed the silver shining in her hair. *When did that get there? Must be new.*

Oblivious to his stare, his mother smiled. "That enough light, ya think? There's a box of emergency candles in storage, but I have no idea where your father put them."

"He probably doesn't either, Ma." Mikie chimed in. "Well, guess that's it for the night. Thanks for dinner." Mikie bent down and dropped a kiss to her cheek. Chase did the same.

She wrenched in her seat to look at them. "Y'all ain't leaving, are you? What about the game?"

"Another time, Ma. I'm hoping the power outage is isolated, but if it's not, I'd say Mary Ellen's about to have a cow. You know she hates the dark and Caden is probably having a field day with her."

"That boy! He's getting as bad as Chase. Always pranking and scaring and being ornery. I do believe your boys have Mason beat."

Mikie and Mason both frowned at their mother.

"Until they outgrow it. This one was a lost cause." Mikie jabbed a thumb in his brother's direction. "But I have hope for his protegés."

Their mother laughed lightly, glancing from Mikie to Mason and back again. "Leave them alone, Mikie. Nothing wrong with having a little fun."

"Sure, Ma. Whatever you say." Mikie patted her back softly and walked to the door.

"See you after school, Mimi." Chase hugged her shoulders again and followed Mikie into the darkness. As the pair left, his mother rubbed her eyes and yawned, looking ready for a long winter's nap.

Mason stood, took her hand, and pulled her up to a standing position. "Head on upstairs, Ma. I'll let Dad in when he makes it home."

"Bless you, child! That warm bed is calling my name, especially now that there's nothing to do but sleep." Her eyes crinkled in the corners as she laughed, deepening the creases the years had made.

"Hop to it, then."

With slow, measured movements, she hugged Mason. Then, Lily Anne, squeezing her tighter than she had him.

"I'm so glad you came tonight, Lil. You be careful going home and don't be a stranger. Anything you need, wedding or otherwise, you holler. Hear me?"

"Yes, ma'am. I will. Goodnight." Lily Anne sat back down and crossed her legs primly at the ankles.

Ma strolled softly to the steps. "G'night, you two."

Mason waved her on, thanking God he was home. He loved his work, but without his family to share it with, he was half a man.

Scooting to the edge of the couch, Lily Anne readied herself to stand. "I guess I better go, too."

"Hey, what happened to our game night?" Mason gently touched her shoulder, hoping to stay her leave.

"Not many games we can play with two players."

"Right." Mason let his hand drop between them on the couch. His date was a bust. It wasn't as bad as the engagement party, but it wasn't like he'd hoped, either. He waited for her goodbye, half deflated, with both hands on his thighs. When she made her move, though, it wasn't to get up. Instead, she scooted a little further on the couch, widening the distance between them, and grabbed the deck.

"Still remember how to play Smack?"

Mason didn't answer the hypothetical question. They both already knew the answer. Instead, he settled back into his spot and let her deal, thinking to himself there was hope for the night yet.

Two games in, that hope dissipated, as the king of diamonds mocked him. The candles flickered from the corner of the living room closest to the window, casting shadows and painting ambient light across the pane. Flurries outside lit up for a split second before the flakes fell back into the darkness and out of sight. The air around them grew colder by the minute.

Mason narrowed his eyes and stared at the stack of cards in his hand, willing an ace to appear. Better yet, a queen or a jack. He flipped the first of three cards over, each an opportunity to match Lily Anne's royalty with one of his own. A nine of diamonds appeared and he groaned. He turned the second of the three cards allotted him. The nine of hearts landed with a soft thud on the center pile. He gave it the stink-eye but before he had a chance to lay down his third and final card, Lily Anne smacked the cushion, covering the pile with her palm.

"Doubles, Mase. The smack gets them."

"Come on, Chief. I still had a card to flip."

Lily Anne's grin grew wider. "Had being the key word in that sentence, past tense. You *had* a flip before the doubles and the smack. Now, you've got none."

Mason set his cards down and crossed his arms in dramatic fashion. No woman should be able to look adorable and evil at the same time, but she pulled off both with her primly crossed legs and candlelit eyes. He'd lost two-thirds of his deck so far, but knowing Lily Anne was right stung worse. Those were the rules and his fiancée, the avid rule-follower, knew them inside and out.

"I sure didn't peg you for a sore loser, Mason. Let me refresh your memory as to how this game works since it looks like you've forgotten."

Instead of goading her, Mason sat there pretending to listen while she rattled off the directions they both knew by heart. In truth, though, she could have been singing the phone book and he still would have found her fascinating. The graceful way she moved her hands, pointing to one card and then another, combined with the melodic tone of her voice hypnotized him, so much so he almost missed when she stopped talking. He would have, if not for the sudden gasp when she turned over a jack of spades.

"Thank you, Lily Anne, for that riveting rule citation." With a simple smile, Mason turned over a card and resumed play.

The silence stretched between them as they played, except for the occasional holler of victory or groan of defeat. With just the two of them, Mason didn't feel the need to

overdramatize every move he made like he did when Mikie was in the room. Running at warp speed got old after a
while. So did chasing the next laugh and pulling the next
prank. But having nothing to contribute to the family and
feeling helpless was more than tiring. It was exhausting to
the point of soul-sucking.

With Lily Anne beside him, though, he could be himself.
Not the jokester or the wise guy that everyone expected.
Not the boy that people refused to forget, but the man he
desired to be.

"So, is Chase as much like you as he seems?"

Mason squeezed the back of his neck and shifted in his
seat, thinking over the question. "Yeah, I guess. Kind of."
He eyed her like she was thin ice and he was an elephant.
Then, he shook his head. "He's more like the me you used
to know."

"Right." With a nod, she gathered the cards she'd won
into her deck. "Because you're not 'that' Mason anymore.
Gotcha." Her fingers made air quotes as she spoke.

With his free hand, he splayed a palm over his chest and
fell back into the couch, slipping into the playful persona he
wore like a shield.

"You wound me, madam."

"Stop it!" Lily Anne rolled her eyes. "You know what I
mean."

"I know I do. I'm still me, but a grown-up version. Mason
2.0, if you will."

"Mason 2.0? Okay, I'll buy that. You're still trouble,
though." Lily Anne glanced at the window. Outside, the
snow continued to fall, harder than when the game had
started. Upon seeing the quarter-sized flakes, her face fell.
"Mason, I've not really driven too much in weather like this.
Mom usually insists we carpool and it's really coming down
out there. I better get h—"

A door slammed, stopping her sentence short. They both jerked toward the sound.

"Mrs. Montgomery? Please tell me you've got a room tonight?"

Mason grabbed a candle and walked toward the entrance, holding Lily Anne's hand tightly as she followed him. When they were close enough to illuminate the foyer, a familiar form leaned against the door facing.

"Clay?" Mason's eyes widened. "What are you doing here?"

"Looking for a room, man. My flight got canceled. You got somewhere I can crash?"

"Yeah, sure. Hang on just a second and I'll get you checked in." Mason dropped Lily Anne's hand and rounded the counter.

Clay handed him a credit card. "Thanks, Mase. I owe you,"

"Put that away. Ma'd kill me if I tried to charge you."

Clay stared at Mason, screaming for him to take the card without so much as opening his mouth. Mason retaliated, silently telling him to put the wallet away and no one would get hurt.

"Well, I'll go and let you take care of him." Lily Anne's small voice broke through, ending their wordless battle as it did.

"Hold up, Chief. The game was getting good."

"I know, but it's bad out there and Mom will worry." Lily Anne flashed a quick smile, but the slack in her shoulders revealed her disappointment.

Clay took a step forward, tossed an arm around Lily Anne, and gave a quick squeeze. "Say, how is Danny Jo these days?"

"She's good. Running around like a chicken with its head cut off most days, but that's nothing new."

Clay inclined his heard toward Lily Anne. "Like mother, like daughter. Well, looks like I'm stuck here at least for a day or two while I rearrange my tickets. Maybe I'll run by Country Confections and pay my respects in the morning."

"That'll tickle her pink." Lily Anne rummaged through her purse and held up her keys, a sure sign there was no changing her mind about leaving. "G'night, Mase. I'll text you when I get home."

"Sounds good, Chief." Mason hugged her tight. Before letting go, he kissed the top of her head like he'd done the night of the engagement. The fruity smell of her hair rose up and Mason inhaled deeply, not wanting to let her go. But he did. "Be safe."

"Yes, sir, sir!" With a two-finger salute, his signature farewell, she left his side and stepped toward Clay. She leaned in for a side hug.

Clay returned the embrace. "If I don't see you again before I head back to Chicago, I'll see you in a few weeks at the wedding. This lug roped me into being a groomsman." Clay clapped Mason's back and grinned, a knowing grin that reminded Mason what a lucky man he was.

"I know." Lily Anne smiled. "I approved the choice. Don't make me regret it."

The three of them laughed as Lily Anne waved and stepped into the night. When Mason turned around, Clay let out a loud whistle. "You got it bad, man."

"That's where you're wrong, Clay." Mason shook his head. "I got it good."

Chapter Eight

A cold gust of wind greeted Lily Anne as she stepped outside the inn. She hunched her shoulders but the chill of the night air ran deep, settling around her snug as a scarf. As she shuffled down the sidewalk, she surveyed the roads. The blacktop was covered with a thin layer of white, but didn't seem to be frozen underneath. She'd make it home easily.

Though she wouldn't admit it out loud, she had her dad to thank for that. A frown formed at the errant thought and the faded memories it conjured. Her and Dad in a beat-up Mustang in the school parking lot. She was still years away from testing for her permit, but he insisted she learn the basics. Together, the two of them did laps, practiced backing up, and attempted to parallel park, until she got too close to the baseball coach's pick-up that one time. Neither of them told her mother about the lessons. The secret time they spent together was sacred and the most fun she had all middle school.

Snow pelted Lily Anne's head as she tried to get a hold of herself, rubbing her arms over her coat while she walked to her parking spot. When the action did nothing to calm her, she hugged her stomach as a shiver ran through her. Despite the freezing temperature, the tremor had nothing to do with the big wet flakes kissing her face and everything to do with the loneliness and anger that clung to her father's memory like a glove.

Bitter tears pricked her eyes as she unlocked the car door. *Not gonna cry, not gonna cry.* No matter her protests, a drop rolled down, catching on her lip. She licked it away, focusing on the salty taste rather than her disposition.

Get it together, girl. He's not worth it.

Lily Anne scolded herself for caring. She should be past the hurt and disappointment already. The fact that she wasn't burned her to the ground. She didn't need to waste another second thinking about the man who shared her last name, especially not when there was a wedding to plan and an article to write.

Lily Anne started a mental list of things to work on when she got home, ending with an email to Mrs. Campbell. After writing the amendment on her freelance contract and scanning it over to the magazine, she had immediately received a rejection via email. However, the response seemed to be a form rejection rather than a personal message, most likely sent by an assistant or intern. Lily Anne wasn't taking no for answer until she heard it, or read it, directly from Mrs. Campbell herself. Tonight, she'd type up a better memo explaining her case. If that didn't work, she'd simply call Mrs. Campbell and lay it all on the line.

"Lil?"

At the sound of her name, Lily Anne skidded to a stop, finding Logan staring back at her.

"Logan, what are you doing here?"

"A few minutes ago, I was having dinner with friends. Right now,"—Logan paused, snatching the keys from her grasp and closing them up in his fist—"I'm driving you home."

"That's not necessary. I'll be fine."

"Don't doubt that a bit. If I take you home, though, I can sweet talk Danny Jo into letting me stay the night and save myself the cost of a hotel room. Agner Hill just shut down."

"Oh." Lily Anne ceased her efforts to pry open his fingers. "Okay, but only because it works out better for you. What about your car?"

"You get to repay the favor and bring me to pick it up."

"Sure thing, since I open the bakery in the morning. Waking you up at the crack of dawn will be payback for all those hours of beauty sleep you deprived me of when you and your buddies watched night games in my living room in Lexington."

"Yeah, yeah. Just get in, Lil."

Lily Anne hurried over to the passenger side and climbed in. Without even giving the engine time to heat up, Logan turned the windshield wipers on and backed out.

"You surprised me, sis. I wasn't expecting to run into you tonight. Are you chasing down a story?"

Logan adjusted his grip on the steering wheel while Lily Anne contemplated her answer. She'd been waiting for the perfect time to tell Logan about her engagement, but doing it while stuck in a car with him hadn't been what she imagined. Running with the "no time like the present" motto, she inhaled deeply in preparation. Instinctively, she thumbed the back of her engagement ring, working the band up and down the little wiggle room left from the recent sizing.

"Actually, Logan, I was visiting my fiancé, Mason." Lily Anne pulled off the glove and held up her left hand, the pearl shining in the white gold setting as the car went under a streetlamp. Logan tapped the brakes and slowed the car to a stop in the middle of the country two-lane. He seized her hand and pulled it to his face, inspecting the ring like it was a mirage ready to disappear.

"You big goof, let go of me and drive!"

Logan loosened his grip. "I will, just let me get over the heart attack you gave me first."

"Stop being so dramatic." Lily Anne yanked her hand back and pointed to the road. "I'm not saying another word until you start driving."

Scowling, Logan pressed the pedal and the car puttered on. "All right, I'm going. Now, talk."

"Well, it happened at our high-school reunion. Mason made good on a promise that if neither of us were married, we'd tie the knot on Valentine's Day. He proposed in front of everyone and I accepted. It was spontaneous and crazy and not like me at all." Lily Anne rubbed her lips together as a dreamy feeling swept through her. "But I'm happy."

Mason had unexpectedly barged into her life with the grace of a new calf on a frozen pond, knocking her flat on her butt instead of sweeping her off her feet. He was the last man she'd pictured being with. Yet, in the short time they'd been a couple, he'd solidified himself as the someday she never let herself dream of. *Until now.*

Logan checked the mirror, looking back toward the inn. "Wow. Okay. Mason? He was the guy I met at the bakery, right?"

"Yup, that's him." Lily Anne tugged her other glove off by the fingers and twisted her hands. Having something to hold on to while her insides fell apart helped, not much, but hopefully enough to get her through explaining Mason's identity to her well-meaning, albeit overprotective, brother.

"And you two were already engaged, then?"

Lily Anne slowly nodded. "Yes, we were."

"So why didn't you tell me?"

"I w-wanted to, but I needed to make sure it was safe first." Half expecting Logan to stop in the middle of the road again, Lily Anne scooted to the edge of her seat and angled herself toward him.

"Safe?" Logan shot a sideways glance in her direction, but kept driving. "Lily Anne Dawson, what's going on? Did he hurt you? Because if he di—"

"He didn't," Lily Anne wrung her hands harder. "At least not since he proposed. Do you remember that time I broke my nose?"

"Yeah?"

"Mason was the one I thought planned the prank that caused me to fall, the guy I told you about when it first happened. Mason Montgomery. That's why his name sounded so familiar to you and why I waited to tell you about us."

Logan gripped the steering wheel tighter and snapped his mouth shut. His eyes were narrowed on the road, but Lily Anne squirmed as if he were staring at her. After several excruciating seconds of silence, laughter, loud and exuberant, bounced from one side of the cab to the other.

"Oh, Lil, that's rich." Logan slapped his knee like he was in a comedy club instead of driving on snowy roads. "You, what? Thought I was going throw down right then and there?"

Lily Anne gasped and pointed to the wheel. "Well, yeah. You did try to hunt him down after I told you my suspicions. What was I supposed to think?"

"Relax, sis. Not my first time on snow." Logan made a show of putting his hands back. "You're unbelievable. I mean, sure, I was a hothead back in the day, but I'm not going to beat your fiancé up for being a stupid teenage boy."

"You're not?" Feeling a little like a fool and a lot on the defense, Lily Anne jerked her gloves back on and folded her arms across her chest. It wasn't that funny, nor was it illogical, based on past experiences.

"No. Not in a million years. Well, maybe if he broke your nose on purpose, I might. But I wouldn't go after him for no reason. The guy looks like he can take me. Besides, I might be switching jobs and losing insurance, so getting in a fight with your fiancé isn't a smart move."

"Stop it, Logan." If the two of them were anywhere other than a slushy country backroad, Lily Anne would have smacked him on the shoulder, but as flakes the size of nickels fell around them, she merely pointed instead.

Logan slowed the car to a stop as the light switched from yellow to red. "Okay, okay." Beneath the streetlight, his green eyes brightened as he turned to face her full on. When Lily Anne met his gaze, she expected more laughter. Instead, Logan took her hand and squeezed lightly. "All jokes aside, I know better than anyone how dumb young guys can be and how much damage their idiocy can cause. I was just like Mason at that age, but I grew up and I'm betting he has, too."

A sudden green flash lit up the cab and Lily Anne turned her face toward the road. *Perfect timing.* Talking about Mason was new and discussing him with Logan, even newer. The dark made it easier. "He has. Mason is nothing like the boy I remember. He's so much sweeter now."

"That's good, but you guys are just getting reaquainted. Are you sure you're ready to get married?"

Knowing she wasn't entirely sure, she answered Logan as honestly as possible.

"As sure as I can be without walking the aisle. I think marriage is one of those things a person can grasp conceptually but never be fully prepared for, like a tattoo. You know what to expect when you sit down in the chair, but no amount of research can ready you for the physical pain of the needles. Likewise, no matter how many times you stare at the design, you can't fully comprehend its beauty until it's part of you forever. That's when it takes your breath away." Lily Anne was sure that marriage to Mason would do exactly that—leave her breathless.

"In that case, I'll skip the sage advice and go straight to the congratulations." Logan released her hand, patting it a few times before letting it go. "Now, when did you say the wedding is?"

"Valentine's Day."

"I'll clear my calendar."

"I appreciate that." Lily Anne took a deep breath and rushed on before she changed her mind. "Especially since I want you to walk me down the aisle."

Logan's mouth opened obscenely wide, but he closed it quickly and covered the reaction with a smile. Slowly, he pulled in the driveway, put the car in park, and angled himself in the seat, making him eye to eye with her. His face reflected a humble air she didn't know he was capable of and the tiniest hint of pity she wished wasn't directed at her.

"Are you sure you don't want to at least talk to your dad first?"

"No, you've cared for me more than my dad ever did. I know Dad's different with you and your mom. I'm glad he is, but I'm his daughter in name only."

Logan gripped her headrest. "Does Mark even know about the wedding?"

"Not at the moment, and I'd appreciate it if you kept this between us. I'm gonna tell him, but not yet."

"I won't say anything." Logan paused, lifting his index finger between them. "*If* you promise to invite him."

"I promise. It's not like he'll make time to come, but sure." Lily Anne battled the urge to cross her fingers and nullify the words. She didn't, but she wanted to.

"Thank you." Leaning further over the console, Logan laid a hand on her shoulder. "Lil, you know I love you. If you're sure about this, it'll be my honor to give you away."

As the snow continued to fall outside around them, Lily Anne blinked back the unshed tears dying to slip past her lash line. Her father might have abandoned her, but Logan's words proved the existence of good men. Men that stick around when they're free to walk. Men that show up when they're expected to bow out. Men that go the extra mile instead of skipping town.

Men that love unconditionally, not from a place of duty or responsibility, but from choice.

Unable to hold back, Lily Anne gave her brother a tight hug. "Thank you."

Logan simply nodded in response and looked straight ahead at the house while the car grew cold. Apparently, he thought the conversation was over. *Oh, but no.* She still needed to introduce everyone.

"So, now that I'm sure you're not going to beat up my fiancé, I want to get everyone together. I don't think he even knows who you are. You had me so rattled the other day when the two of you met, I didn't even think to explain. Can we all do dinner instead of that lunch you promised?"

Twirling the car keys around his finger, Logan smiled. "Of course. Text me a day and time that works and I'll be there."

"M'kay. Will do. And, Logan?"

"Yeah?"

"Thanks for not freaking out."

Another nod was all she got, but that was enough.

Lily Anne opened her door, glancing back when her feet hit the pavement. "Come on, I'll let you in. Mom is probably already asleep and if the power is out here like it was at the inn, you'll need some candles or a flashlight."

With nearly frozen fingers, Lily Anne unlocked the front door as quietly as she could and the two of them stepped inside. She toed off her shoes, kicked them beside the mat, and flipped the switch on the wall, just in case the electricity was still working. Light flooded the room and she breathed out a sigh of relief.

"Lily Anne? Is that you?"

"Yeah, it's me, Mom." Lily Anne cringed, wishing with all her might she'd have let Logan fend for himself instead of walking him in. Since crashing her engagement party, her mother had not stopped talking about the wedding. More specifically, about calling the ceremony off.

"Is that Mason with you? Because I've got something to talk to you two about."

"No." Lily Anne sighed. "It's Logan. He got stranded for the night, so he's hoping you'll take pity on him and offer him a room."

"Yeah, Danny Jo. What she said." Logan laughed and strolled over to the couch where he proceeded to pull Danny up from her seat and into a hug.

"Hello, darlin' dear. How are you?" Danny Jo wrapped her arms around Logan, finishing the embrace with a prodigal-son-like fervor.

"I'm good. How are you?"

Danny Jo held her hand in front of her, making a see-saw motion. "So-so. I'll be better once I talk some sense into that daughter of mine. Do you know she's engaged?"

"Just found out tonight, ma'am. It seems like she's thought it all out, though. I approve."

"You're madder than she is." Danny Jo jerked a thumb toward Lily Anne. "But the guest room is still yours."

"Thank you." Logan yawned and stretched. "I'm going to turn in. You two have fun, now. G'night."

Her mother smiled. "Goodnight. Sleep tight."

"Don't let the bedbugs bite." Lily Anne interrupted, finishing the phrase while Logan walked off. In a few quick motions, she yanked off her socks and dropped on the couch, tucking her legs underneath her, the way she did when she was little and waiting for a bedtime story.

Danny Jo sighed as she took the seat beside her. "Lily Anne, I know you're tired of hearing my two cents' worth about your wedding, but we need to talk."

"Mom, we've gone over everything. There's not much left to talk about. Mason proposed. I accepted. End of story."

Danny Jo blinked a few times and reached for Lily Anne, sandwiching her newly bejeweled hand between both of hers. Like always, her mother's hands were warm and soft to the touch, despite the worn skin that had weathered more and more the last few years. "What are you thinking, darlin'? Really thinking?"

"I'm thinking there's a man willing to spend his life with me and let me spend mine with him, and that chance doesn't come along too often. Did you know that even with divorce rates dropping, a little over one in three couples will eventually call it quits? Those aren't great odds, Mom." Lily Anne knew her words were as far from sonnets and love stories as Pluto was the sun, but that didn't make them any less true. Dealing in facts was safer than emotions that changed like the weather.

Danny Jo stared at her as if she'd lost her mind. "Hun, I don't want to hear statistics. This is when I want you to tell me he looks at you like you hung the moon and that you got so tongue-tied when he dropped to a knee, you nodded to answer. I want you to say if you searched the world a hundred times over, you'd never find another man to make you feel the way he does. Can you say that? Anything even close?"

"No, Mom, I can't." Lily Anne locked eyes with her mother, willing her to see the truth behind them. "But that's not what I'm looking for in a relationship, either."

"What are you looking for exactly?"

"A kind heart. A shoulder to lean on. A family man who stays." Lily Anne pulled her hand from her mother's grasp and grabbed a throw pillow, squeezing it tight. "I don't need a fairytale, Mom. Mason checks the boxes that are important to me. With him, I have a chance for a happy life, and that's enough for me."

"That's good, sweetheart. So, how about you walk down the aisle when that chance changes to certainty. No need to rush it, baby."

"No. I gave him my word we'd marry this Valentine's Day and that's what I plan to do."

Lily Anne knew she owed her mother a better explanation, but the real reason was hard to face. Dr. Branham's suspicions were educated guesses that were sure to make her worry. She didn't want to share anything before having her bloodwork done, and the ultrasound, if necessary. Before, there'd been no rush to get the tests done, seeing as how she wasn't romantically involved, but now that she was with Mason, maybe calling for an earlier appointment might not be a bad idea. The results determined the fate of his future family, too. That is, if he still wanted to marry her once he knew about her potential infertility.

Danny Jo sighed, shifting on the couch. "Postponing the wedding isn't saying goodbye. It's giving you both time to make sure this is what you want."

"You mean it gives Mason time to change his mind. Mom, not all men are looking for a reason to tuck tail and run." Lily Anne covered her mouth, shocked by the low blow she'd thrown. Danny Jo flinched but remained quiet. When Lily Anne tried to back pedal, her mother shook her head.

"Baby, I know you think you've got it all figured out, but don't make assumptions. Just because your father and I didn't work out doesn't mean the same thing will happen to you."

"There's no guarantee that it won't. At least I know I can trust Mason. That's more than most couples start out with."

"You're right, but there's so much more to marriage than that. Are you sure it's enough?"

"Yes, Mom, I am." Lily Anne smiled, hoping to appease her mother. When Danny Jo smiled back, she knew she hit the mark.

"If it's good enough for you, it's good enough for me." With that, her mother strolled into the kitchen. Lily Anne followed close behind, amazed she'd let the subject drop so easily. "But I'm not sure Pastor Clemens will be so easy to convince."

"Pastor Clemens?"

Danny Jo didn't elaborate. Instead, she opened a top cabinet door and scanned inside a moment before shutting it quietly. Then, she moved on to the bottom one, directly under the sink, and huffed, not bothering to shut the door back. Placing her hands on her hips, she glanced around the room.

"Aha." Danny Jo snatched what looked to be a pocket planner from off the kitchen table and handed it to Lily Anne. "You need to look through that. All the dates are circled for you."

"Dates?" Lily Anne flipped through the book, finding red circles strewn all over the first few pages. "For what?"

"The couples counseling I signed you up for. You're not the only one who does research. Therapy during the engagement substantially increases the chance for a successful marriage." With that, her mother smiled sweetly and returned to the sink.

Lily Anne blinked back the red blurring her vision. Armed with a colorful array of responses, she took aim at her mother and opened her mouth, ready to fire. But she took too long. Danny Jo beat her to it with an ear-splitting scream.

Within seconds, she recognized there were no actual words coming out of her mother, but unintelligible noises laden with fear. Showing more athleticism than ever before in her in entire life, Lily Anne ran to her mother's side, where she was backed against the dining room wall. Somewhere behind them a door shut.

"Do I need to call the poli—Oh, boy. Is that what I think it is?" Logan pointed as a small gray creature, about the size of a Pomeranian, with a white face, rat-like tail, and narrow snout, padded out from under the sink in front of them.

"Mom?" Lily Anne whispered, terrified if she spoke too loudly the animal might pounce on them. "Is that an opossum?"

"Yup." Danny Jo nodded. "First time I've seen one this close. Looks like a baby."

Logan crossed his arms over his chest and stared at the animal, wide-eyed. "How do we get it to leave?"

Danny Jo pointed to the living room. "Hand me that umbrella over there by the front door. I'm going to swing it a few times, maybe jab its leg. My daddy always said if you scare 'em a little, they'll pretend to be dead. The poor thing should go limp. Then, I'll scoop it up with a snow shovel and throw it outside."

"Maybe we should call an exterminator," Lily Anne said, offering a final out to everyone in clawing and biting distance as Logan gave her mother the umbrella.

Danny Jo shook her head. "At this time of night? No one will be on call. This is our best shot. Now, are you two gonna help me or what?"

Logan stood up straighter and rubbed his hands together. "What do you want me to do?"

"Open the door for me when I say to." As Logan nodded, her mother turned to her. "Lil, while I'm scaring the poor thing, grab the snow shovel on the back of the door that leads into the garage and hand it to me."

Blowing out a breath, Lily Anne bobbed her head up and down. "O-o-kay."

"On the count of three, I'm gonna fake my attack. Logan, you open the door. Lily Anne, you sneak and grab the shovel." Danny Jo stretched her neck from side to side as she repeated her instructions. "Got it?"

"Got it." Lily Anne and Logan answered in unison.

Her mother nodded. "Okay. Here goes. One. Two. Three!"

All at once, the three of them swung into action. Danny Jo barreled toward the baby opossum, swinging the umbrella wildly. Logan opened the front door, just in case the varmint made it that far. With bare feet and hurried steps, Lily Anne raced around the table and toward the garage door. She had it cracked, her hand still around the knob, when Logan yelled her name.

"Lily Anne, watch out. It's coming straight for you."

"What?" Lily Anne snapped her head in her mother's direction. "I thought it was supposed to play dead."

Her mom shrugged, still swinging the umbrella in wide-sweeping strokes. "Me, too. But I don't think it's old enough to know that yet. Get out of the way."

Danny Jo lunged to push her out of the path of the hissing opossum, but little paws scurried right across the top of Lily Anne's feet before she could, slicing the skin wide open. She shrieked and jumped, startling the creature. In a panic, the animal quickly snapped its mouth shut. Sharp teeth clamped down around her pinky toe before the opossum juked and leaped, clearing the open door and scampering into the garage. Blood trickled atop her foot and dripped off her toe as Lily Anne hobbled back around the table.

Lily Anne sucked in a breath as Logan handed her a wad of paper towels and helped her to the couch. "Ouch. Oooh. That hurt."

In seconds, her mother was by her side. Gently, Danny Jo inspected the wound. When her fingers landed too close for comfort to a scratch, Lily Anne flinched. She tried to cover the wince with a fake cough, but her mom caught the action.

With measured movements, Danny Jo eased her foot to the floor. "Do you think you need stitches?"

"Probably not." Lily Anne took a second look at the scratch and changed her mind, realizing it was longer and deeper than she first thought. "Maybe."

Danny Jo pointed at Logan and jerked her head toward the hallway. "Can you grab the butterfly bandages from the medicine cabinet in the bathroom?"

"On it."

As soon as Logan was out of sight, her mother wrapped her in a hug. "Lily Anne, I'm so sorry."

"It's not your fault." Lily Anne smiled as she lifted her shoulder in a half-shrug. "Besides, it's just a flesh wound."

Her smile turned to a grin as her mother pulled her hand away in mock disgust at the awful Monty Python rendition.

It had been Lily Anne's favorite movie growing up, much to her mother's dismay.

Danny Jo continued to stare at Lily Anne's foot. "Still, I want you to see Doc Kendrick in the morning and let him take a look at you, in case you need a rabies shot."

Rabies? Lily Anne quickly decided to trust her mother's judgment.

"Okay, Mom. If it'll make you feel better, I'll go."

Her mother smiled in that all-taken-care of way of hers, making Lily Anne equal parts grateful and annoyed. She'd been raised by a strong woman. A strong, stubborn woman that didn't take no for an answer or accept any excuses. She was smart, too, and probably right about the opossum.

Hopefully, she'd be right about the counseling.

Chapter Nine

Mason chuckled as he reread the bizarre string of text messages staring back at him.

SORRY IT TOOK ME SO LONG TO TEXT, BUT I'M HOME.

WELL, LET ME REPHRASE THAT, I WAS HOME. BUT THERE WAS AN OPOSSUM UNDER THE SINK. I'M STAYING THE NIGHT WITH EMMA LOU. I HAVE TO GO TO THE CLINIC IN THE MORNING FOR A POSSIBLE RABIES SHOT, BUT IF YOU CAN MEET ME AT THE CHURCH AROUND NOON, I'LL EXPLAIN EVERYTHING.

After agreeing to her request he'd studied the conversation numerous times, but no matter how many times he tried to fill in the blanks, he had no clue what went down after Lily Anne left the inn. Seemed like she had quite the story to tell, though, and he could hardly wait. So much so, that he found himself itching to call her while he walked the short distance from the inn to the church.

Fortunately, the beauty of the morning took his mind off the mystery and planted his thoughts firmly on the serenity of the landscape. On either side of him, snow glistened in the morning light. The sun was bright as a new bulb in a white washroom but the strength behind it was too weak to warm water, let alone the frozen ground crunching under his feet. A good snowfall didn't come often in eastern Kentucky, but when it did, the town transitioned from pretty to breathtaking. Trees of all shapes and sizes littered the hillside behind the inn, beads of water dripping from bare branches or evergreen needles as the flakes melted. A burst of wind shifted his feet into high gear and tickled his nose with the smell of pine and wet soil.

Mason wished he had his camera. He ran through a list of potential publishers and magazines in his head. Breaking into the industry had been tough, but with each shot, he'd earned their trust. Now, a contract came without so much as a glimpse at the composite. Sighing, he shook off the artist's urge and focused on getting to the church on time with his game face on.

As Mason's feet hit the parking lot pavement, he smiled, spying a familiar baby-blue four-door. Lily Anne sat inside. A leatherbound book rested lightly on the steering wheel in front of her while she chewed on her pen. The sight took him back. How many times had Mason walked to the gym, only to find her scribbling feverishly in the driver's seat? Too many times to count. Back then, he seized the opportunity to scare her each time she ventured too deep into her world of words. Yanking the door open on her, pounding on the glass, or diving into the back seat with a shout. Now, he simply smiled and tapped lightly on the window.

Despite his gentle knock, Lily Anne jerked. Wide eyes shone like new pennies back at him through the window. In a handful of seconds, her shoulders relaxed as she shot him a shy smile. Mason waved and then held the door open for her.

"Good morning, Chief." Mason chirped louder than he'd intended, putting the cardinals still flitting to shame. His voice hadn't sounded that high since puberty.

Lily Anne stepped away from the door. "Morning. Thanks for meeting me here."

For a breath, he thought about a kiss on the cheek, but Lily Anne had other ideas. With a brief nod, she started up the walkway, leaving Mason still in his tracks. A few quick strides later, he was walking beside her.

"Anything for you, Lil, and my curiosity. I'm dying to know why we're here and how an opossum got into your apartment. Spill." Mason rubbed his hands together in front of him, preparing for the juicy story.

"The opossum was under the sink at my mom's house. When we tried to get it out, the crazy animal ran into the garage below my apartment, but not before slicing my foot open and sinking its teeth into me."

"What? Are you okay?" Mason slowed his pace, noticing for the first time the slight limp in her gait.

"Yes, but it was deeper than I thought. Dr. Kendrick put in a few stitches this morning and gave me my first rabies shot as a precaution, and to make my mom happy. Apparently, I have to have three more to finish out the schedule. Did you know it's extremely rare to get rabies from an opossum? They have a lower body temperature or something that makes it difficult for the virus to live."

"No, I didn't know that." Mason fought the urge to shake his head at the fun fact. *How was she so calm?* "I'm so sorry you had to find out the hard way. Is there anything I can do to help?"

"Not unless you can catch the rodent in my apartment. Actually, it's not inside my apartment yet, that I know of, but I'm sure that weaselly little thing can find its way in."

Mason scrunched up his nose and shook his head. "I didn't major in wildlife, so best leave that to the professionals."

"Yeah, that's what I said, too." Lily Anne slowed as she tucked a stray curl behind her ear. "Mom's calling around today to get someone to come out. I'm just going to stay with Emma until the thing is caught."

"That makes sense. So, that answers the opossum conundrum, but why are we at the church?"

"The church is my mom's idea."

With that, she stopped and hung her head, drilling holes into the pavement with her stare. Mason knew nerves got the best of her, but he wasn't having it, not when hours ago her laugh lit up his living room to the point of blinding, despite the power outage. Gently, he took her hand in his before he spoke.

"Danny Jo?" Mason laced their fingers together and she finally raised her chin. Dark circles shadowed her bloodshot eyes. Apparently, she hadn't slept nearly as well as he had.

Lily Anne darted her eyes back to the ground. "Mom thinks we should go to marriage counseling."

Mason expected her to laugh and yell "gotcha" at him, but she didn't. Her face was devoid of all humor when her head popped back up, leaving little doubt to her seriousness.

"Marriage counseling?" Mason managed to parrot back around the lump growing in his throat.

Lily Anne nodded slowly, as if doing the action at half speed might make the words sink in better. "Apparently, our marriage is worrisome for her and an hour a week with Pastor Clemens will ease her troubled mind. She sprung the sessions on me last night between lecturing me about our engagement and finding the opossum under the sink."

"You guys were arguing about me?" Mason had known Danny Jo since he'd moved to Pine Valley in middle school. She'd been a warm hug in the form of sugary dough during that transition into his teen years. Contrary to popular belief, guys eat their feelings, too, and Mason did so at Country Confections with a donut or two dozen.

"N-no, not arguing, per se. We were voicing our opinions. She likes you, Mason, but she thinks we're rushing things."

"Right." With his free hand, Mason kneaded the back of his neck. "I guess her finding out about the engagement like she did made it worse, huh?"

"Maybe. She didn't say, just gave me a planner marked up in red ink with the dates we're supposed to be here. I'm so sorry about this." Lily Anne eyed him through her thick lashes like Ol' Yeller had died a second time, and the mounting frustration inside him crumbled.

"Nothing to be sorry about, Lil. It'll be fun." Mason dropped Lily Anne's hand and charged up the church steps, bent on showing her just how fun counseling could be. *Fake it 'til you make it. Right, Lord?* "If therapy proves to your mom"— *and you* —"how serious I am about us, then bring it on."

The words were no sooner out of his mouth than the door to the church opened from the other side. Mason and Lily Anne stood still on the landing, deer-in-headlights style, until Pastor Clemens greeted them.

"Mason! Lily Anne! How nice to see y'all. I hear congratulations are in order." The gray-haired man of God stood before them in a royal blue dress shirt *sans* tie, charcoal dress pants, and a pair of black suspenders attached—his trademark accessory. A wide smile split his face, brightening the dark brown eyes that sat beneath bushy brows. He looked every bit the part of country preacher. More importantly, he acted the part, not just in the church house, but wherever he went. Among the sermons etched in Mason's memory, more than a few belonged to Pastor Clemens, and Mason knew he was a better man for them.

"Thank you, sir." Mason stood straighter as he spoke. Being in the presence of a preacher had that effect on him, always had from the time he was old enough to understand what being behind the pulpit meant.

"Certainly. Now, let's get you two out of the cold and into the hot seat." Pastor Clemens patted Mason on the back the way he did every Sunday, but this time it made Mason's heart race. From the looks of it, he wasn't alone. Lily Anne's breathing shallowed at an alarming rate, making Mason inwardly groan. *Fun.* Yeah, nothing about this was fun so far and they weren't even in the office yet.

Pastor laughed as he motioned for them to follow him. "Y'all, come on. I'm kidding."

Lily Anne intertwined her fingers with Mason's. The simple gesture squashed his anxiety and made him stand taller than when Pastor Clemens had greeted them. Putting on his bravest face, Mason winked at Lily Anne before tugging her down the hallway behind Pastor Clemens.

"Sit down and make yourself at home."

Music filled Mason's ears as the door to Pastor Clemens's office opened. To his surprise, it wasn't hymnals or worship songs like he expected. Not country or bluegrass, either, but definitely loud and old, maybe the Eighties?

"Let's get down to it, shall we?"

Lily Anne leaned back in the chair and crossed her legs at the ankles. "S-sure."

"Mason, you ready?" Pastor Clemens asked.

Mason nodded, unable to speak. The old man surveyed the two of them, top to bottom, like he had an eagle-eye view even though they were all seated level. Mason wasn't sure what he was looking for, but he must have found it because the gentleman tilted his head ever so slightly, crossed his arms over his chest, and smirked knowingly in his direction. Mason shifted in his seat but didn't look away. If Pastor was skeptical of Mason's intentions, he needed to change his mind and shrinking beneath his stare was no way to do that.

"Okay. We'll start in the garden of Eden. You probably know the story, but humor me. When God saw His creations, he said it all was good, except for the loneliness of Adam. That displeased Him, so He put the man to sleep and formed woman using Adam's rib. Eve was made to be a helpmate. Lily Anne, when you and Mason marry, that will be your role. Is that something you're comfortable with?"

"Y-yes, I believe so." Lily Anne covered Mason's hand with her own as she spoke, a welcome surprise. She was full of those around him and Mason loved knowing he was the reason.

Pastor leaned across the desk. "Mason, that goes both ways. Are you comfortable serving Lily Anne as her help-mate?" His smile flashed friendly, but his eyes remained wary, the same expression Lily Anne sported the night of the reunion.

The preacher's disbelief cut deep. *Lord, does no one see me?*

Mason squeezed his neck, took a breath, and turned to Lily Anne. To anyone but Pastor Clemens, the shift might have come across rude, but there was a shadow of a smile on the old man's face. Convincing the preacher of his sincerity was important, but not nearly as pivotal as convincing Lily Anne.

Mason placed his other hand atop hers. "Absolutely."

The simple word filled the space between them, clear and unwavering, chasing away the shyness from Lily Anne's gaze. With even breaths, she stared harder than before. Mason did the same, opening himself up to her like a book waiting to be browsed. Ever the avid reader, her eyes never moved from his until Pastor Clemens started speaking. Mason missed the heat from her gaze immediately.

"Good to hear it. It's my understanding this engagement happened rather suddenly after a large time apart. With that in mind, today's goal is to get you two better acquaint-ed and—oh, I love this song, especially when it's unexpect-edly used as an intro. The game I've got for you today is called Two Out of Three. Paul wasn't kidding when he wrote all things work for God's glory, huh? Even Meatloaf." Pastor snickered and shook his head, clearly amused with the way things were playing out. "Here's how it works. You each are going to make three statements. Two will be true and one will be a lie, and your partner will have to guess which is what."

"That sounds simple enough." Lily Anne chimed in, angling her body more toward Mason's chair. He expected her to pull her hand free, but she tightened her grip. Mason pressed his lips together to keep from grinning.

The pastor, however, smiled wide as he wagged a finger at them. "Don't think I'm going easy on you today. I want you both to really open up, start a conversation that will last a lifetime." Without warning, the preacher planted both hands on his desk and pushed to his feet. "I'm gonna step out and give y'all some privacy. Get in as many rounds as you can and be ready to tell me all about them next time."

Pastor Clemens ambled to the door, catching Mason's eye before he left. A silent discussion ensued. The preacher telling Mason to step up his game, Mason promising he had it under control, preacher saying he'd better. Then, he was gone and Mason was alone with Lily Anne, music still ripping through the room.

"I'll go first." Lily Anne took Mason's other hand. At her touch, Mason's pulse picked up. He was beginning to expect the Churchill Downs racing rhythm whenever he was in her presence, but had yet to find a way to stifle the reaction. Seeing how it had been going on for over a decade, he didn't think he could.

"Okay," said Lily Anne. "Number one: I have a t-shirt addiction. Number two: Skipping backward is my hidden talent. Number three: I am allergic to fish."

Mason wriggled a hand free and stroked his chin, pretending to think long and hard about the statements. He knew the answer, but acting as though he didn't gave him longer to look at her. Though Lily Anne had always been pretty with her baby-doll wide eyes, slightly crooked nose, and pale pink lips, sitting across from Mason as his future wife, she stole his breath. Her copper eyes shone bright and the longer he stared at them, the deeper the color grew. Flecks of amber burned around the pupil and the outer rim, mimicking the heat expanding in Mason's chest. Afraid the impulse to kiss her might take over any minute, he clucked his tongue a few times to anchor himself firmly in Pastor Clemens's office instead of his romantic fantasies.

"Easy, Chief. You're lying about the fish."

"Oh, yeah? How do you know that?"

"Because you cooked last summer at the annual fish fry. I was home for the weekend and I distinctly remember you sneaking a few samples. I'm sure it was for quality control, right?" Mason leaned his head in her direction and watched a pretty pink color her cheeks.

Lily Anne rolled her eyes but kept smiling. "That's precisely what I was doing. Besides, don't you know it's impolite to comment on a lady's eating habits?"

Mason shrugged innocently. "I'll try to mind my manners from here on out. Your turn. Two truths and a lie? Okay. Here goes. I burn any bread I put in the oven. I'm a mama's boy. And I spoke with a realtor today."

Mason watched closely for any sign of anxiety at his confession. This might have been a game, but it was more than that, too. It was an opportunity to gauge her reactions about a topic he desperately wanted to tackle but hadn't found the gumption to yet.

"Y-y-you burn bread?" Lily Anne stammered. "Guess I know to keep you out of the kitchen, then."

"Nope, that's the lie, Lil. Ma prefers my garlic bread to hers any day of the week."

Pulling back, Lily Anne released Mason and folded her hands in her lap. "Oh."

"And I'll be Ma's baby and proud of it until the day I die." Mason wiped his hands down his jeans and rushed on while he still had the nerve. "Here's the thing. There's a house on the outskirts of town I'd love to look at with you. You remember Ol' M—I mean, Mr. Rowe, don't you? From Forget Me Not Photography?"

"It's been years since I spoke with him, but, I remember him. I hated to hear about his mother's passing back in the summer. How's he holding up?"

"He'd doing good, as far as I know. It's actually his mother's place I wanted to go check out. If we like it, I thought we might have dinner with him some evening, too, to discuss things. How does that sound?"

Lily Anne pressed her hands tighter together. "A little out of my comfort zone, if I'm being honest. I don't know the Rowe family well, and I'm not the most graceful in intimate settings with strangers."

Mason faked a cough to cover his jaw drop. Lily Anne—private, reserved, bashful—had opened up to him about her anxiety, willingly, for the first time since he'd known her. Mason wanted to shout hallelujah at the gift she had given him, but he settled for an unspoken prayer of thanks to keep from scaring her.

"Thank you for telling me that, Lil. Would it be easier if it was a quick lunch at the inn instead?"

She nodded. "I think so. But can we keep the meeting on the quiet side? I don't want to get anyone's hopes up about the house until we know for sure."

Translation: I don't want to let them down if you change your mind.

Mason cringed as her unspoken fear gutted him. How could she still think he'd leave her hanging? After his very public proposal? After signing her formal proposal? He thought they were past that, but her reaction said otherwise. No matter. Mason was a man worth counting on and he aimed to prove it, to Lily Anne, to his brother, and to Ol' Man Rowe.

"Sure. That'll probably be better anyway, since I want to talk business with him. He's looking to sell his studio."

Lily Anne sat up straighter. "And you want to buy it?"

Mason tried to keep calm, but the thoughts of moving his career back home made him giddy. A smile broke free. "More than just about anything. We've had one meeting already, but Mr. Rowe wasn't convinced I was right for the job. I'm hoping to change his mind."

"Well, I'll try not to hurt your chances, but I make no promises." Lily Anne averted her eyes. "I'm a bit awkward."

Mason brushed two fingers beneath her chin and raised her head. Her fallen face reeked of sadness, so deep he had to fight the urge to wrap both arms around her. Since he couldn't, he did the next best thing and threw the attention back on himself.

"So what? I'm loud and obnoxious. It doesn't make me a lost cause. It makes me human. And, you, Lily Anne Dawson, are a beautiful human, inside and out, an asset not a liability. Having you by my side makes me look better, not worse."

Unable to keep from touching her, Mason pressed a kiss to her forehead and took a good long look at the woman he wanted to keep for a lifetime. Her eyes were shiny with unshed tears and her breath had gone shallow, but Lily Anne was still the most gorgeous, creative, capable creature he'd ever seen. *Lord, how can she not see the person you made her to be? Help me show her what I see.*

She opened her mouth to argue, but Mason pushed a finger to her lips. "Case closed, Chief. You're up again. Give me your best two-out-of-three."

"Okay." Lily Anne took in a deep breath. "I cried when the Chicago Cubs won the World Series. The beach is my favorite vacation. I need to have kids as soon as possible if I want to be a mom. Even then, I might not be able to."

Mason swallowed down a gasp. "You've always hated the beach, Lil. You skipped the senior trip, remember?"

"I do, but I wasn't sure you did." She hugged herself as she spoke, shaking a strand of silky blond hair loose from her bun. Mason pushed the stray curl away from her cheek softly and rested his hand on her knee, willing himself to remain facing forward instead of bowing his head beneath the weight of her truth.

"Lily Anne, is that why you want to get married?"

"Yes. No. Maybe. Look, Mason, I wasn't trying to trick you. The doctor ordered some tests the week of the reunion and then you showed up on one knee like my knight in shining armor with a pop-bottle ring. So, I took it as sign, an answer to a prayer I hadn't said yet. But I can't let you go through with the wedding without knowing all the facts."

"What are we up against?" Out of her line of sight, he flexed his fingers on his free hand to keep from reaching out, knowing the touch would be seen as pity, and pity was the last thing she needed.

"My, uh, *irregularity*. Dr. Branham thinks it could be hypothalamic dysfunction, but we're not sure yet. She mentioned the possibility of an ultrasound to get a good look at my ovaries and fallopian tubes to be on the safe side, but she wants the bloodwork done first. Which I'm having done two weeks before the wedding. All signs indicate that ovulation is happening, just maybe not as often as in a healthy female reproduction system. Pregnancy is still possible, but the older I get, the lower my chances become." Lily Anne laid her hands on her lap, looking more vulnerable, and more beautiful, than he'd ever seen her.

Mason scooted his chair closer to hers and wrapped an arm around her. "Listen, Lily Anne. You, me, and God got this. You said yourself a family isn't impossible. Maybe a little harder, but doable. We'll figure that out when the time comes, okay?"

She bit her trembling lip as her eyes filled with tears. "O-okay."

Mason reached out and rubbed her cheek just as the first drop fell. Gently, he swiped it away. "It truly is okay. I appreciate you telling me, but kids or no kids, we're a team now. Let's go one last round. Want to?"

She wiped another tear away and tried to smile. "Sure, why not?"

"Okay. No laughing!" Mason wagged a finger at her. "Promise?"

Lily Anne bobbed her head in agreement. His girl was so brave and now he needed to be brave, too.

After a long exhale, Mason pushed on. "Here goes. I can't drive a stick shift. Anything wool gives me hives. And I've had a crush on you since the tenth grade."

"Stop it, Mason." Lily Anne playfully smacked his forearm. "It's supposed to be two truths and one lie. Not the other way around."

"I know and I'm playing by the rules. Scout's honor."

"That can't be. Your Ford Ranger was manual. I remember because you said all the start and stall of the homecoming parade would kill the transmission. So, we rode your bike instead."

"Yup." Mason confirmed she had the facts right, but Lily Anne's pinched brows and tight lips told him she didn't follow. He rephrased the answer. "You're right about the stick shift. And wool? I'm really allergic." He nodded again to drive the truth home.

Lily Anne's eyes widened. "But that makes the crush true." Her hands flew over her mouth as she shook her head and mumbled, "No."

"Yes."

"W-w-why didn't you say anything?" Her copper eyes swept across him, turning his cheeks hot under her intense perusal.

"I think your reaction now answers that, doesn't it?" Mason crossed his arms over his chest, trying to protect his fragile heart until she blushed.

Lily Anne eyed him like hot chocolate in the middle of winter. "Is that why you made the pact? Why you proposed?"

Mason wanted to answer honestly, but didn't know how. While his longtime feelings for Lily Anne were a huge factor in the equation, the straw that broke the camel's back had been Ol' Man Rowe's laundry list for a successor. But telling Lily Anne that made him look every bit like the impulsive boy she'd known in high school. Ratting himself out? No, thank you. But lying? That was a no-go, too. So, he did what he was best at—laughed it off.

"Why else would I propose?" Without missing a beat, he threw up his hands and flashed his best what-do-you-think smile. Sensing she needed more, he dropped the act and brought out the big guns, the truth, minus the business end of things.

"Chief, listen. I want to be the man beside you, for better or worse, through failure and success, joy and sorrow. I get that you're not there yet. Heck, I've got a decade head-start in this relationship. But if that's not what you want *ever*, I'll step back and root for you in secret like I've done all these years. I can live with being your closet cheerleader. I can handle being your *someday*. But I can't be your safety net, Lily Anne. I won't let fear walk you down the aisle, not even if it's me waiting at the altar."

Lily Anne sat stunned. Mason wasn't sure how to handle her silence, so he pecked her cheek and laced his fingers with hers, hoping that might bring her out of her stupor.

She blinked and dropped her eyes to their joined hands. Softly, she wiggled her fingertips and relaxed as an alarm went off on her phone. "W-w-well, looks like we made it through our first session."

With that, Lily Anne let his hand go and headed for the door. Mason was at her heels in no time at all. Like always.

Before leaving the office, she glanced over her shoulder and smiled. "You know, Mason, fear is powerful, but so is hope."

"Indeed, it is." He nudged her into the hallway, ignoring the knot of guilt forming in his gut.

Mason tried to map an escape route from the corner he'd backed himself into. There was no doubt he cared more about his fiancée than about the business that pushed them together, but knowing that and proving it to her was entirely different. He'd tell her about Mr. Rowe's original rejection when the time was right, after his last name was tied to Forget Me Not Photography and Lily Anne was no longer a Dawson.

As usual, Lily Anne sped ahead, making it out the front door before Mason could even blink. How she managed to walk so fast with those short legs, he'd never know. *She's probably halfway through the parking lot by now.* Imagining her speed walk, he chuckled and paused on the landing for a moment. When Mason looked down, however, he was shocked by what he saw. Lily Anne stood at the bottom of the steps. He watched her carefully to see if she adjusted her sweater or checked her phone or wrangled a stray curl, but she didn't. Instead, she looked back and motioned for him to join her with a big wave of her hand.

Jogging down the steps, Mason felt less like a puppy and more like a partner. *Finally, Lord.* He held onto that feeling as the two of them walked back through the parking lot, focusing on it instead of the question settling in the back of his mind.

Did Lily Anne really see him? As the man that adored her?

As a husband to love?

Chapter Ten

Lily Anne surveyed the kitchen in the back of The B&B Inn, amazed by what she found. The space rivaled that of the bakery with the dual ovens set in the wall, a walk-in cooler the size of a small office, and the industrial stovetop boasting eight burners. Stainless-steel appliances shone under the lights like mint nickels in the sun. Along the back wall, a nice three-tub sink sat ready and waiting while a small, seemingly forgotten, low-end dishwasher hid away, tucked beneath a countertop in an alcove off to the right side.

At the creak of a door behind her, Lily Anne turned around. Mrs. Montgomery strolled in, wearing a black-and-white checkerboard apron and a welcoming smile. Grateful for the company, she went back to the dining room to meet her soon-to-be mother-in-law with a hug.

"Hey Mrs. M." Lily Anne counted to three, the appropriate amount of time for a friendly embrace in her mind, then slipped free, assuming her previous position. She studied the various vegetables spread across a cutting board before plucking a potato and positioning it for a rough chop.

"Are you sure you don't mind me doing this? I know cooking with the dishwasher is a little unconventional."

"Not at all, but I do think you're off your rocker."

Lily Anne held up her pointer and thumb, leaving a small space between them. "Maybe a little. But it's a neat trick, especially for those stretching every second they can. Cooking with the dishwasher is convenient because you can set it and leave it. While the meal is 'cooking' you can do whatever you need to. Plus, it's nutritional and delicious!"

Mrs. Montogmery raised her eyebrows. "I'll take your word for it, darlin'."

"I've never tried it before, but I've read a lot about it. You just put your veggies and meat in one jar, your dessert in another, place them on the top rack, and turn the dishwasher on. After it cycles, the meal is ready. I figured the readers would get a kick out of it, you know?"

"I'm sure they'll think it's something." Mrs. Montgomery eyed the mason jars suspiciously for a few seconds before a giggle escaped her. Lily Anne joined in, laughing until she snorted, which only made both women laugh harder.

When Mrs. Montgomery had caught her breath, she untied her apron and hung it up. "Is Mason joining you?"

"Yes, he'll be here after he wraps up his nature shoot for GeoWorld." Lily Anne couldn't keep from smiling at the mention of her fiancé's name. The man was growing on her, like kudzu up a mountainside. With every glance, soft-spoken word, or sweet touch, another sprig shot up around her heart. Soon, it'd be entirely covered.

"I forgot he was taking those today. Well, I'll get out of your hair and leave you to it. Y'all have fun tonight." Mrs. Montgomery swung the dishtowel at her elbow before returning it to the rack and heading for the door. A snap of her fingers later and she was looking back at Lily Anne. "Oh! I spoke with Danny Jo earlier. The exterminators have a trap set for that overgrown rat but said it might take a while to catch the little rascal. Are you staying with her until then?"

"Nope. No way. Her house and my apartment are connected by the attic. The whole property is compromised and I'm not taking a chance on waking up with that, that *thing* beside me in bed." Lily Anne cringed at the imagined visual.

Mrs. Montgomery knocked her knuckles against the door facing. "Where are you staying, then?"

"On Emma Lou's couch." Lily Anne paused as Mrs. Montgomery pursed her lips. "Don't do that! It's more comfortable than it sounds."

With a shake of her head, Mrs. Montgomery planted her hands on her hips. "Nonsense. You'll stay here until the beast is caught."

"T-t-that's so sweet, but n-n-not necessary. I'm fine where I'm at."

"I'm sure the couch is great." Mrs. Montgomery walked back over, placing a hand on Lily Anne's shoulder. "But you and Mason are engaged, sweetheart. I insist you stay here."

Lily Anne nodded, unable to sneak a word past the emotions clogging her throat. She was quickly realizing that in saying yes to Mason, she'd gained a whole new family. That realization both thrilled and humbled her.

"Glad that's settled. I'm going to sort a little laundry while you cook." With that, Mrs. Montgomery excused herself, leaving Lily Anne alone with her work.

Refocusing her attention to the dinner prep, she grabbed another potato from the pile and went back to chopping. The clock ticked in the corner, reminding her she was running out of time to get the dinner going. Mason would be home soon.

Picking up the pace, Lily Anne slid the boneless chicken strips into the remaining mason jars, setting them to the side with the potatoes. A quick rinse and slice job later, two more sealed containers stood full of strawberries sprinkled with cinnamon and drizzled with honey, a substitute for the suggested maple syrup. After shaking to perfection, she scooted them to rest with the other prepared glassware. She left them there while she went to inspect the dishwasher.

Lily Anne yanked the dishwasher door down. Everything seemed to be in order, but worry ricocheted inside her head. *How sanitary is this dishwasher? When was the last time it was cleaned? How often is it recommended for a wash cycle?* It hadn't occurred to her to check. Besides, even if it had, she'd have never worked up the nerve to ask Mrs. Montgomery about the maintenance schedule or cleanliness of her machine.

Though she knew deep down the dishwasher was fine, she needed to make sure. Being a guest in the kitchen, she had no idea where the dish washing packets were, so she did the next best thing. Lily Anne swiped the bottle of dish-washing liquid from the counter, squirted the packet cubby full, and started 'quick wash' to ensure a germ-free cook-ing cycle. As the rushing of water filled her ears, she rolled her shoulders. She'd spent hours scouring the internet for the perfect date-night recipe to share with her devoted life-hackers—and Mason—so the last thing she needed was for the meal to be soiled by leftover gunk in the dishwasher.

"Hey there, Chief."

Lily Anne jumped at the sound of Mason's voice, step-ping onto a rogue potato peel. Her foot slid, propelling her forward, right into Mason. He dropped whatever was in his hands and took her by the waist, steadying her with a strong grasp. The thud from the fallen items filled her ears, and just like the night of the reunion, her head ended up tucked beneath his chin. Not missing a beat, Mason kissed her hair and chuckled lightly. The rich tones and vibrations echoed through her and her belly turned to mush.

"Hey, Mase."

Lily Anne cleared her throat and took a step back. It was then she realized what he'd been carrying when she'd nearly bowled him over. Luggage, a brown leather suitcase cracked from years of use and a make-up bag dotted with sunflowers, about the height of a family-size cereal box and twice as thick. *Her* luggage. Her luggage that had been left with Emma Lou. "How'd you get these? Wait. How'd you *know* to get these?"

Mason held up his phone. "Ma texted me and Emma Lou met me at the community center. Any other questions?"

"Um, no. Thanks for grabbing them for me. You saved me a trip."

"Not a problem, Lil." Mason strolled forward, invading the personal bubble she attempted to always maintain.

Strangely, Lily Anne didn't mind his nearness. Since sharing the doctor's suspicions with Mason at the church, she caught herself replaying their conversation, reliving his reaction, and reveling in the quiet calm he managed to ignite within her. She didn't know what to make of them as a couple, but she looked forward to finding out.

Staying under the same roof would definitely help with that. *Unless he doesn't want you here.* The idea wormed its way under her skin, breaking open old wounds infected by her father's abandonment, until finally she had to ask.

"You don't mind if I stay, do you?" Lily Anne dropped her hands to her side. "If it's any trouble, I know Emma Lou will take me back. If she won't, I bet Eliza Lee would. She's vying to be bridesmaid and letting me crash at her place would certainly seal the deal."

Mason stepped toward her. "Do I mind if my fiancée, who I'm obligated to dine with at least four nights a week—your stipulations not mine—and who I must meet for date night at least once a week—again, not my rules—lives in the same house until the opossum of death is caught? Let me think about it." Mason touched his forefinger to his temple a few times for good measure. "Okay. I thought about it. I guess sharing my space is the first of many sacrifices I'll make for this marriage. It's a burden, but I'll bear it."

With eyes brightening, Mason grinned and leaned in close, so close the warmth from his breath heated her cheek. The warmth mingled with his fresh ocean scent kicked her senses into overdrive. He inched in even further, his lips brushing against the shell of her ear as he whispered, "Gladly."

Lily Anne's eyes went wide. *Why was he bent on embarrassing her?* The better and more puzzling question: *why did she like it so much?* There was no logical explanation and she hated it. Facts made sense. Statistics were responsible. Plans reduced error. Mason? He did none of those things and, yet, she was falling for him. *Oh, Lord. Falling? Help me, sweet Jesus! I don't know how to love someone like that. Please don't let me fail him while I'm figuring it out.* Needing space, Lily Anne scurried away, plucking the stray peeling off the floor as she hurried around to the opposite side of the table. She tossed the potato skin into the garbage bowl Rachael Ray had taught her to keep close by.

"C-c-counseling went well this morning, don't you think?" She drummed her fingertips against her thigh as she spoke, desperate to expel the nervous energy building within her.

Mason's eyes honed in on the action and a slight frown tugged his mouth down. As quick as it appeared, though, it was gone and a bright smile replaced it. "I do. It was nice to get to know one another again."

"It was. You surprised me with how well you handled everything. Very mature." *And sweet, kind, charming.* Lily Anne smiled as she kept the string of adjectives going in her head.

"Slow down there, Chief. You don't have to build up my ego. I already proposed."

"Mason, I mean it." She rolled her eyes. "Anyway, why don't you grab your camera and take a picture of the jars before I stick them in the dishwasher?"

"Okay, okay, taskmaster. If I didn't know better, I'd think you were just using me to better your column. You wouldn't be the first."

"What?" Lily Anne drew in a sharp breath and planted her hand on her chest. Beneath her palm, her heart galloped as she thought of the article for the magazine. She'd been putting off telling Mason about the assignment until Mrs. Campbell agreed to the retraction.

After their last phone conversation, Lily Anne was sure she was close to cracking. Apparently, Mason's whirlwind wedding was highly sought-after gossip, giving Lily Anne nice leverage to barter the retraction. Without an agreement in writing, though, the magazine could back out. No way did she want to get Mason's hopes up, only to let him down. Her father had taught her lasting love wasn't easy and a failure of such magnitude might be the bump in the road that wrecked them as a couple.

Lily Anne picked up a mason jar and twisted the lid. "You really had women fake affection to get ahead at work?"

"Once or twice that I'm sure of. Way more that I can only speculate on. After The *Belle's* feature, it seemed to get worse." Mason ran a hand along his bearded jawline. "Just another reason I keep ignoring Mrs. Campbell's calls. Has she been pestering you, too?"

"Me?" Lily Anne tapped her sternum. "No, not at all. She, uh, actually gave me the name of a consultant for my gown."

"See? That right there proves she's got a good heart." Lifting his chin, Mason's gaze lighted on the stairs. "Be right back. I'm going to take your bags up to your room and grab my camera."

Mason carried the luggage while Lily Anne paced in place. She needed to come clean about the article and her plan for the retraction, but it was still too soon. *A little more time, Lord. Please.* She was still pacing when he made it back.

Situating the strap around his neck, Mason gestured to the dinner prep. "Okay. You point and I'll click."

Lily Anne nodded while she double-checked everything. She pointed at the chicken, the potatoes, and the strawberry dessert. The ingredients were all accounted for. Mason walked around behind her a few times, first left, then right, then back again. Finally satisfied with the angle, the shutter blinked in rapid succession as Mason shot the daylights out of the jars.

"Got 'em. Ready for step two?"

Partially hypnotized from watching Mason work, Lily Anne bobbed her head. Carefully, she gathered the jars in her arms and hugged them close to her. Now that she thought about it, a serving tray would have made transporting everything from the dining room into the kitchen much easier. *Too little, too late.*

She turned the corner to the nook hiding the dishwasher and stopped. Well, she tried to stop, but soap suds covered every inch of the floor and it was impossible. With the jars still pressed against her, Lily Anne worked to keep herself upright by imitating the ice skaters she'd admired all her life. When her foot ran across the air conditioning vent, though, it was game over as her balance bottomed out. With a scream and a wince, she went down, hard.

"Lil? You okay?" Mason's footsteps followed close behind the question.

Lily Anne, still stunned from the impact, turned her head toward the entrance. Brown boot tips came into view, bringing her back to her senses. "Mason, wait. Stay b—"

"Whoooaaaaaaaa!" Mason went flying beside her, hoisting his top-of-the-line camera as high in the air as his arm allowed.

"Back. Stay back." She deadpanned as Mason landed with a thud beside her. He was laughing, still holding his camera high.

Lily Anne shook her head at the sight they must have been and then giggled. Her butt was cold from the bubbles she'd busted, the jars were still clutched to her chest, and there was no way her dishwasher dinner was happening. With that thought, her laughter died mid-snort, and tears sprung in her eyes. *What about the column*? No respectable journalist lets their readers down. The first drop fell. *What about dinner?* Another tear rolled down her cheek. She wiped it away as she sat up, tucking her bent knees beneath her.

"Hey." Mason raised up slowly. With a single glance her way, his laughter screeched to a halt. "What's wrong?"

Lily Anne put the jars she'd been holding on the floor—*no need to worry about food contamination now*—and stood on wobbly knees. She didn't have time to answer him, not with her insides shaking. Closing her eyes, she tried to focus on her breathing. *Deep breath in. Hold. One-Mississippi. Two-Mississippi. Three-Mississippi. And out*. The measured air flow did little to help, but she tried it again. Still nothing. On her third attempt, darkness streaked her vision. She didn't pass out often, but when she did? *Oh, boy!*

Lily Anne bent her knees to minimize the impact, but before she went down, two warm hands wrapped around her. A minute later, those same warm hands caressed her arms, racing up and down the length of them. The friction sent a jolt to her system, forcing her eyes open.

As her vision came into focus, a familiar face surfaced. "Mason?"

"Hey, there, beautiful." Reaching out, Mason brushed a curl away from her cheek. "Glad to see those pretty peepers again. I thought I'd lost you there for a second."

"Y-y-you almost did." Lily Anne took hold of Mason's biceps as she glanced around, gasping when her gaze landed at their feet. "The floor!"

"Shhhh. We'll get it in a minute." Mason took her hands in his and squeezed, his eyes widening as he did. "Lil, you're like ice. Let's get you warmed up."

Mason let her hands go and stepped back to turn off the dishwasher. When the machine had gone silent, he resumed his place beside her and draped an arm around her shoulders. Lily Anne opened her mouth to argue, to assure him she was fine and could clean up the mess, but she didn't have the strength it took to lie. Instead, she leaned into Mason, soaking his warmth up like a sponge. Suds dripped off him, too, but somehow, he radiated heat that seeped deep into her bones. Together, they climbed up the stairs to Mrs. Montgomery's room. Lily Anne half listened as he explained there'd been a mishap with the dinner and asked his mother to order a pizza. She agreed and ran off to call it in.

As Mrs. Montgomery went downstairs, Mason helped Lily Anne to her room. Without a word, he started the shower and adjusted the temperature. When the stream ran strong and hot, he led her to the bathroom with a promise to leave her suitcase by the bed and that he'd lock the door behind him. Lily Anne mustered another nod, the best she could offer. Mason accepted it like a Pulitzer Prize and hugged her tight.

After a quick shower, Lily Anne slipped into her favorite pair of pajamas and headed downstairs, bent on cleaning up the mess she'd made. To her surprise, Mason and Mrs. Montgomery were nowhere to be seen. In their place stood her mother, holding a mop.

"Mom?"

Danny Jo leaned the mop handle against the counter and opened her arms wide. "Hi, baby. C'mere. You look like you could use a hug or two"

"I could."

As Lily Anne stepped in the embrace, her mother ran a hand down her hair, smoothing the wet curls the way she always did after a bad dream. "I had a feeling you needed me."

Lily Anne stiffened. "A feeling? Or a phone call?"

"Both." Her mother released her and began filling up the mop bucket with hot water. "Don't get mad at Mason. He knows I worry about you."

Lily Anne raised an eyebrow. "How does he know that, Mother?" Mason and her mother being cohorts? That was a scary thought.

"Since the engagement, we might chitchat from time to time. Apparently Country Confections has the best breakfast pastries in town. He's probably tickling my ear to win over his almost-mother-in-law, but I do believe that boy could eat his weight in Long Johns. He loves those things."

"He does, doesn't he?" A lazy smile stretched across her face as Lily Anne realized she knew Mason's favorites. Long Johns, Diet Coke, steaming black coffee, canned peas but never fresh, corn on the cob cut onto the plate, fuzzy blankets instead of cotton, polos instead of colla—

"So, are you gonna tell me what happened? Or am I gonna have to pry it out of you?" Her mother's voice interrupted Lily Anne's thoughts as she emptied the contents of the mason jars into the garbage disposal. She knew she could save the food and try again later, but what if suds got in somehow or the meat had spoiled from being left out or the jars had cracked from the fall? No, the best thing to do was admit defeat and scrap the whole thing.

Lily Anne sighed as she grabbed another towel from the linen closet. "I can't write my column this week."

"Okay, and?" Her mother urged her on as she wrung the mop out over the sink. Then, she started another figure-eight on the floor at the end of the room while Lily Anne dried the portion she had already done.

"And I ruined dinner. I've got jars of raw chicken and a floor full of suds instead of the homecooked meal I wanted to wow Mason with. I'm a failure."

Lily Anne dropped her head. Disappointing herself was one thing, but disappointing Mason? Her readers? Nothing made her feel more worthless. She wanted to give them everything she had to offer. If she gave them her best, maybe they'd stick around. Maybe she'd be good enough. Maybe they'd love her. The mentality didn't work on her father, but with Mason she still had a shot.

Her mother pointed at the dishwashing liquid near the sink. "Hush that kind of talk before I wash your mouth out with soap."

Lily Anne rolled her eyes even as her nerves kicked back up. "But it's true. I failed Mason and I failed my readers. I don't even know why I bother. I try so hard, but every day is like ramming my head against a brick wall. I end up with a mess and headache." Lily Anne started rubbing circles to her temples, more preemptively than for show. The pain would come. It always did after one of her episodes.

"Take some medicine then." Her mother slid the mop into a bucket by the door and went to the table. While she rummaged through her purse, Lily Anne continued to dry the last of the tiles. She had just finished when her mother rejoined her, handing her a blue-and-white acetaminophen bottle with a smile.

Less than amused, Lily Anne shook her head and set the bottle on the counter "Thanks, Mom.".

"You're welcome. Baby, when are you gonna realize you don't have to be perfect? Tonight flopped. So what? I guarantee you Mason doesn't care one iota about that chicken you're frettin' about."

"Maybe, but what about the paper?"

"It'll survive. If I know you like I think I do, I bet you'll have a new article idea before morning. You'll do your thing and by the time the paper comes out, tonight will be water under the bridge. Am I right?"

Lily Anne cut a side-eye in her mother's direction. "I might have a few backup ideas I can pull out. But that's not the point."

"What is the point?" Her mother threw up both hands, clearly at a loss to the problem. She didn't get it. How could she, when Lily Anne never showed her the black hole her thoughts spiraled into it?

Lily Anne grasped her fingers and squeezed. *Here goes nothing.* "Maybe I'm not cut out for this. Writing. Being a wife. Marriage."

Lily Anne's mind stuck on the idea of marriage. If she were honest with herself, the conversation from the church had left her rattled. When Mason had warned he couldn't be her safety net, Lily Anne dismissed the idea as an impossibility. But was it?

Her mother held up a hand, dishtowel still in her grasp. "Okay, I'm gonna stop you right there. I don't know a good article from a hole in the ground, but I watch you light up when you pick up a pen. What you lack in talent, *if* you do, you make up for in passion. You're cut out for it, but the timing has to be right. The same is true of marriage. Did I ever tell you why I married your father?"

Lily Anne inclined her head toward her mother. "N-n-no, but I'm going to go out on a limb and say because you loved him."

"I did, but our marriage was pushed along by the accident." Her mother raised her eyes toward the ceiling and drew in a sharp breath.

"The house fire your parents died in?"

"Yes, baby. I was months away from graduating, but I was only seventeen and homeless. Child services had no one local to place me with so they gave Aunt Betsy temporary custody, even though she lived in Ohio. I didn't want to move and your father knew that, so the day after the funeral, he proposed. Aunt Betsy was furious, but I begged and pleaded with her until she signed for me. We got married the same day he proposed. The next day, I moved in with him and his parents. Your father's quick thinking saved me from leaving the only town I ever called home."

Lily Anne balled her fists. "Yeah, and he left you in that same town, too." She wished forgetting her father came as naturally as loving him, but even though years had passed, she still cared. From the look on her mother's face, she did too. That didn't sit well with her. Her father didn't deserve her mom's love. Or hers, for that matter.

Her mother's shoulders sagged. "Darlin', I know you've got issues with your daddy, but, believe it or not, he's a good man. We just rushed and got in over our head. That's why I was so angry at the engagement party and adamant about counseling. I don't want the same thing to happen to you and Mason. Be honest with me and with yourself. If failing wasn't an option, would you still be marrying Mason?"

Lily Anne inhaled deeply, clenching her fists tighter. *Would I be marrying him, Lord?* She racked her brain, but came up empty.

"I don't know. If you'd asked me that the night of the reunion, I would have said no. But he's not at all what I expected, Mom. Mason's dependable and caring and knows how to make me laugh when I want to cry. It's so weird the way he can read me. The fact that he called in reinforcements tonight is pretty impressive."

Her mother laughed lightly as she reached out and tugged on a curl. "You're right about that. Sweetheart, you've got a good head on your shoulders and an even better heart. Maybe it's time you start letting your heart do the thinking for you and give your brain a rest."

"I'll try," said Lily Anne, thinking to herself how much easier that was to say than do.

Her mother nodded, smiling wide. "Good. Now, I'm gonna get out of here before Mason gets home with that pizza."

"Wait." Lily Anne caught her by the arm, stilling her movement. "Before you go, will you help me make some peanut butter no-bake cookies? Mrs. Montgomery told me

I can use whatever I want from the kitchen and I thought I could make some for dessert, as a way of saying thank-you."

For a few long seconds, her mother searched Lily Anne's face. Then, she smiled and set the cleaning supplies away. "I sure will, darlin'. Point me to a saucepan."

Lily Anne held up a finger and went in search for a cooker. While she plundered the cabinets, her mother's question sprang back into her mind. Would she be marrying Mason if she wasn't scared of failing at marriage? At motherhood?

Was Mason a safety net?

Chapter Eleven

"**W**ell, are you up for the job?" Richard brought a coffee cup to his lips while the few stragglers of the committee trickled out of the conference room.

Smiling at the familiar Cut-Through Mining logo on the mug, Mason extended his hand. "Absolutely. It's an honor to do this brochure for you. Thank you for trusting me with it."

Richard accepted, shaking with the enthusiasm of a satisfied customer. "As if we'd want anyone else. You know better than that. The last pictures you took of the horses and trails were extraordinary. I've never seen reclaimed land look so good. No one would believe strip-mining could turn into something so beautiful, but you proved it. I have no doubt you'll do right by our new herd, too."

"Yes, sir. I walked around the barn and stable addition before the meeting to get a feel for the lighting and backdrop. This time of the day will produce some stunning shots."

"That's what I like to hear." Richard took another sip from his cup before pointing at Mason. "Anything new with you?"

"How much time do you have?" Mason made a show of looking at his watch and the two men chuckled. "Hey, Richard, would it be okay to visit the grounds prior to the shoot? Maybe tonight? With a friend?"

"A friend, huh?" Quirking a brow, Richard smacked Mason's back like they were buddies shooting the breeze. In a way, they kind of were.

Mason laughed at his covert tactics and leveled with him. "Actually, with Lily Anne, my fiancée."

"I was wondering when you'd fess up to the engagement. Sure, you can." Setting his coffee cup down, Richard unlocked his phone and tapped on the screen. "I sent security a message, so they won't cart you off in a cop car."

"Thank you, sir. I don't think a jail cell would make for a good date."

"Don't knock it 'til you try it. That's how I met my Lucy." With a sly grin, Richard walked away.

Mason wasted no time as he raced to his car. Tonight was date night and he was pulling out all the stops with a moonlit picnic. Sure, it was going to take some work—heaters, a couple of camp chairs, a few thick blankets—but he had time to get everything in place, if he hurried. His fingers flew as he typed out a to-do list in the notes section of his phone. With so many stops to make, he checked each one off before heading to the next, saving his brother's general store for last. Mikie would probably talk his ear off.

Sure enough, he did, keeping Mason at the register a good twenty minutes after paying for the supplies. While the two of them argued over who needed to pick up Ma's dry cleaning, Pastor Clemens shuffled up to the counter, his arms full of hand-warmers.

"Hey, Mason." Pastor set down the hand-warmers, stretched out his suspenders and smiled. "I'm so glad I ran into you."

"Really?"

"Yup. The heat pump at the church went out yesterday so I'm afraid we won't be able to meet this week for counseling. But, never fear, I've got a backup plan. Here. Take this." Pastor Clemens pulled a folded note from his shirt pocket and handed it to him.

Mason eyed the paper like it was cheese on a mouse trap but finally took it. "What is it?"

"A couple's exercise. You and Lily Anne need to complete the assignment separately and then exchange your response sometime before the wedding."

"Thank you, sir." Mason shoved the assignment into his pocket. "Hope you get the heat fixed soon."

"You and me both. See you next week. You, too, Mikie. Don't think I didn't notice your absence last Sunday."

Mikie nodded a silent apology and turned to face the register. In seconds, his cheeks matched the red fabric of the camping chairs Mason held. While Pastor Clemens explained the importance of church attendance to his brother, Mason snuck out of the store and hightailed it to the picnic site.

When he was happy with the set-up, Mason rushed back to the inn and planted himself on the couch. He wanted to be ready and waiting for Lily Anne before she made her way down. By some miracle, he made it mere minutes before she walked in.

Lily Anne waved a hand up and down in front of her. "Hey, Mason. I got your message. Are these enough layers?"

Mason took her in, starting with the fleece beanie atop her head and moving toward the wide cotton scarf tied at her neck. A mess of curls pulled into two pigtails sprung out from either side of the hat. Beneath the floral print scarf, a thick cableknit sweater the color of a plum peeked out at him. Below its hemline, jeans hugged her legs until about midcalf when black fuzzy boots took over. *Beautiful* didn't touch his girl.

"Yeah, yeah. You should be good, but take your peacoat in case the temperature drops again."

Lily Anne made a beeline for the hall closet. "Okay. Want me to get yours, too?"

"Yes, please." Mason met her at the door and took the coat, draping it over his arm as they left the inn. With Lily

Anne walking her normal breakneck speed beside him, he hurried to the vehicle, tossed the jacket into the backseat, and swung the passenger-side door open.

"You seem jumpy. Are you okay?" Lily Anne slid in the seat and wiggled against the cold leather.

Mason rounded the vehicle and climbed in, wanting to kick himself for not turning on the seat-warmers for her.

"Yeah, fine." As he spoke, Lily Anne bent over to click the safety belt and a burst of peach filled the cab. The aroma lingered so thick and sweet, Mason curled his fingers around the steering wheel to keep from pulling her close and covering her with kisses.

"If you say so." Lily Anne shrugged, clearly unconvinced. "Where are we going tonight?"

Mason volleyed his gaze from the road to her and back again. "You'll see."

"Please, tell me." Lily Anne fluttered her eyelashes his way. "You know I hate surprises."

"Yeah, so you say, but I'm sure you're gonna love this one." Almost sure, or, he had been when he'd thought of the picnic initially. Now that his plan had transitioned from thought to reality though, an inkling of doubt had worked its way through his enthusiasm, making his palms sweaty.

"Yeah, and why's that?"

"Because I know you." Mason smiled through his worries. He knew Lily Anne better than she thought he did. Maybe it was time to lay all his cards on the table and show her the depth of his attentions.

Lily Anne laid her palm on top of Mason's hand that rested on the console. "Oh, do you now?"

"I do." Weaving their fingers together, Mason decided it was time to get real. "Wanna hear how *much* I know you?" Baiting her might blow up in his face, but he needed to show her just how deep his teenage crush ran.

Lily Anne scooted toward him, her thigh hitting the middle console. "Lay it on me, Mase."

Mason parked the jeep on the side of the two-lane backroad they were on and took both her hands in his, swirling small circles on her skin to calm himself as much as to comfort her.

"Well, I know you love the color yellow because it reminds you of smiley-face stickers and sunshine. You think flowers as a gift are a waste of money. Your closet is filled with dresses, but only of the sleeved variety because you don't like showing the birthmark on your right shoulder."

"How did you know th—"

"Shhh." Mason held up a hand and she closed her mouth. "Leggings are a must, but you don't do heels. You're more of a flats and flip-flop kind of girl. Scary movies aren't your thing, but you think the storylines are fascinating. You're a whiz at trivia and the best baker at Country Confections, unless Danny Jo asks. Then it's her, hands down."

That made her giggle, and Mason took the time to sneak in a breath before continuing.

"Buttered toast is your go-to breakfast but sometimes you swap the butter for strawberry jam. Never both, though. You think that's insane. You're a perfectionist with a stubborn streak you prefer to call determination because it's more professional. Your biggest dream in life is to land a national byline. Your favorite animals are horses and you hate opossums. How am I doing so far?"

"W-wrong."

"*Wrong*?" Mason tried not to panic, but his voice still shook. "About what?"

"I-I don't hate opossums. I just don't want to live with one." Lily Anne grinned and Mason closed his eyes, refusing to steal her signature eye roll, even though he wanted to.

"So sorry. My bad." Mason smiled as his gaze met hers. He thought about stopping while he was ahead, but the deep waters that ran inside her soul called to him. Sink or swim, he had to try.

"I know you tap your fingers against your thigh when you get nervous, just like I know you've been battling anxiety for a while now. You hide your panic attacks from everyone because you can't stand the thought of talking about it and you've been using self-help tips and coping mechanisms to get through them. Most days, that's enough. Sometimes, it's not, though." Mason closed his mouth and let the weight of his words sink in. He knew the moment they did.

Lily Anne went stiff in her seat. "You *know*?"

Her head whipped around, and she stared at the window. Seeing her in so much pain gutted Mason, but it was too late to turn back now. Gently, he cupped her jaw, turning her face back to him.

"It's nothing to be ashamed of, Lil. It's o—"

"When did you figure it out?"

Mason squirmed in his seat. "In high school." Praying she left it at that, he tried again. "But that doesn't matter."

"When *exactly*?"

Mason took a breath and cursed his luck. He'd never been on the winning end of a fourth-quarter touchdown before and, from the looks of it, his streak was safe with Lily Anne. *So much for wanting the deep end.* Mason took another gulp of air before he answered her question, sinking further into the muddy water he'd stirred up.

Chapter Twelve

*T*he day we made the pact.

Mason's answer hula-hooped through Lily Anne's mind long after a curt nod prompted him to pull back on the road. It took a few miles for her heart to catch up to her head, but when it did, curiosity got the best of her.

"Is that why y—"

"Why did the t—"

Lily Anne and Mason both spoke at the same time, breaking the silence they'd been resigned to. She smiled shyly at their childish behavior before motioning for him to continue.

"Why did the teddy bear turn down dessert?" Mason tried again, without so much as a breath in her direction.

Lily Anne raised both hands from her lap, palms up. "What?"

"Why did the teddy bear turn down dessert?" He repeated himself, slower and sharper, as if her hearing and not the sudden shift in conversation fueled her confusion. He made no sense, but she decided to play along anyway.

"I don't know. Why?"

"Because he was stuffed." Mason deadpanned and poked her side across the middle console. "Get it?"

Lily Anne shook her head but giggled all the same. "Yeah, I get it."

This man! Exasperating, annoying, and corny beyond belief. If the string of superlatives stopped right there it might be hard to fulfill their agreement, but the more time she spent with him, the more she saw *him*. Lily Anne realized the boy he'd been in high school shrank in the shadow of the layered man he had become. Like scratch art, colors exploded beneath Mason's surface: vibrant, brilliant, captivating colors impossible to unsee. Only a fool would walk away from such splendor, and Lily Anne prided herself on her intelligence.

Mason cocked his head her way. "Your turn. What were you saying?"

"It's, uh, just...Well, what I mean is... Shew, what I wanted to know is if that was why you wrote our agreement. Did you come up with it because of my anxiety? Out of pity?"

"What?" Mason squealed as loud as his brakes. "No, I already confessed my crush, Lil. I just wanted to make you smile. Plus, I thought you might finally see my feelings for you."

"I think I was too freaked out that day to know my own name, let alone pick up on your secret flirting. I'm sorry I was too wrapped up in myself to see it, Mase."

"No worries. You see it now." Mason snatched her hand and kissed it in a single motion. Her skin warmed at the point of contact. "In a few minutes, you'll see our destination, too."

Sure enough, in less than a mile, a familiar landscape revealed their location: Cut-Through Trails. Even with the location revealed, Lily Anne was as lost as ever.

She pointed to the red-and-white reflective rectangle on the side of the road. "I-I don't think we're allowed back here. That sign said, 'no trespassing' and I'm pretty sure us being on this side of the gate makes us delinquents. *Criminals*—as in the orange-jumpsuits-and-handcuffs kind of criminals."

"C'mon, Lil. Live a little." Mason side-eyed her, his grin softening. "Do you trust me, Chief?"

Lily Anne blinked as the question processed. Did she trust him? With this date? With breaking the rules?

With her heart?

Her insides screamed yes. After all, her entire defense against her mother's worries hinged on trust. Heck, her willingness to marry Mason revolved around her trust in him, that he'd be able to look past her anxiety and stick around in spite of her failures. In the dark, Lily Anne nodded.

"Yes, I trust you, Mase. But if we get caught, I'm not only throwing you under the bus and flooring it, but I'll kick it in reverse and gun it a second a time, too."

Mason laughed and killed the ignition. Then, he raised her hand to his lips once more, this time twisting it gently and kissing her wrist. His lips were like a worn blanket left in the sun, warm and comfortable, familiar in the best possible way despite the newness of their relationship.

"Lily Anne, if I get you arrested, I'll lay down willingly." Mason held her hand as he spoke. His gaze remained steady and unwavering, a collage of friendly forest hues blending together, so deep she didn't know if she was sitting still or free falling. Before she lost herself entirely, Mason clicked her seat belt release. "C'mon. Your dinner awaits."

With that, he jumped out of the jeep. Before Lily Anne had time to blink, Mason opened her door.

Lily Anne climbed out. "Thank you, but did you say dinner?"

"Sure did, Chief." Mason looped his arm with hers and jerked his head toward the path. A small metal firepit and two camp chairs stood like a beacon in the night. In between the chairs, a fold-out card table rested, covered by a red-and-white gingham tablecloth with a picnic basket sitting on top. A propane heater blazed adjacent to each chair while a pile of throw blankets sat off to the side. Hidden behind the bedding was a cardboard box full of extra tanks of propane and a bundle of firewood.

Lily Anne gasped. It was a scene ripped straight from the pages of a romance novel, the kind that ended with a couple in love looking forward to forever. In all her twenty-eight years on earth, she'd never seen herself in those kinds of books. With each date Mason planned, though, her belief in happily-ever-after grew.

"Grab a seat, Lil, and I'll get a fire going." Mason released her arm and turned the heater nearest them on high. She sank into the nylon chair and watched as he went to work. A few chunks of wood, a Firestarter, and a click of the lighter sent flames to dancing in the fire pit. While the fire continued to catch, Mason plopped down and began unpacking the basket. He passed a sandwich bag to her, along with a can of ginger ale, a fudge round, and snack-size bag of chips.

"You still like peanut butter and banana sandwiches?" Mason squeezed the back of his neck, offering a shy smile instead of the near-permanent smirk he'd managed to perfect.

"W-with honey?" Lily Anne squeaked out the words, feeling every bit as nervous as Mason looked. How did he know what to pack? Did she forget telling him her favorite food?

Mason smiled, his eyes burning brighter than the fire in front of them. "Is there any other way?"

Lily Anne melted from the warmth of his gaze. So did her nerves, leaving in their place a set of tingles in her belly. "Not in my book." Licking her lips, she lifted her sandwich to her mouth.

Mason stretched his leg and opened his chips. "I was hoping you still loved them as much as you used to. It was all you ever ate in school."

"I was a weirdo. What can I say?" Lily Anne brushed a few crumbs from her lap as she spoke, hating the way the words made her feel but knowing they were true.

With a shake of his head, Mason grabbed a bottle of water from the basket. "No, you just knew what you wanted. With lunch, with school, with life. You had it all together, you know that?"

"Hardly." Lily Anne laughed dryly. "I was so naïve."

Mason pointed the water her way. "Nah, Lil. You were impressive."

At Mason's words, heat unfurled within her chest, sprinting up her neck and peppering her cheeks. She had no idea the former class clown had paid such close attention to a nobody like her.

"Um, no. Far from it. I was a kid who had dreams I liked to call plans. Too bad none of them panned out and I had to run back home to Mom." Lily Anne took another bite, trying to replace the aftertaste of regret, but the sandwich wasn't near sweet enough.

After snagging a few napkins, Mason scooted his chair close. "What made you leave Lex-Post?"

"Downsizing." Lily Anne sighed. "I tried to find another position in the city, but no one even offered me an interview. I guess I wasn't good enough." Refusing to spare anytime for a pity party, Lily Anne opened her chips and rushed on. "No job meant no money for rent, so I came back home. I hadn't been in town but a week when Howard contacted me about copy editing. I've been at *The Vine* ever since. That was six months ago."

"I hate that Lex-Post didn't work out for you, Lil. But I, for one, am happy you're back in Pine Valley." Mason stuck a finger in his chest and chuckled lightly. "And I'm even happier that I'm home, too. God has a way of putting us where we need to be."

Lily Anne chewed his words as she chomped a chip. As happy as she was to be sitting next to Mason under a sky full of stars, the fact she had to come crawling home stung. Could God really take her mistakes and turn them into masterpieces? *Maybe.* She sighed. "I know the Bible says He works all things for our good, so maybe me being here is His way of salvaging the mess I've made of my life. Don't get me wrong, Mason. I trust God's plans for me, but this isn't where I saw myself ending up ten years ago."

"You didn't see yourself back in Pine Valley?" Mason stared at her, deep and long like the other day at the church, his eyes turning to mossy green in the firelight. "Or engaged to me?"

"Both." Lily Anne set the empty baggie on the table, and folded her hands in her lap. Before she had time to work out what she wanted to say, a high-pitched neigh shattered the silence. "D-d-did you hear that?"

"Yup, sure did." Mason stood and looked both ways. "Let's go check it out."

Mason offered his hand and she took it, slowly but with a vice-like grip. He tightened his hold in response as they made their way down the path and through the darkness like a wanna-be-journalist on the heels of an informant. She struggled to keep up and without his direction to watch for a break in the ground here or to take a sharp left there, she'd have face planted numerous times. Mason's steps never faltered, almost like he knew the way.

Mason halted his steps and Lily Anne slammed into him, nearly sending them both toppling. The only thing that kept them upright was his firm footing and Lily Anne wrapping her arms around his chest, a move similar to the Heimlich maneuver but higher on the body. It didn't jar Mason, but succeeded in knocking the breath clean from her lungs.

"Oomph."

"Y'all right there, Chief?" Mason stared back at her from across his shoulder and Lily Anne nodded, taking a deep breath in through her nose and out through her mouth.

Another neigh sounded, but this time no running was necessary. The noise was directly in front of them. Lily Anne dropped her arms from around Mason and peeked around his shoulder. For the second time since they started their date, she gasped, following it with a schoolgirl squeal.

"Hello, there, sweet fella. Aren't you gorgeous?" No longer scared for her life, Lily Anne skipped to the fence a few feet away where a white-and-black speckled foal stuck its snout through the gap. Soft and gentle, she slid the tips of her fingers down its mane as the animal nuzzled in closer.

Mason sidled up beside her and stuck his hands in his pocket. "His name is Cupid."

"That suits him perfectly, with those big black eyelashes he keeps batting at me." Lily Anne rubbed Cupid's neck again and smiled. "Did you know Cupid shot two different kinds of arrows, one of gold and one of lead?"

Mason blinked rapidly at her randomness. "I can't say I did, Lil. Where'd you hear that?"

"Shakespeare. One of the plays from college had a footnote that explained it. While the gold-tipped dart produced romantic feelings, the lead-tipped dart resulted in strong dislike and the desire to run away."

Mason covered her hand with his, helping her pet Cupid. "Which have you been hit by, Lil?" As he spoke, the intoxicating aroma she'd come to associate with him swirled around her, ocean waves on a nighttime breeze. His hand was comforting, warm and a little rough, but not too rough. A man's hand, the kind capable of leading in the dark, like he'd just done. The kind capable of holding her up, wiping away the tears, and joining in prayer, if only given a chance.

"Both." Lily Anne peeked over her shoulder. "I never pictured myself back in Pine Valley and definitely not as your fiancée, but I'm glad I'm here. I think the arrow I was hit with was double-dipped, gold covered in lead. The time we've spent apart has given the outer coat time to dissolve and now the gold's coming through." She shrugged, attempting to skip past her confession, but when Mason's eyes met hers, she knew she didn't have a chance.

Mason reached around with his free hand and cupped her cheek. "Gold, huh? I'm no Olympian, but I'll sure take it if that's what you're handing out."

He caressed her like she was Sunday-after-church fine china and it was his first supper at the table. It was an awkward angle with her looking over her shoulder and him leaning around, but Lily Anne didn't dare move, afraid if she did, her nerves might ruin the moment. Mason slid his hand along her jaw and worked his fingers into the hair at the nape of her neck while at the same time tugging her near him. Hot breath skimmed her cheek as Mason's mouth ventured closer to hers. Overcome with a boldness she'd never experienced before, Lily Anne pushed up on her tiptoes, erasing the space separating them.

Mason might have gasped, or it may have subconsciously come from her as reaction to her newfound courage. Either way, the sound died between them as her lips fused to Mason's in a fairytale kiss she knew she'd relive before falling asleep. The kind of kiss that ran clean down to her toes, an explosive, tingling, you've-got-the-right-stuff kind of kiss that made her dizzy. Mason massaged her scalp gently and when the tip of his tongue begged entrance, she welcomed it, falling deeper still into the moment and the man she never saw coming.

"Break it up, now! Did you two not see the sign? You're not allowed back here."

Lily Anne froze, staring at Mason. She watched with Frisbee-sized eyes as Mason pulled back and dug beneath his collar. Silently, he slipped a thin lanyard up and around his neck. Without breaking their gaze, he handed the badge to the security guard. Lily Anne squinted in the low light, trying—and failing—to make out the ID as it passed by her face. It was too dark. When the man handed the badge back to Mason, she still had no clue what it said.

The officer bounced his stare between them, jabbing his thumbs through his belt loops. "Oh, shoot! Sorry, Mr. Montgomery."

"No problem." Mason stuck out his hand and the security guard graciously shook. "Thanks for asking questions before you carted us off."

The guard jerked his head toward the badge Mason still held. "I'm glad I did. Rich would have killed me. He told us we'd have visitors tonight, but I didn't know you'd be all the way down here."

"We needed to stretch our legs. Right, Lily Anne?" Mason winked as she fought a blush.

Not wanting to be rude, Lily Anne kept her gaze on the officer instead of inspecting the ground for cracks like she wanted. "R-right."

"Well, stay as long as you like. Y'all have fun, okay?" The security guard tipped his hat toward them.

With a two-finger salute, Mason bid the man farewell. "Will do, man. Be careful tonight."

As the security guard went on his way, Lily Anne exhaled loudly, stepped back from Mason and Cupid, and bent at the waist. With frenzied swipes, she pushed her palms up and down her jeans. When they were more dry than wet and her heart rate had leveled to a normal pace again, she raised up to find both of them staring at her.

Mason took a step toward her, watching her like a wounded animal in the woods. "Sorry about that, Chief. I didn't kn—"

"You did so!" Lily Anne wagged a finger at him and advanced until she was directly in front him, pressing her pointer into his chest. "You knew all along we had clearance to be here and instead of sharing that information with me, you let me think we were breaking the law."

Mason opened his mouth but before he could say a word, Lily Anne kissed his cheek. "You're trouble, but the best kind. This is the most fun I've had since I moved back home. Thank you."

Smiling, she grabbed his hand and pulled him ever so slightly back the way they'd come. Mason reciprocated the tug, but in the opposite direction.

"I thought you might wanna hang out here for a bit. Pet Cupid some more, share some coffee, do some star gazing." Mason motioned with an open palm to a grassy area on the other side of the path where two sleeping bags, a couple of thermoses, and a shepherd's hook with an unlit fishing lantern lay in wait.

"You thought of everything." Lily Anne shook her head. "Who knew class clowns could be so considerate?"

Mason shrugged and slipped a hand into his pocket, his cheeks turning a pale pink as he did. "No, Chief. I thought of almost everything. I forgot our assignment from Pastor Clemens."

"How did you get our assignment already? Counseling isn't until tomorrow."

"I ran into him at Mikie's store. The heater's out at the church so we won't be meeting this week. He gave us home-work instead."

"Oh." Lily Anne took the paper and started walking in the direction of the second camp site. "You look at it yet?"

Mason inclined his head to the paper. "Nope, I figured we'd do it together. You do the honors, Chief. Let it rip."

Lily Anne unfolded it and read the directions to her-self quickly. More than satisfied with what she found, she cleared her throat and reread them aloud to Mason.

"Write a letter to your partner reflecting on your rela-tionship thus far. The letters will be exchanged at a later date."

As Lily Anne refolded the paper, Mason laughed out loud. "*Psssht*. That's right up your alley."

"Lucky me." Lily Anne grinned as Mason led her to their stargazing set-up.

As soon as she wiggled her way into the sleeping bag, she rejoined their hands and raised her eyes to the sky. Stars darted in every direction, splattering the sky like white paint against a velvet backdrop. Lily Anne's fingers itched for pen and paper. The picture was perfect inspiration for her letter.

The letter she was certain *As the Belle Told* readers would love.

Chapter Thirteen

I t had been a week since their first kiss and Mason couldn't stop thinking about it. That kiss had knocked his socks off. Sweet but eager, shy but passionate, and well worth the decade-long wait. He was still walking on cloud nine. Well, he would have been if the issue of a wedding venue didn't keep pulling him back down to the earth. Time was running out and he was beginning to get desperate. They all were— him, Lily Anne, his mother. The very same mother currently staring at him.

"You can't have an outdoor wedding." Ma spoke in her most polished listen-to-your-mother voice, each word coming out more stilted than the last. "For one, it's February. For two, it's freezing. For three, I forbid it."

Mason patted her arm as he walked around to the empty chair. "Ah, you can bundle up." A tickle in his throat worked its way into a cough, making him reach for his coffee. He took a big gulp and pointed at the newspaper his father was reading. "Besides, the forecast is predicting a rise in temperatures."

"To what, Mason? The fifties?" His mother shook her head, but her wide eyes never left his face. Mason didn't so much as blink. Even though his love for his mother had grown in spades over the years, his fear of her had done the opposite. Looks that had once leveled him no longer scared him senseless. They did, however, make for a most amusing breakfast at the inn.

Without raising his head from the paper, his father chimed in, answering his mother's question for him. "Low sixties, if we're lucky."

Mason and Ma stared holes in his hair while his dad reached for his mug. He paused, with the coffee halfway to his mouth. "What? That's what the extended forecast says. It might be doable with the right game plan."

Ma crossed her arms over chest. "It's too late for a game plan. The wedding is three weeks away and we don't have a venue or a marriage license. They had to print, 'Text or call for directions' on the invitations, for crying out loud."

Knowing she had a point, Mason frowned. "I know, Ma. But I'm squaring away the wedding license as soon as I leave here. Lily Anne already filled out her part yesterday so I just have to drop in and sign. As for the location, I'm working on it, but it's slim pickings. The community center is booked up and so is the church." With a screech, he pushed away from the table and stood.

His mother joined him, giving him a quick hug. "Awww, sweetie, I'm not trying to discourage you. It'll work out, you'll see." As she pulled away, she ruffled his hair, reminding him of test days growing up. Sure, she pushed him to study hard, but she always soothed him with a touch or a hug when his studying didn't pay off as much as he'd hoped.

Mason let out a deep breath. "Thanks, Ma."

"Just nix the outdoor option, okay?" Ma went up on her tiptoes and pushed a shock of hair away from his forehead.

"I make no promises, except to come back with a marriage license and a decent location, walls withstanding." Mason kissed his mom's cheek and waved at his dad. "I'll see you at dinner."

His father turned the page, lifting his chin toward Mason. "Good luck, son."

"Thanks. I'm gonna need it." Mason nodded and headed out, determined to find a wedding locale come heck or high water.

But, first, he needed to square away the marriage license. Mason hopped in the jeep and drove around town to the county clerk's office, his thoughts straying to his soon-to-be-wife. Lily Anne was a dream come true, the chosen one in his heart's game of duck-duck-goose, the girl he'd compared every woman he'd ever dated to and found them lacking. Knowing the legal permission for their marriage was hours away from being granted was surreal.

With his mind stuck on his fiancée, Mason parked the car and followed the steps into the county clerk's office, whistling an old song about going to the chapel as he did.

The man directly ahead of him in line started to sing along, turning to Mason abruptly. "Are you going to the chapel sometime soon, son?"

Mason chortled at the question, but cleared his throat quickly as he realized the patron in front of him was none other than Mr. Rowe.

Rocking back on his heels, Mason kept his gaze steady as he answered. "Yes, sir, on Valentine's Day, as long as the clerk here grants me the license we need."

"Good to see things are right on schedule for you," said Mr. Rowe. "If you're looking for a photographer, I know a guy that'd be interested." With that, he waved a hand with his suggestion, like it was an afterthought, but his eyes were eager.

"Wow. Thanks, Mr. Rowe." Mason balled his hands into fists as his side. *I forgot the photographer. How?* "I don't want to cause you any trouble, though. Are you sure you're free?"

"I am. I kept hoping you'd holler at me, but since I've been, what's that word the kids nowadays use when someone stops calling or messaging them? Ghosted? Yeah, that's it. Since I've been ghosted, I'm desperate enough to put you on the spot. What do you say?"

"Yes, definitely. I'm so sorry I haven't called before now, about the pictures and that lunch we talked about."

Mr. Rowe dismissed the apology with a wave. "No worries. I'm happy to help with your wedding. It'll be my last hurrah before I hang up the ol' camera for good. That is, as long as I've found the right person to turn the studio over to by then."

"Have you found him yet?" Mason gulped, knowing the answer might be a two-edged sword.

"I think I'm looking at him. I was going to wait until we had that lunch meeting, but I've been watching you since you've been home, and I'm convinced you'll do the studio proud. If you still want it, the business is yours." Mr. Rowe took a step closer, offering his hand.

Mason accepted it and shook wholeheartedly. "Thank you so much, Mr. Rowe. I won't let you dow—"

"Next!" The cashier behind the counter stood up and beckoned the line to move forward.

Mr. Rowe released Mason's hand and took a step forward. "Gotta go, but we'll discuss this more later. Lunch, next Sunday?"

"Sounds great." Squaring his shoulders, Mason stood up straighter. "Thank you, again, Mr. Rowe."

"The pleasure's mine."

With that, Mr. Rowe made his way to the counter, leaving Mason alone to celebrate. All the pieces of his life were falling together. The studio, his family, the wedding. With adrenaline coursing through his veins, Mason held back the urge to jump up and down. Instead, he rolled his shoulders to burn off the excess energy. Mid-roll, the line moved up.

With hurried steps, Mason took his place at the counter. The lady explained the sections, where to sign and date, and what to leave blank. He thanked her and stepped to the side to complete the form. A sudden sneeze caught him off guard. Before he knew it, one sneeze had turned into three, then, four, and the tissue box on the counter sat half empty.

Surprisingly, the allergy attack distracted him from the task at hand. In no time at all, Mason completed the license and was back in the jeep and on the lookout for a venue. He drove straight to Shelby Jane's cabin. As new manager of Happy Harvest Orchard, he hoped she'd be able to help him. In fact, his list of possible locations started and ended with her.

"Please let this work," Mason murmured as he knocked on the door.

As it opened, a smiling Shelby Jane came into view. She propped a hand on her hip and leaned against the door. Her ponytail swished behind her as she moved. "Hey, stranger. What are you doing here?"

"Sorry to show up on your doorstep like this, but I was wondering if the orchard might have a plan in place for winter weddings?"

"Eh, that's a big fat negatory."

Mason felt the color drain from his face as he stood in Shelby Jane's doorway. He'd never believed blood could truly run cold, but the moment convinced him otherwise.

Shelby Jane laid a hand on his shoulder. "Aw, Mase, don't look like that. Come on in and tell me what you had in mind. If we put our heads together, maybe we can figure something out."

Mason obliged, not wanting to be rude, and followed her into the living area. His eyes lingered on the jagged lines of the exposed wood surrounding the room. Family pictures—past and present—hung on the wall on either side of the fireplace. Above the mantel, an antique frame held a landscape view of the orchard. Reds, yellows, and rusted oranges burst from the foliage. Rows of corn stood tall on one side while vines and pumpkins dotted the other. Hay bales lined the rickety fence in front of the well-worn barn. He recognized the framed photo as one he had taken several years back.

Mason lifted a finger to the picture. "Looks good there."

"That's some compliment coming from the photographer himself." Shelby Jane adjusted her hair tie and slid into an armchair. "Now, tell me what you're looking for exactly."

Mason took a seat on the couch across from her, letting his hands hang between his knees. "I'll be real honest, Shelby. I don't have a lot of requirements. Beggars can't be choosers, and I'm nearly at the begging stage."

"I kind of figured that when you asked about outdoor weddings." Shelby Jane chuckled as she folded her hands in her lap. "I wish the orchard was a viable option, but, at the moment, it's not. I'm working on a project to change that, but it's still a long way off. Does the wedding have to be outdoors in the wide open or would you be willing to settle for the woodsy feel in an enclosed area, like a barn capable of powering portable heaters?"

"Either," said Mason. "I'm past the point of being picky." A sneeze surprised him and he covered his mouth.

Shelby handed him a tissue. "Bless you."

"Thanks." Mason worked to hold the next sneeze in. *What is with my allergies?*

Shelby Jane tugged on her ponytail and sighed. "As much as it pains me to say this, you should check out Sun and Fun Farms over in Hickory Hills. They've been around longer than we have and might be able to pull off an event like what you're planning."

Wiping his nose again, Mason nodded. "I don't know if Lily Anne wants to travel that far from home for the wedding, but it's worth a shot, I guess. She left me in charge of the venue and I don't want to let her down." Mason wiped his hands down the thighs of his jeans and pushed off the couch. "If I'm headed to Hickory Hills, I better get a move on. Thanks for your help, Shelby."

"Anytime," she said, joining him where he stood. The two of them walked to the door. "Let me know how it goes." Shelby waved goodbye as Mason jogged back to his vehicle.

"Sure thing," yelled Mason over his shoulder as he pulled the driver's side door open.

After a quick stop for a bathroom break and more coffee, he was on the road again, scowling at himself with every glance in the rearview mirror. Going home with a venue was imperative, partly because of the time crunch, but mostly because he needed to prove himself responsible to Lily Anne. And to Mr. Rowe, his family, and the rest of Pine Valley who pegged him as the class clown of yester years.

Unlike Happy Harvest Orchard, Mason didn't know the owner of Sun & Fun Farms personally. Thankfully, the operation was more structured with an office that stayed open all year round. The place had an online presence, too, with a phone listing and turn-by-turn directions to the Hickory Hills stable. Following them led him straight to the property.

Mason parked and scanned in every direction. The need to freeze the frame consumed him. The landscape stood like a masterpiece incarnate. A light blanket of frost shimmered off the naked trees peppering the surrounding mountains. In the distance, out past the cornfield, fog rose from a pond. Behind the water, rows of evergreens stretched deep into the horizon and when the sun shone just right, shadows breathed through their needles, bringing the scene to life with their movement.

Several shelters scattered across the land, some modern but most aged to perfection. The contrast between them—new and old, smooth and rough, sturdy and shambled—produced a balance even the most detailed and precise staging could never replicate. It was natural with the tiniest hint of cultivation, a blending that made it raw and exquisite by the same token. As a photographer, the scene made his blood pump harder and his heart race.

He'd never forgive himself if he didn't at least try to capture the moment, so he dug out his phone and started snapping. He didn't intend to veer off the walkway, but before he knew it, he stood behind the office, well off the beaten path.

"You're not supposed to be here!" A sprig of a boy yelled out the back door, startling Mason out of his awe-filled stupor. Behind him, a lady yanked on the child's shirt collar.

"Noah, get back inside." She threw a thumb behind her as she spoke.

"But, Mom."

"No buts unless you want yours busted."

"Fine." The boy backed away from the door, but not before giving Mason the evil eye.

The lady turned to Mason with a wry smile. "He's rotten, but he's right. This area is off limits until the season opens up."

"Sorry about that, ma'am. I got lost in the beauty of this place and my camera lured me back here." Mason held up his phone as proof and strolled toward her. "I was hoping to talk to someone about holding a wedding ceremony here."

"That'd be Mr. White." Her eyes softened as she pointed over Mason's shoulder. "Go around front and I'll meet you there."

"Thank you." With a spring in his step, Mason walked back to where he'd wandered from and waited. The door swung wide after a few seconds and the lady from before ushered him through.

She pointed to a seat along the back wall. "Make yourself comfortable and I'll get the manager for you."

Mason lowered himself in an armchair and looked around aimlessly. "Thank you. Take your time."

If he were in Pine Valley, he would've been able to strike up a conversation about work or her parents or the little boy running around. Even with living away from the town for so long, a few days was all it took to catch up on the gossip. In Hickory Hills, that wasn't the case. Mason was essentially a stranger, having met very few residents other than Janice from the jewelry shop where he'd purchased Lily Anne's ring. The lack of familiarity set him on edge.

To settle his mind, he picked up a magazine from the end table and flipped through, stopping on a recipe for cookies-and-cream fudge that made his mouth water. He knew for a fact The B&B Inn had the listed ingredients stocked up, so he took a picture of the page, intent on sweet-talking Ma into making a batch before the night was over. If he came home with a venue, he wouldn't have to beg too hard.

"Hey, there. Sorry to keep you waiti—Mason? What are you doing here?" With a smile, Logan stepped forward, red hair flaming beneath the bright lights of the foyer.

Mason jumped to his feet. "You're Mr. White?"

"To anyone else, sure. To you, we'll stick with Logan."

Mason wasn't sure how it happened but in the blink of an eye, Logan had his arms around him in a bear-hug, clapping his back. "How you been, man?"

"Good, good." Mason stepped back and told himself not to stare but his mind had short-circuited. Logan was the last person he expected to talk wedding plans with. At least he had an in with the farm, now. Or an out, depending on Lily Anne's relationship with the guy. The conversation might be a piece of cake or it might go over like Lily Anne's dishwasher chicken. Hoping for sweet instead of sour, Mason smiled. "Your day going good?"

"Decent. What can I do for you?" Logan sat down and motioned for Mason to do the same.

He did. Leaving a chair in between them. "A friend of mine said you might be able to help me out with a wedding venue. We're needing a place for a ceremony on Valentine's Day. Can you do it?"

Logan shook his head. "Afraid not. I'd love to have you and Lily Anne tie the knot here, but we don't do winter weddings either."

"Don't or can't?" Mason didn't want to be rude by questioning him, but desperate times called for desperate measures, and he was about as desperate as he'd ever been.

"Can't. There are some electrical issues in the barn we're trying to get fixed. I've been working on it since I started. Last Monday was my first day, but so far, I've struck out. I'm sorry, Mason. I wish there was something I could do."

As hard as it was, Mason had to admit sincerity shone in Logan's eyes. Mason still didn't like him, but the guy was growing on him, as long as Lily Anne was nowhere in sight.

"I understand. Thanks for taking the time to talk to me."

"Are you kidding? Of course. Say, does Lily Anne know you're here?" He smiled and Mason clenched his fists. His fiancée's name coming from Logan's lips twisted his gut. Irrational? Yes, but it was an involuntary reaction.

"Do I know who's here?" Lily Anne's melodic voice chimed from somewhere behind them. "Am I interrupting something, Logan? I didn't mean to barge in, but your text said to come as soon as I could, so here I am. Wait. Mason?"

Mason felt the exact moment Lily Anne saw him. His skin grew hot beneath her stare as sweat beaded along his brow and under his collar.

"Mason? What are you doing here?"

Mason chuckled without the least bit of joy. "That's funny, I was about to ask you the same question." He had no idea what was going on but there was no chance he was heading back to Pine Valley without an explanation.

Lily Anne nudged Logan with her shoulder. "Brother here texted me an address and asked me to meet him. So here I am."

"What did you say?"

She tilted her head as she slowed her speech, the words coming out a question more than a repetition. "Logan texted me an address and asked me to meet him here?"

"Not that." Mason shook his head. "The first part."

Lily Anne's eyes brightened like a light switch had been flipped. When she started tapping her thigh, he knew she understood what he was asking.

"I said, 'brother here texted me.' Stepbrother, if you want to get technical about it, but we dropped the 'step' years ago, right after I thought you broke my nose."

Mason's body flashed hot all over, making a new row of sweat pop out along his hairline. "Come again?" It was a strange reaction to learning Logan was a friend—no, family—not a foe, but Mason chalked it up to shock.

"You need some water?" Logan's brows pulled down as he touched Mason's shoulder. "You look kind of pale."

"No, I'm fine," Mason said, using the universal adjective meaning the exact opposite of how it sounded.

"Ya know, why don't we all move into the kitchen and talk? There's some fresh coffee and a few brownies left over. Sound good?" With a thumb pointing over his shoulder, Logan motioned the way he'd come from while bouncing his gaze from Lily Anne to Mason and back again.

Lily Anne clasped her hands in front of her and squeezed tight. "T-that's fine by me. That okay with you, Mase?"

Mason debated saying no, but Lily Anne's discomfort cut him to the quick. He simply nodded in agreement while a myriad of questions leapfrogged in his mind. Logan motioned for them to follow as he led them down the hall away from prying eyes and listening ears.

The kitchen boasted a stove in the middle of the back wall, a run-of-the-mill refrigerator, a long rectangular farmhouse table with bench seating in the middle, and a counter on the other side of the room. A deep sink broke up the counter with a drainer on one side and a microwave on the other. Mason seated himself on the end closest to the door while Logan grabbed a mug for each of them. He pointed to a covered aluminum pan next to the microwave and Lily Anne snagged it, dropping it on the table before sliding onto the bench beside Mason.

While Logan poured the coffee, Lily Anne took Mason's hand with a shy smile. Once everyone was seated, Mason blurted the question swirling inside his mind.

"Logan is your brother?"

"Yes, he is." Lily Anne answered with an unwavering gaze. Her copper eyes shimmered, warm and welcoming, giving the appearance of poise and etiquette, but when she pulled in her bottom lip and began to chew, Mason saw the nerves behind the façade.

"Why didn't you tell me who he was when we met in the bakery?"

Logan touched Lily Anne's shoulder. "I got this one, Lil."

First, Logan reached across the table, plucked a brownie out of the pan, and placed it on a paper plate in front of Lily Anne. Then, he did the same for Mason before taking a big bite of the chocolatey goodness himself and washing it down with a gulp of coffee.

"Mmmm." Logan wiped his mouth with a paper towel. "It's my fault she didn't tell you who I was. When I remembered your name, she freaked out thinking I'd remember the rest of the story, too."

Mason massaged the back of his neck, begging the ache that had started there to fade. "What story?"

"The part where she blamed you for her broken nose and I went looking to break your nose as payback." Logan shrugged and went back to eating without a care in the world. Man, if Mason looked like that after one of his jokes, he understood why Mikie couldn't stand him.

Lily Anne dropped Mason's hand and folded her arms over her chest with a huff. "I didn't say I was positive Mason was responsible, just almost positive."

"Almost positive was enough for me." Logan managed to get out around a mouth full of brownie.

"Back up." Mason held up his hand like a crossing guard. "How did I cause you to break your nose?"

Lily Anne shook her head and took Mason's hand in her own again. "You didn't. But I thought you did. I was sure you pulled the fire alarm that started senior skip day. Remember?"

Of course, Mason remembered, seeing as how he *did* pull the fire alarm. At the time, he had no idea the principal would go so far as to threaten expulsion for the perpetrator. Mason couldn't get expelled so close to graduation. He'd already been accepted to Kentucky School of Photography on scholarship, a scholarship contingent on a 3.5 GPA and an unblemished record. The whole thing made for an unforgettable experience as Mason worked to stay under the radar while the faculty tried to smoke out the culprit.

Under the table, Mason ran his free hand down the thigh of his pants, hoping to dry his palm. "Yup, who could forget?"

"Definitely not me." Lily Anne speared a bite of brownie with her fork before turning her eyes on Mason. "Someone pushed me from behind when I was trying to get out of the student center. A stool broke my fall, and my nose, in the process."

"You were serious when you asked me about the prank?" Mason blinked in rapid succession as a furious eighteen-year-old Lily Anne surfaced in his memory. She'd demanded to know if he pulled the senior prank. Now, he knew why. "You really broke your nose?"

Lily Anne chewed her brownie, swallowing before she spoke. "Yes, I really broke my nose. Why would I lie about that?"

Shrinking to the size of a grasshopper, Mason scrubbed a hand down his face. "I thought you were trying to help Principal Burke find the guilty party. I don't remember seeing you bandaged or anything."

"It was only a hairline fracture, so it didn't bleed." Lily Anne lifted her shoulder in a half-shrug. "I didn't even know it was broken until a week after it happened. By then, the bone had already started healing so the only way to straighten it was to rebreak it and set it. I decided to live with a crooked nose instead."

"No wonder Logan wanted to beat me up," Mason grunted, angry at his younger self's stupidity. *A broken nose!* How had he not realized the pain he'd caused? Or the grace extended by Lily Anne with her 'yes' at the reunion. More than ever, Mason realized what a miracle her agreement to his proposal truly was.

Logan went over to Lily Anne and threw an arm over her shoulders. "I'm glad I didn't. It would have made giving her away at the wedding a lot more awkward."

"That it would." Lily Anne smiled, wide and bright, looking every bit the part of an excited bride.

Mason slouched in his seat, wishing he could disappear. He wanted to confess right then and there, to tell her the truth about the part he played in the prank and her broken nose, but fear stopped him. Fear and a series of sneezes.

Mason stood and jerked a paper towel off the roll behind the sink. "Hey, Logan, where's the bathroom?"

Leaning around the door facing, Logan pointed. "Back down the hall, through the lobby, and to your right."

"Thanks."

Mason nodded and walked with heavy steps. He deserved the blame for what happened all those years ago and Lily Anne needed to know that. How could he tell her though? She'd all but written him off back in school when she just suspected him to be guilty.

What would she do when he confirmed her suspicions?

Chapter Fourteen

L ily Anne smiled brightly at the turn of events that had led to brownies and coffee in the middle of the day. The proper introductions had been completed and been much less awkward than she had anticipated. In fact, the impromptu meet-and-greet with Logan and Mason was going great, until Mason took a sneezing fit and excused himself.

With Mason still in the bathroom and Logan gone to take a phone call, Lily Anne pulled her notebook out of the tote she'd brought with her and opened it to where she'd been working on her letter previously. She read silently, trying to reacclimate to her prior train of thought.

> *Mase,*
> *Growing up, I never read you as a love story. You were comedy and satire, with a little suspense mixed in. You and I weren't even in the same genre. You were loud to the quiet I craved, stormy to the calm I chased, and chaos to the control I created. The funny thing is, not much has changed. You are still all those things. Yet, in your eyes I read the most riveting romance ever penned: Ours.*

Lily Anne tapped her pencil as she thought about her next lines. She needed to get words on the page, and fast. Mrs. Campbell had moved the deadline up, making the feature due at midnight. When Lily Anne read the change, she'd nearly stroked out, but after a few breathing exercises and a vent session with Emma Lou, she had a plan that started with clearing her day from work. Neither her mother nor Howard were happy about that, but with the Saturdays she'd agreed to work in exchange, they both got the better end of the deal, no question.

Earlier, Lily Anne had just found her writing rhythm when Logan texted. Knowing she had the rest of the day to finish the assignment, Lily Anne had hopped in the car and driven over without another thought. Apparently, Logan wanted to show off his new job at Sun and Fun Farms, which was indeed a surprise, but not as much as finding Mason talking with him in the lobby. It had all worked out for the best, though, and as soon as they were finished, Lily Anne planned to steal away into a study room at the library and write until closing.

"Hey, sorry I took so long."

Lily Anne smiled at the sound of Mason's voice as she closed her notebook and returned it to the bag. But the smile died as soon as she got a good look at him. His cheeks were red as cherries and his nose was even brighter. His forehead glistened with sweat. Mason wiped his mouth with the back of his hand as he leaned against the wall, drawing Lily Anne's attention to his dry lips.

Lily Anne rose from the seat and placed her hand on his arm. "Mason, are you okay?"

Instead of answering, Mason's eyelids dropped to half-mast as he flailed to the left, knocking Lily Anne square in the nose and right into Logan. Tears sprung to her eyes and her head throbbed from the impact of the blow, but none of that mattered when she saw Mason's body slide down the wall. Gently, she placed a hand on his cheek and gasped.

"He's on fire, Logan." Lily Anne ran back to the table, grabbing her keys and tossing her bag on her shoulder as fast as she could. "I think he needs a doctor. Can you help me get him into the car?"

Logan nodded and squatted down beside Mason. With him on one side and Lily Anne on the other, they pulled Mason to his feet and out the door. Even with both of them working together, it was a chore getting him in the car. When the safety belt finally clicked, she sent up a silent prayer of thanks. As she did, Mason sneezed again, barely covering his nose in time to keep the snot from flying.

"Bless you." Lily Anne reached across the middle console and rubbed his back. The cotton was soaked with sweat. *Not a good sign.* "Close your eyes and rest. We'll be at the clinic soon."

Lily Anne wasn't sure how many speeding laws she broke, but in the time it should have taken her to get back to Pine Valley, Mason was already in and out of the clinic. Doc Kendrick diagnosed Mason with a nasty case of the flu, and gave him an arsenal of prescriptions and strict orders for rest. Thankfully, the pharmacy on site rushed Mason's medication because of his high fever. By the time they pulled up to The B&B Inn, Mason had already downed the first dose of cough syrup and a bottle of water, making Lily Anne a little more confident in her inferior nursing skills.

The steps to the front door looked more like Mount Everest than the few concrete blocks they actually were, especially with the weight of Mason bearing down on Lily Anne's shoulders. At least he woke up long enough to help. Still, in his weak and groggy state, it took all her strength to help him into the inn where Mrs. Montgomery waited to offer her motherly services.

"Heya, Ma." Mason's eyes drooped and his words slurred.

Mrs. Montgomery looked her son over and frowned. "Oh, my poor boy. You look awful. Let me help get you to bed."

"Nah, that's okay. Lil's got me, don't ya, beautiful?" With a smile, Mason attempted a wink that came out more like an incredibly slow blink.

The two women shared a look that spoke volumes, Lily Anne asking with her eyes if medicine always had this effect on him and Mrs. Montgomery's stare answering with a re-sounding yes.

"Yes, Mase," cooed Lily Anne in appeasement. "I've got you, but like you said before, you'll always be a mama's boy, so let's give her a chance to help."

With that, Mason wrapped his free arm around his mother and the three of them ascended the stairs at a much faster pace than Lily Anne had mustered getting into the inn. Mrs. Montgomery readied his bed while Mason and Lily Anne stood in the hall. When finished, Lily Anne helped Mason into his room and sat him on the bed. Still in jeans and a polo, he was the picture of uncomfortable

"Mrs. M, do you know where he keeps his pajamas? His shirt is soaked with sweat and it can't be good for him to sleep in it."

"In the top drawer, dear."

Lily Anne plundered in the dresser, finding the t-shirts in the first drawer as Mrs. Montgomery had suspected. The pants, though, were another story. After coming up empty handed in the dresser, Lily Anne moved to the nightstand where she finally struck gold with the bottom drawer.

"I'll help you get the new shirt on and then go get Mr. Montgomery to help with the pants."

Mrs. Montgomery nodded and smiled, but it didn't crinkle her eyes the way it normally did, causing Lily Anne to pause. Searching her face, pink stains on both cheeks jumped out at Lily Anne, especially against her blanched skin and pale lips. Lily Anne touched her palm to Mrs. Montgomery's forehead, jerking back at the warmth radiating from her skin.

"Okay, new plan." Lily Anne jerked her gaze from Mason's mother to his bedroom door. "I'm going to get Mr. Montgomery right now and as soon as you guys are done helping Mase, I'm calling Mikie to take you to the clinic, too."

Lily Anne rushed to the next floor of the inn and knocked, softly at first. When no one answered after the second knock, she rapped a bit harder. The door remained shut, though, causing her rapping to turn to pounding which finally roused a sweaty-browed and sallow-skinned Mr. Montgomery. This time, Lily Anne didn't even bother checking his head to determine he, too, had been hit with a fever.

"Mr. Montgomery, I'm sorry to bother you, but Mason needs a little help getting dressed. The cough medicine the clinic gave him has some strong pain medicine in it and he's a bit loopy. Can you help Mrs. Montgomery get him changed?"

"Sure, sure."

"Thank you. I'm pretty certain you and Mrs. Montgomery need to be tested for the flu, too. She's running a fever already and, from the looks of it, so are you, or will be before long."

Mr. Montgomery laid the back of his hand on his cheek and then his forehead. "I do feel a bit under the weather, now that you mention it."

"That's what I was afraid of." Lily Anne nodded slowly. "I'm going to call Mikie to take you both over to Dr. Kendrick's."

Mr. Montgomery stepped out of the room, closing the door behind him. "Okay, go ahead. It'll take me that long to convince that wife of mine to go to the clinic. She hates doctors."

"I understand. Mom is the same way. Thank you, Mr. Montgomery."

He nodded a "you're welcome" and headed down the hall.

Lily Anne dialed Mikie's number and waited. When a voice on the other line finally came through, Lily Anne explained the situation all in one breath. The clinic would close soon and the Montgomerys needed to get a move on if they were going to make it in time to be seen.

Within minutes, Mikie had both his mother and father in the car and ready to go. Lily Anne watched from the entrance, expecting him to pull out any minute, but instead he came barreling back up the steps, taking them two at a time.

"The inn's supposed to host the town council dinner in the kitchen. Can you call and cancel? I would, but cells don't get great reception on the road to the clinic."

"Uh, yeah, I can do that." Lily Anne closed her eyes and took a breath as Pastor Clemens's voice rang in her ears, describing the biblical picture of a helpmate. She'd understood those words with her head when the preacher had first said them. Now, it was time to let her heart do the work. "Wait, Mikie. What time is the committee meeting?"

"Six o'clock sharp."

"Are they bringing the meal? Or was your mom cooking?"

"Mr. Hart is having it catered. The food should arrive about fifteen minutes before the dinner starts. Why?"

Lily Anne looked at the time. The clock on the wall had nearly two hours to count before go time, plenty long enough for Lily Anne to sanitize every inch of the dining room and first floor restroom *if* she abandoned her writing. She took another deep breath and nodded. "Listen, Mikie. What if I scrub everything down and have Emma play hostess? That way, no one is exposed but you don't have to cancel."

"Lily Anne, I can't ask you to do that."

"You're not asking. I'm offering."

"Are you sure? Do you really have the time to do all this?"

Lily Anne bit her tongue to keep the answer at bay. She didn't have time, not really. She did, however, have a duty to her fiancé and his family, soon to be their family, and she wasn't about to let them down. Her father had demonstrated time and time again how easy dropping the ball could be, but in doing so, he'd also showcased the power of the clutch play. Digging her heels in as if they were cleats, Lily Anne pasted on a smile and stood up straight, ready to catch the third out in the ninth inning.

"Don't worry about that. I got this, Mikie. Just get your parents the medicine they need and leave the rest to me."

"Thanks, Lil." Mikie blew out a long exhale. "You're a life saver. If you need to know where anything is, just call Mary Ellen."

"Will do. Now, go before the clinic closes." Lily Anne wrapped him in a quick goodbye hug before bolting back inside.

With her phone to her ear, she slid her notebook onto the counter and made a mad dash for the kitchen.

"Hello?"

"Hey, Emma Lou. What are you planning this evening?" Lily Anne opened the hall closet door as she listened to Emma prattle on about pizza and a movie and maybe a book before bed. As soon as Emma paused to take a breath, Lily Anne interjected with a new itinerary.

"Yeah, all that sounds wonderful, but I know something that sounds better."

"Oh, yeah?" Emma huffed in that I-don't-believe-you tone.

Lily Anne could almost picture her, hand on her hip and one eyebrow raised. Instead of laughing like she wanted to, she took a breath and laid it all on the table. "Chaperoning the town council dinner at The B&B Inn."

"I think I'll pass, Lil."

"Please, Em. Mason and his parents have the flu and I've been with him all day, so I can't do it. I'm going to clean like a demon and then turn the reins over to you. It won't be hard, I promise. Dinner is being catered so you won't have to do anything but smile and keep an eye on everything." With her free hand, Lily Anne crossed her fingers. *Can't hurt.*

"Before I say yes, answer one question. Is Mr. Hart going to be there?"

"Yes." Lily Anne tried to cross her toes, too. "He is, but you two will hardly see each other. Besides, it's been forever since you and Clay broke up. You're past the point of needing to avoid his father now."

Emma exhaled loudly. "I may not need to keep my distance anymore, but I want to. I'm sorry, Lily Anne. I just c—"

"What if I promise to have a lesson-planning party with you next weekend, complete with those scones and sweet rolls you love?"

Rustling came through the speaker, like Emma was situating herself, like maybe she was getting shoes and a coat. "That's not fair! You know I can't say no to the scones."

Lily Anne smiled. "That's what I'm counting on."

"Fine. I'll be there."

"You're the best, Emma Lou," said Lily Anne, meaning every word to the nth degree. "I owe you."

"You definitely do."

With that, the line went dead and Lily Anne went to work.

Chapter Fifteen

Mason massaged his temples, attempting to fend off the mountain-sized headache building behind his eyes as he scooted up against the headboard. The sliver of light passing between the lowered blinds and the window looked much too bright to still be morning. Slowly, so as not to worsen the pressure inside his head, he turned his neck to check the clock on the nightstand. The time there proved his theory. At two in the afternoon, he'd slept the day away, which really didn't matter since he had no idea what day it was anyway. The last thing he remembered was Doc Kendrick telling him to drink plenty of fluids as Lily Anne guided him out the door.

"*Achoo.*" Mason covered his face with one hand while he felt around the bed for a tissue box. After three passes, he thought he might have dreamed it until he felt a pointy corner against his palm. He cleaned his face, wadded up the paper, and shot it toward the garbage can in the corner. It missed the trash, but hit the door as Lily Anne opened it, peeking her head around to look in.

"Hey, Chief."

"Good to see you awake." She smiled, stepped in, and closed the door behind her. "Are you up for a while or do you want to try to get some more rest?"

"Up, I think."

"Good." With measured steps, Lily Anne ventured into the room, turning a lamp on in the corner farthest from the bed. Her corkscrew curls took on the color of natural honey beneath the muted light, a brilliant shade of golden yellow that gave off an ethereal glow while the spirals bounced across her shoulders. When she turned around, Mason noticed the horn-rimmed glasses she was wearing instead of her usual contacts. Behind the lenses, tired eyes stared back at him. Had she stayed with him throughout the night? Judging by the dark circles make-up did little to hide, it was a definite possibility. Mason swallowed hard, causing a tickle to crawl up his throat and ignite a coughing fit.

Lily Anne's eyes rounded as she held up a finger. "Let me get you some water. Be right back."

Still unable to talk, Mason nodded. Moments later, she reappeared carrying a lunch tray. Carefully, she deposited the tray on the accent table along the back wall before joining him. She handed him the water and sat on the edge of the bed.

"How are you feeling?"

"Like I got hit by a truck." Mason tried to laugh, but the sound came out more like a wheeze.

"Not a truck, but the flu. At least your fever broke." Lily Anne placed the back of her hand against one cheek, then the other, before finally laying her palm across his forehead for several seconds. With the hint of a smile, she dropped her hand between them. "Still gone, thank God."

"I don't remember the last time I woke up, so I'm guessing my temp's been down a while." Mason shrugged as he sipped. He held the water in his mouth longer than necessary, letting the cool liquid soothe his dry tongue.

Lily Anne looked at her watch. "Since about 3:30 this morning."

"From the way I feel right now, that sounds right. But I honestly don't remember." Mason took another drink before balancing the glass on his thigh.

"You were in and out of it. Because of the medicine, I think." Lily Anne laughed, not loud but hard enough to shake her slight shoulders. "I don't know what kind of sleep aid was in that cough syrup Doc prescribed, but it threw you for a loop."

Mason scrubbed a hand down his face, hoping to hide his heated skin. "Medicine has always knocked me out."

"I kind of figured that when your mom had to help me change your shirt last night." Lily Anne's eyes went wide and her cheeks pinkened. "Y-you were soaked in sweat and I was afraid the wet material would cause you to chill."

Mason interrupted with another coughing fit and took a giant gulp of water. *How attractive.* He shuddered to think how awful he must have looked. Another rush of blood ran to his cheeks as he chugged the water faster. After he'd drank half the glass, his throat felt more like sandpaper than a desert, but his face still flamed.

Seemingly unfazed by his disheveled appearance, Lily Anne continued. "By the way, you really need some more clean clothes. We took the last tee from your drawer. If you're okay with it, I'll throw whatever is in your hamper in the wash with mine when I do them today."

"Don't you have to be at the bakery?" Mason blinked in confusion. "Or the paper?"

Lily Anne shook her head, curls bouncing as she did. "No. Mom's covering my shift and I called Howard to let him know I wouldn't be in today."

"Awww, Chief. You didn't have to do that." Mason searched her face, expecting a furrowed brow or drawn lips. Instead, he found only tired eyes smiling back at him.

"I know I didn't have to. I wanted to. Taking care of you—it's my job, now—and my work ethic is exemplary." Lily Anne leaned in and kissed his cheek, letting her lips linger until a sudden string of coughs shattered the moment.

"Besides, I'll be working on my life-hack today as part of your treatment. Ever had a hot toddy before?"

"Can't say that I have, Chief. Heard of them, but never drank one."

Lily clapped her hands and rubbed them together, looking like an evil genius with a trick up her sleeve. "Well, today's your lucky day. I've got my mom's recipe and all the ingredients ready to go."

"If it will make this headache go away, bring me two."

"It will. I've had a few in my life. Believe me when I say, it cures what ails you."

"Thank you. For everything."

"Of course. I can't have my groom sniffling at that altar, or at the tailor's, for that matter. Logan already has an appointment at Southern Man on Saturday, and I thought you might want to go with him. If I can nurse you back to health, that is."

"I'll be better by then." Mason straightened in the bed as he mulled over how best to broach the topic of Logan. The fact that she had hidden away this huge part of herself stung worse than a red wasp. In a matter of weeks, they'd be married. As her husband, he needed to understand her family situation in order to navigate himself around them.

Realizing his head hurt too much to cipher out a plan of attack, Mason lead with the question burning a hole in his heart.

"Speaking of Logan, why is he walking you down the aisle, Lil?" Mason watched as her face grew hard and the warmth in her eyes dissipated.

"Why don't we talk about this when you're feeling better?"

Sick, tired, and, if truth be told, annoyed at her hesitancy, Mason snapped, "Because we're running out of time."

At his raised voice, Lily Anne met his gaze. Reflecting in the darkened copper, Mason saw a frustration that matched his own, but beneath that, hurt glimmered. Deep hurt, the kind that leaves scars and alters lives. Seeing Lily Anne in such pain, he tried again, resorting to a softer, more comedic approach.

"For goodness' sake, Lil, I thought Logan had the hots for you until, like, yesterday." Mason chuckled. He knew it landed flat, but when Lily Anne tossed him a bone with the lightest of laughs, he rushed on. "I don't want to mistake your dad for an old science teacher or something. Pretty sure I'd flunk Husband 101 if that happened."

"Maybe."

Unable to keep quiet, Mason huffed and mock-glared until she raised her hands in an I-give-up motion.

"Fine. I see your point, and I want to explain. I do. It's just hard. Dad is a sore spot for me."

Mason watched as Lily Anne drew in a deep breath and shut her eyes. Without caring about germs or bacteria or even residual snot, he reached over and took her hand in his. At the feel of her trembling, Mason sent up a silent prayer for strength, for her and for him.

Opening her eyes, Lily Anne nodded—once, twice, three times—before blowing out a lungful of air in a loud exhale. "Mom and Dad divorced when I was in middle school, right before you moved here, I think. When he left, I was wrecked. In my head, I knew it wasn't my fault, but my heart didn't believe that, especially when all I got was radio silence from him. I didn't understand why he didn't want me around. I still don't."

Lily Anne paused, shifting her line of sight from the blanket to a landscape painting high above the bed, but she kept talking.

"I tried to be a good daughter. I kept my room clean, didn't talk back, not much, anyway, made good grades. But when Mom and Dad divorced, it felt like none of that mattered. Dad promised to visit, but, week after week he never showed up. I started thinking that maybe I wasn't good enough for him, especially after he married Sherry, Logan's mom. Why would he want to spend time with me when he had a ready-made family in Hickory Hills?"

Furrowing his brow, Mason tightened his hold on her hand. He wanted to interrupt, to set the record straight about the value of her company, but when she continued staring at the picture over his shoulder, he realized that she was lost in reverie.

She went on, not sparing him a glance. "Right when I'd given up hope, Dad did a complete turnaround. Everything changed. He started calling and wanting visits on the weekend. It took a while, but I eventually forgave him. I got my dad back, and a second family in Hickory Hills, complete with a pain-in-the-butt big brother in Logan and a family dog. It was nice."

"By senior year, life was good with all of us. Dad seemed proud of me for my writing, even talked to some old buddies of his that worked at Lex-Post about my journalism. Things were looking up, until the bottom fell out and Dad bailed again. The mine where he worked shut down and he lost his job as a surveyor. Logan was in college by that time, but Sherry didn't want to move so Dad compromised. He took a position a few counties over and stayed with a coworker during the week. Our weekend visits tapered off until they became nonexistent. He blamed it on overtime and double shifts, which was probably true, but it didn't make it hurt any less. The day you found me crying in journalism class was the day he told me he wouldn't be coming to graduation. I was crushed, totally panicking, in the middle of an attack, actually."

"I remember. If I'd had a paper bag handy, I'd have chucked it at you, but I had no idea where to find one." Mason laughed but it was void of any real joy. "I've never forgotten that day. Your hair was down, like it is now, which caught me off guard, until I realized you were using your curls to hide your tears. I hated it. I wanted to fix whatever was wrong, but since you refused to acknowledge me, I sat down, hoping to make you laugh."

Lily Anne smoothed the blanket at the end of the bed. "Oh, Mason. I'm so sorry, but I was beside myself. I kept thinking it was my fault, that I wasn't up to par, that I'd failed him somehow. It's dumb, but I think I gave up on finding love that day. If my own father didn't love me enough to stick with me, why would anyone else? Then you came up with our Valentine Proposal and I thought, why not? I had nothing to lose."

"Gee, thanks." Mason barely mumbled the words, but it was clear Lily Anne heard him when she rolled her eyes.

"Come on, Mason." Tilting her head in Mason's direction, she patted his cover-clad ankle. "You know you were definitely not my favorite person back then, especially after you broke my nose. Well, after I thought you broke my nose."

Realizing what she'd said, Mason remained quiet. He still needed to come clean about the prank, but hadn't figured out the right words or built up enough courage yet. He closed his eyes and took a few breaths. Maybe if he focused on breathing instead of his confession, telling her would be easier. The bed shifted, forcing his eyes open.

Lily Anne stood up and grabbed his tray. "Hey, sleepyhead. Try to eat a little before you're too tired. Then, after your nap, I'll bring you the hot toddy. Sound good?"

Mason nodded as Lily Anne set the lunch beside him on the mattress. Knowing there would never be a good time to explain his prior sins, he decided to push pause on the conversation. A few more hours, or days, wouldn't matter, not after a decade had already passed.

Hopefully not.

Chapter Sixteen

*M*usic?

Lily Anne's eyes fluttered open. The darkness made it impossible to see her hand in front of her face, so she laid there while her body adjusted to the low lighting. The tune kept playing.

Where was it coming from? And why wouldn't it stop?

The notes of a muffled melody continued to ring, but her semi-wakeful state kept her from making out the song. *It's too early for this.* With a groan, Lily Anne slapped above her head in search of her pillow.

The music started up again, but this time Lily Anne recognized it as her phone ringing—the tone assigned for Emma Lou.

What on earth?

The dusky light filtering through the windows resembled dawn, early dawn, like waking-up-with-the-roosters dawn, which did not match Emma Lou's MO. The break in character pushed Lily Anne's senses to high alert as she grabbed her phone off the nightstand.

"Hello?"

"Hey. Remember when you said you owed me?"

Lily Anne swept the sleep from her eyes, wondering what she'd gotten herself into. "Which time, Em?"

"Doesn't matter, pick one. Either way, I'm cashing in the favor right now."

"Now, as in, later *today*?" Lily Anne rested her head against her pillow.

"Now, as in, this minute." A loud bang sounded from Emma Lou's side of the line followed by a jingle. Car keys, maybe?

At the sound, Lily Anne opened her eyes. "Emma, what's going on?"

"Davey's coming home."

Lily Anne sat up. "That's great. When?"

A smile broke lose. She hadn't seen Davey in years. If it wasn't for Logan's teasing at the bakery a few weeks ago, it would have been that long since she even thought of him. Was he still in Alabama? Or was he overseas now? She couldn't remember, but she knew he was serving as an army mechanic wherever he was. *Maybe he'll come to the wedding.*

"He's hurt, Lil. A crush injury. The jacks gave way on him."

Hearing that, the heart in her chest plummeted. In high school, Davey was her baseball buddy. Their mutual love for the sport had fused them as friends. That and the fact Emma dated Clay all through school. Davey and Clay had an unmatched bromance, so more times than not, the four of them ended up sharing tables at school functions and moving in the same circle. She'd even attended his going-away party when he entered the military. Seeing Davey's father, Jim, struggle to keep from crying, Lily Anne knew what a father's love should be like.

"H-h-how bad?" Lily Anne closed her eyes, picturing father and son together. She couldn't imagine the tailspin Jim must be living through.

"Bad enough to need rehab. Are you still staying at the inn?"

In her sleepy state, Lily Anne nodded before realizing she needed to answer Emma with words. "I am. This opossum is a tricky one, apparently."

"Seems like, but it works out better for me this way. Get Mason and his camera. Can y'all meet me at Pine Valley Healthcare and Recovery?"

Lily Anne threw the cover off her. "Yeah, sure. We'll be there as soon as we can. Want me to pick up anything else?"

"No, I've already called in the calvary. We're going to make his homecoming a happy one!"

"All right." Lily Anne wasn't sure of that, but she pretended to be. "Text me if you end up needing something from the store and I'll grab it."

"Thanks, Lil. Bye."

"Bye, Emma."

Before she had time to lock her phone, a knock sounded on her bedroom door. Without bothering to check her reflection, Lily Anne ran to the door and opened it while she tried to steady her breathing.

"Is everything okay?" Mason took her hand in his and laced their fingers together. *How did he know what to do to calm her?* No longer needing to count Mississippis, Lily Anne rushed to explain.

"That was Emma asking us to meet her at the rehabilitation center. Davey Barnes? He's injured and deserves a hero's homecoming, so we're going to give him one. She wants you to take pictures. Can you do that? I mean, do you even feel up to it? Your sched—"

"Is now clear. And that hot toddy yesterday afternoon fixed me right up."

"Okay, good. I'm going to go get ready." Glancing at the phone still in her hand, Lily Anne checked the time. "Meet you downstairs in a half hour?"

"Half hour." Mason hugged her tight before leaving her to her own devices. She watched the door open and close to his room before entering hers.

Lily Anne went straight for the shower, turned it as hot as she could stand, and let her tears mix with the water. She cried for Davey and Jim, for their time apart and the tragic circumstances surrounding his return home, for their pain, past and present. She cried for the uncertainty of their future, the rehab, the possible setbacks. She cried for the hard parts of life for both of them.

Lily Anne cried for herself, too, for the little girl who longed for a daddy to love her. The loneliness she had tried to lock away busted free thanks to the gold-star example of a father like Jim shining bright in front of her. How many times did she reach out for the gentle touch of a daddy's hand only to find thin air? How many father-daughter dances did she ignore to keep from sobbing? How many birthdays did she blow out her candles with a single wish—a father to love her—only to go another trip around the sun still wishing?

If she were in Davey's shoes, who would come for her? *Mom?* Definitely, cinnamon rolls and coffee in tow. *Logan?* Probably, if for no other reason than to hit on the nurses. *Mason?* Yes, barring no changes to their relationship. *Emma?* Without a doubt, likely dragging Eliza Lee along like the night of the engagement party.

But her dad?

The question mark flashed neon in her mind. What about her father? Would it be like every other big moment in her life when he went AWOL? Or would he find time to check on his only daughter. She didn't know, but past experiences forced her to tic the box in the 'no' column, which made the tears gush harder and faster than before.

Oh my gosh! Lily Anne Dawson, get it together. Quit being a drama queen and get over it. Today is not about you. It's about Davey. She stepped back from the stream of water and pulled in as much air as she could through her nose. *Hold. One-Mississippi. Two-Mississippi. Three-Mississippi. And out.* She repeated the counting until the memory of her father's shortcomings sunk to the bottom of her heart, out of sight and out of mind. Then, she prayed as she washed herself clean and toweled dry. Her prayers were still going strong after she dressed and met Mason.

"Ready to go, m'lady?" Mason bent his arm, elbow out. The gesture, sweet and silly, lightened the mood while still respecting the situation. She smiled immediately, wondering how on earth she'd been so blind as to miss the swoony side of Mason Montgomery.

"Yes, kind sir." She threaded her arm through and let him lead her to the car. Mason opened her door, like the gentleman he was proving to be.

A split second before she slid in, he took her hand and tugged her close. Warm hazel eyes stared down at her, so warm her cheeks burned from his heat. The flames spread lower, drying out her lips. Needing relief, Lily Anne licked them. As she did, Mason's eyes darkened and he leaned in. The tip of his nose skimmed her skin as he pressed his mouth to hers. His lips moved slowly and Lily Anne matched his pace, savoring him like the finest chocolate. The breath between them melted with the kiss. For a moment, she was his air and he was her oxygen. And then, the moment was gone. Mason pulled away slightly and released her hand.

"Why did y—"

Before Lily Anne could finish her question, Mason laid a finger on her still tingling, swollen lips. Lily Anne turned her head slightly and his finger fell away.

"You live for punctuality, Chief." Mason traced her jawline until he reached her chin and tipped her head with the same finger he'd pressed against her lips. "If I don't stop now, I can guarantee you we're gonna be late."

"Oh, o-okay." Lily Anne stammered, her face on fire. Mason pulled the door open wider and Lily Anne hopped in. Mason went around to his side and did the same, adjusting the heat as he slid in the seat. He left the radio off, but tapped out a short rhythm on the steering wheel as he drove. Every few minutes, their eyes met and he grinned.

When Emma Lou met them in the parking lot, Mason was still grinning.

"Hey, guys. Thank you for coming. It'll mean the world to Jim. He was a wreck when I talked to him this morning."

"Of course." Lily Anne hugged Emma. "There's nowhere else we'd rather be. What can I do to help?"

"I've got the stuff to make some punch in the staff lounge. They said we could use it while we get everything set up in the lobby here. Eliza Lee's bringing a banner, Mary Ellen's picking up a few balloons from Goldie's Rods and Blooms, and Pastor Clemens is bringing half the congregation, if not all of it. Oh! I forgot, your mama's coming, too, with Lord knows what kinds of pastries. Scones, I hope."

"And cinnamon rolls." Mason winked at Lily Anne. She side-eyed him, pretending to be perturbed, but inside she swooned at his consideration. Well, that, and cinnamon rolls.

"Them, too. So, we've got the food, friends, and family covered." Emma counted on her fingers as she spoke, then turned and pointed at Mason. "I need you to take care of the photos."

"Will Davey want me taking his picture?"

"That's a good question I don't have the answer for, but Jim requested photos. I ran everything by him as he was rushing around the office making arrangements."

"Okay, as long as you're sure I won't be imposing. I'll stay out the way as best as I can and focus more on what's going on around Davey than the man himself. That work?"

"That'll be perfect." Emma Lou pressed her palms together in a prayer position and rested her chin on her fingertips. "Now, what else am I forgetting?" She squinted as if staring through fog and walked away. Lily Anne started to follow her, but Mason touched her forearm, stopping her.

"I need you to stay nearby with my bag in case I have to change lenses."

"Oh. I can do that."

"Thanks." Mason handed her the carrying case while he slid the camera strap around his neck.

With the bag secure, the two of them ambled into the break room to make the punch. Lily Anne studied the recipe on the table and opened all the juices, dumping them into the bowl. Then, added the rainbow sherbet. No sooner had she thrown away the empty container than Emma poked her head in.

"He's here. It's go time."

Lily Anne closed her eyes and asked God for strength. She reminded herself that He had a purpose and plan for Davey. This was part of it. When she opened her eyes, Mason's head was bowed. She didn't want to disturb him but longed to show her support. With as little movement as possible, she weaved her fingers with his and joined him in prayer. It was short and she had no idea what was spoken between him and the Father, but that didn't matter. When he wiggled his hand free with a whispered *amen*, peace blanketed her. Mason didn't speak, but the light in his eyes reflected the same feeling.

"Welcome home!" A chorus of voices filled the lobby as they walked out. Emma Lou wasn't kidding when she named off all the guests. Nearly the whole church filed in and there were enough hugs and handshakes to break a Sunday-morning record. Mason circled around the group with slow measured movements, careful to stay out of the throng and speak only when spoken to.

Mason put poetry-in-motion to shame while he worked. Determined eyes surveyed the room until they lighted on the exact image he wanted to capture. The flash lit up, over and over again, so fast Lily Anne couldn't keep track. By the time the shutter closed from one shot, he refocused, on the hunt for the next shot. His set jaw looked fierce and when he tilted his chin ever so slightly, Lily Anne had to smile. She'd never seen someone so at home behind the camera.

When Davey finally came into view, Jim pushing the wheelchair behind him, it became obvious why Mason's photographs turned out so amazing. Mason's stare mirrored the pain reflected in Davey's eyes as he continued to snap picture after picture. The rare occasion when Davey smiled, Mason did, too. When Jim placed his hands on Davey's shoulders and squeezed, barely holding back tears, Mason's gaze misted behind the camera. He didn't just catch the moment, he preserved the emotion fueling it, tapping into the feeling himself to find the perfect angle.

After Mason wrapped up the photo session, he returned the camera to his bag and zipped it up. With it secure, he went over to Davey and gave him a bro hug, complete with a shoulder slap. She watched as Davey nodded at what Mason was saying and the two shook hands. When he stepped away, she moved in.

"Davey Barnes, I've got a bone to pick with you." Lily Anne poured all the southern sass she could muster into her I-mean-business voice, but the attempt landed flat to her own ears. By some miracle, though, it seemed to work on Davey as a corner of his mouth twitched slightly.

"Is that so?"

"Yes, that's so. All this time, I was sure you'd been as active as me in spreading the love of America's favorite pastime, but you've failed me with this one." She waved her thumb in Mason's direction.

"What can I say, Lil? The man refused to listen. Maybe you'll have better luck with him after you tie the knot. Congratulations, by the way." Davey's voice sounded the way she remembered it, well-water deep and just as smooth, but there was a sharp edge to it that hadn't been there before. His gray eyes matched the way he sounded, shining with an intensity that almost made her turn away, but she didn't. Instead, she forced a smile.

"Thank you." Lily Anne tapped her fingers on her leg.

"No, thank you for coming today. It means a lot." Davey nodded as he massaged his thigh, wincing once before folding his hands in his lap.

"Hate to break it to you, man, but I came for the food. Seeing your ugly mug was a small price to pay." Mason shoved half a donut in his mouth to prove his point, earning another twitch of Davey's mouth, on both sides and more defined, but not enough to be described as a smile.

Lily Anne searched to come up with conversational topics, but chitchat had never been her selling point. Thankfully, a pair of little old ladies from church swooped in so she didn't have to. They were doting on Davey like crazy while she and Mason snuck away. They'd nearly made it to the front entrance when Pastor Clemens caught up to them.

"I hate to do this to you two, but I have to cancel our session again." The preacher held his hat in front of him, sliding the bill through his thumb and forefinger. His eyes darted from his hands to each of them. It was comical how stricken he seemed over nixing the counseling session and if he hadn't been a man of God, Lily Anne would have laughed out loud.

"No problem. We understand. It's been a long day," Mason caught her eye as he spoke, rubbing his lips together to hide his smile.

"That it has, but I didn't want to be entirely neglectful." Pastor stretched his suspenders as he rocked back on his heels. "I found you some real-world couple's experience, thanks to sweet Miss Ellie. She informed me there's a bookshelf that needs to be put together in the rec room. I volunteered the two of you. Y'all have fun, now."

Chapter Seventeen

"Can you hand me the instructions?" Lily Anne pointed to the booklet.

"Here." Mason slid the directions down. He watched her precise movements as she flipped through pages until a diagram of labeled pieces sprawled out on the table in front of them. It had lettered squares representing the shelves themselves, long rectangles for the main enclosure of the piece, an Allen wrench, and a hardware list naming each screw, nut, and peg.

Lily Anne started reading aloud in a sing-song voice, illustrating her insane attraction to lists and rules and instructions. While she did, Mason examined the wood slats and picked up the closest one to him. It seemed to be a side piece, so he found its twin and stood them up. Next, he found the two rectangles resembling the top and bottom and snagged a bag of hardware. Lily Anne kept going beside him, but as he focused on the shelves, her voice was too distant to make out. It was a simple design, as far as furniture goes, so he started assembling while she continued rambling. When she paused to take a breath, he laid the U-shaped work-in-progress on the floor to attach the bottom piece.

"Mason, what are you doing?"

"Fixing this so that you can get to the paper in time."

"But I've not even made sure all the pieces are here. Have you?" Lily Anne planted her hands on her hips and scowled at him.

"Oh, come on, Lil. Everything's here."

"How do you know? Did you check them off while I was reading?"

"No." Mason gestured to the partially built shelf and mock dusted his palms in front of him in victory. "But I've about got the basic structure finished."

Lily Anne glared at him. "I can see that."

"I'm sorry I didn't wait for you to finish reading, but look at this."

Mason pointed to a picture in the book. It matched the shelf on the floor exactly. She lowered herself to her knees beside him and examined the structure, running her palm along the edge of one of the side pieces.

"It does look right, but how can you be sure it won't fall apart?" Lily Anne's eyes skipped to the instructions and then back to him as she placed the wrench he'd been searching for in his palm.

"I compare the progress with the picture in the instructions. If my results match the image, then I keep going. If they don't, I back up and punt."

"That makes sense." Lily Anne worried her bottom lip between her teeth and Mason closed his eyes, embarrassed for noticing her kissable mouth. But after that kiss at the car, how could he not? Mason shook his head, hoping to get back on task. They were supposed to be working together. Instead, he'd run off and left her at the starting gate. *Helpmate, right, Lord?*

Mason took in a breath and held it. With a slow exhale, he opened his eyes and found Lily Anne still working that bottom lip. Without taking the time to second-guess himself, Mason reached out and pulled at her mouth with his thumb. Lily Anne released the lip she'd held hostage and turned her head, gluing her gaze to the ground. His thumb slipped below her jaw with the sudden movement, so Mason pressed upward ever so slightly until Lily Anne looked at him.

"Read it, again, Chief, from the top. I want to make sure we get it right, too." With that, he let her go and started to loosen the last screw he'd put in, but she stopped him before it worked free.

"No, Mase. I trust you. It's right. Just tell me what I can do to help, and I'll follow your lead."

Slack-jawed, Mason pointed to the piece that looked like it went next. As Lily Anne handed the shelf to him, Mason thanked the Lord for her trust in him and prayed for wisdom.

In less than an hour, Mason's prayer was answered, the shelf was complete, and Lily Anne was on her way to work. Without immediate plans—he always liked to wait at least a few hours before beginning the editing process—Mason had a chunk of downtime to fill. Unsure what to do, he drove back to The B&B Inn to check on his mother. He found her seated at the dining room table, elbows deep in bird seed and mesh.

"Ma, what are you doing?"

She gestured to the mess around her. "What does it look like?"

"It looks like you're working on decorations for the ceremony after me and Lily Anne made plans to finish them tonight."

"Congratulations, Mason, you can skip the eye doctor this year. Nothing wrong with your vision." With a laugh, she slapped the table. The knock wasn't hard, but carried enough force to overturn the bag, letting birdseed spill and dribble off the table.

"Shoot, fire, and light the matches! Grab me the broom and dustpan."

Instead of rushing to the utility closet, Mason slid in beside his mother and hugged her tight.

"Ma, I've got this. Go watch *The Waltons* with Dad or work on your crocheting or take a nap. I'll take care of the front and finish the birdseed bags."

"But Mason, I want to help."

"I know, and you are, but we're going to need you every day until the wedding to pull this off, so you need to rest while you can. The time for burning the midnight oil's coming." Mason kissed her temple, breathing in her unique motherly scent—fresh laundry hot out of the dryer mixed with a hint of cornbread and butter.

"I got this, Mase. I won't let you down."

"Never, Ma. But I don't want you run ragged. Shoo. Vamoose. Scat."

"Okay, okay. Promise you'll holler if you need me?"

"Promise." Mason rubbed her arms a bit and then let her go. He watched as she shuffled from the table and out of sight, thanking God he was home to stay.

After sweeping the floor, Mason slipped into the seat his mother had vacated, determined to finish the bags before Lily Anne got back. Just as he settled into his comfy spot, Mason heard the front door open and shut. Mikie strolled in, took one look at the table and sat down.

"Need some help, Deuce?" Mikie examined the table with a quirked brow. For the first time, Mason realized how much there was left to do and sighed. He needed help, even if it came in the form of his brother.

"I do, but not just with the bags."

Mikie pushed up his shirt sleeves and sat down. "With what?"

While filling up the first bag, the old vulnerability that continually barked for attention any time Mikie was in a room began to howl, louder and longer, until Mason had nearly talked himself out of his brother's help. But before he could tell Mikie not to worry about it, a text accompanied with a headshot of Lily Anne lit up his phone. She was counting on him and seeing her lovely face reminded him of the man he wanted to be, the person she deserved, and the wedding location they needed.

Mason took it as a sign to swallow his pride and went on. "Finding a venue. I've tried, but it can't be done."

"Sure, it can." Mikie picked up a bag and began funneling bird seed in it.

"No, it can't, man." Shaking his head, Mason handed a spool of ribbon to his brother. "The community center is already rented. The church is booked. Happy Harvest is out. The park is set up for Sweetheart Storytime. Where else is there?"

"Here at the inn?"

Mason snarled. "Be serious, Mikie."

"Listen, Deuce. You're making it too hard. Lily Anne seems pretty easy to please." Mikie pointed the tip of his scissors in his direction. "I mean, she did agree to marry you, so she's set the bar low."

Before he knew it, Mason was out of his seat and across the table, punching his brother's bicep.

"Ouch." Mikie rubbed the point of contact and laughed. "Seriously, though, I bet, deep down, Lily Anne's a total romantic. If you find a place that means something to her, she'll be dancing down the aisle. What about where you two met?"

Mikie sunk back into his chair. "Not an option. I'm pretty sure Lily Anne might smack me if I suggested having the ceremony at Country Confections."

"If she didn't, Danny Jo would." Scratching the side of his head, Mikie glanced at the ceiling. "What about where you proposed?"

"I don't think I can replicate the reunion. But you might be onto something." Mason leaned across the table, grabbing Mikie's arm. "Why didn't I think of it before? There's plenty of space for the ceremony in the high-school gym, and the student center can host the reception, no problem. We can even situate the tables around the perimeter, leaving room for a dance floor. It's unconventional and a little crazy, but so what?"

"Crazy suits you just fine." Mikie jerked his arm out of Mason's hold and grabbed another bag. "Deuce, I think you've got yourself a venue."

Chapter Eighteen

The rich notes of brewing coffee wafted from the bank lobby into the loan office where Lily Anne crossed her legs for a fourth time. She turned her head in the direction of the heavenly aroma, making a mental note to grab herself a cup before she left. It had been a little better than a week since Davey Barnes came home, so it had been that long since Lily Anne had taken a whole day off. She needed that coffee.

But, first, the bank needed her signature.

George Hughes, their assigned officer, pointed to the loan papers. "If you would, print your name at the top of page one and sign on the back sheet. After that, you're done. I'll get this processed so you can be on your way to meet the realtor."

"Thank you, George. We appreciate it." Mason scribbled his name on both designated places and slid the packet to her.

With shaky hands and a touch of buyer's remorse, she did as instructed. "Yes, thank you."

George flipped through the document, giving it a quick once over, then tapped the cover sheet with his knuckles. "I think that's it. With your credit scores and Mason's down payment, I don't foresee a problem. Let me know if you put an offer in today and I'll push this through. You've got my cell number?"

"I do," said Mason. "Thanks, again. We'll be in touch."

"Anytime." George rose from his chair and extended a hand toward Mason, who accepted and shook with a wide smile. George turned to Lily Anne and she did the same.

Together, Lily Anne and Mason strolled to the lobby, where Lily Anne grabbed that coffee she'd been dying for, and walked toward the parking lot.

Mason leaned against the jeep, looking more like a model for a magazine than their cameraman. His hair lay in that messy-styled look that Lily Anne had grown to love. As if reading her mind, he ran a hand through it. "Ready to see the house, Chief?"

"Ready as I'll ever be." Lily Anne took a sip of her coffee. *Ah, just what I needed.*

Mason opened the jeep door on the passenger side and she slid in, reaching for the radio as soon as she buckled. While she drank her coffee and bobbed her head, Mason tapped the beat on the steering wheel all the way to Mr. Rowe's property.

The drive was quick and in the course of four songs, five at the most, Mason parked beside an adorable two-story cottage by the lake. Sage-green siding covered a house accented with deep hunter shutters. In front, there was a small porch with a brick landing attached, complete with a hanging swing and two rockers to match. To the left of the porch, a bay window jutted out from the side. Concrete pavers created an adorable little walkway all the way to the drive.

Lily Anne decided she liked the home immediately as a pretty blonde in a suit walked toward her with a wave. "Hey, y'all. So nice to meet you. I'm Laurel with Kentucky Realty."

Before Lily Anne could respond, Mason was at her side. "I'm Mason, and this is Lily Anne, my fiancée. Thank you for meeting us out here on a Saturday."

"No trouble at all." Laurel smiled wide and took a step closer to the house. "You guys ready for the tour?"

"Yes, ma'am. Let's do it." Mason waved his hand in front of him and Laurel led the way.

The three of them filed through the front door. On the left wall, Lily Anne noticed a coat rack and a narrow bench with shoe storage built in. To the right, about midway, a stone fireplace stood with a straw-colored rug in front of it. Restored hardwood ran the length of the room that ended with a bar separating the living room from the kitchen, but still giving the illusion of an open concept.

Mason and Lily Anne followed Laurel further into the home as she pointed out cabinet space, storage, and energy efficient lighting that added value to the home. She filled them in on all the specifics—the year the house had been built, the last time the plumbing had been checked, the internet capabilities, the extended warranties on the appliances—and answered all of their questions without missing a beat.

When the downstairs had been seen, they ventured to the bedrooms on the second floor. The master left nothing to be desired with tall windows, new carpet, and burgundy walls that spoke life into the room without overpowering the space. The bathroom equally stunned. It even had a clawfoot soaking tub and separate shower. The his-and-her vanity had tons of drawers and space for her hair products, too.

The next bedroom wasn't as big, but had the same windows and carpet, only in a dark gray instead of silver like in the master. The walls looked like some shade of café blue, soft and subtle.

"I know this room may be a little on the small side, but it's the perfect size for a nursery. And look at that view! Can't you just imagine watching the sunrise on a Sunday morning with a cooing baby in your arms?" Laurel smiled wide and Lily Anne tried to match it, failing miserably.

She *could* imagine it. But it took more than imagination to make a baby. It took viable eggs and working hormones. Unable to hold the smile any longer, Lily Anne dropped her head as her stomach twisted.

"Hey, Laurel, you mind giving us a few minutes to wander around up here by ourselves? I'd like a chance to talk things over with Lily Anne alone." Mason placed a hand on the small of Lily Anne's back.

Laurel nodded quickly and walked to the door. "Of course. I'll just wait on the porch."

As Laurel's footsteps trailed down the stairs, Mason slid the hand that had been on her back around her waist, pulling Lily Anne into a hug. "Talk to me, Chief."

"It's just, I *can* imagine that, Mason. A baby with your hazel eyes and belly laugh, a little boy or girl to rock at night, a family like I never had, with a mom and a dad that love unconditionally. But what if imagining is all I'm able to do? What if I can't get pregnant? What if I fail at giving you a family?"

Lily Anne swallowed hard as she stared at Mason. The fear that once again she wasn't good enough to keep a man in her life battered her heart, punching holes from the inside out until the hope she'd managed to muster since the proposal spilled out like sifted flour. A single tear slid down her cheek.

Mason brushed it away. "First of all, you could never fail at giving me a family. The day you said 'yes' to marrying me, you became my family. Secondly, I know you're still waiting to hear back from the doctor, but like I told you in Pastor Clemens's office, it doesn't matter. You're stuck with me. If you want to have a baby, then we'll try until the cows come home and if it's God's will, it'll happen. If not, we'll explore other options. At the end of the day, *we* are still a family of five: you, me, and God the Father, God the Son, and God the Holy Ghost. Wait? They're three in one, so maybe we're a family of three? Math was not my strong suit."

"Mason, stop joking." Lily Anne swatted at his finger still hovering over her cheek. "This is important."

With the moves of a ninja, Mason caught her hand, lacing their fingers together. "I know, Lil. Would I love to have a baby with you? Yes, I sure would. Will I be happy with or without one? Yes, I will. Because I love you for you." He kissed the inside of her wrist right above the pulse point. The touch permeated clean through the bone down to the marrow of her soul.

"Mason, you said—"

"I love you? Yeah, Chief, I should have said it years ago. But don't worry. You don't have to say it back yet. Not until you're ready."

Lily Anne touched her forehead to his. "I want to say it back, Mase. I do. I just need more time." She rubbed her lips together, silently praying for the courage to voice the words she felt in her heart. The last thing she wanted to do was hurt Mason, but after seeing how her parents' marriage ended, that statement scared the life right out of her.

Before she had a chance to explain, Mason stepped back and threw his arm around her. Smiling, he led them to the door. As they stepped into the hallway, he leaned in and whispered, "I know."

Lily Anne released a small sigh as she pushed her fears aside, focusing instead on Mason's admission. He *loved* her? *How* did that happen? *When* did that happen? She didn't know, but she knew the same process was working in her, too. She felt it, even as the two of them descended the stairs and rejoined Laurel on the porch.

With a bright smile, Laurel stretched her arms wide as she glanced at the house. "Well, what do you think?"

"I picked the place out, so you know I'm happy with it." Mason turned, his gaze lighting on Lily Anne. "Do you like it, Chief?"

"Not really, Mason." She shook her head and watched his face fall, as she expected. Now she understood why he joked so much. It was fun. Unable to keep the charade going, she grabbed his hand and squeezed. "I don't like it. I love it."

"Really?"

"Really, Mase. It's a good size to start out with and the location on the lake can't be beat. Plus, it's close to the bakery, the paper, and The B&B Inn, but not in either of our parents' backyard. It checks all my boxes, which, I admit, is hard to do."

With a nod, Mason turned to Laurel. "Well, then, you know what they say."

"What's that?" asked Laurel.

"A happy wife, a happy life. Put in an offer a couple thousand less than the listing price and let's get the ball rolling."

"My pleasure. I'll text you when I hear back." Laurel shook both their hands and went on her way, a little extra pep in her step as she walked to her car.

Mason plopped down in the driver's side seat and raised his hand for a high-five. Lily Anne smacked a loud one against his palm as she wiggled in her seat, doing an impromptu happy dance. She wasn't sure how it started, but laughter bubbled between them as Mason turned the ignition. As she tried to catch her breath, a snort broke free. Instantly, her cheeks heated and she covered her face.

As Mason veered onto the road, he cupped her knee softly. "You're beautiful, you know that?"

Lily Anne mumbled a thank you and turned to face the window. He called her beautiful after she snorted? What kind of man did that? *Not the boy who snapped wise cracks like a Slim Jim, that's for sure.* Her entire life, she'd chased perfection, allowed her flaws to shame her, and hidden her heart away for fear of failure. But with Mason, she didn't have to hide. He got her, all of her, and crazy as it was, he loved her.

Before long, the motor grew quiet, the sudden shift jolting Lily Anne back to the present and The B&B Inn. She'd been so engrossed in her musings, she'd failed to notice they'd returned. Realizing Mason was waiting in the drive, she rushed out of the car to meet him. Taking him by the hand, she led them to the steps and began to climb. As she did, her cell phone rang.

"Hello?"

"Hello, Lily Anne. This is Pastor Clemens."

"Hang on just a second and I'll put you on speaker." Lily Anne hit the button and held the phone between her and Mason. "Okay, go ahead."

"Listen, I've been roped into Sweetheart Storytime and I need to move tonight's session to the square. Is that workable for y'all?"

Beside her, Mason nodded while Lily Anne did the same. "Yeah, that's fine, sir."

"Great. I'll meet you guys under the shelter. Oh, and bring your letters."

Lily Anne stared at the screen, her nerves mounting. She still hadn't found the right time to tell Mason about the article and since she'd meshed the two assignments together, she was bound by copyright laws. She'd emailed the signed contract, which promised a retraction for Mason, and the rough draft earlier in the week. After the scolding she'd received from Mrs. Campbell for missing her deadline, Lily Anne ensured smooth sailing until publication. Asking permission to read the piece out loud at a public event? Not smooth sailing.

Realizing her current situation had no easy resolution, Lily Anne tried another approach to get out of the assignment. "Pastor, can we listen tonight and share next week? I really need more time for mine."

"Nonsense. Whatever you've got will be fine. If you have to, improvise. No one will ever know. Ah, shoot! Here comes the dead spot. I'm gonna lose y—"

The screen reverted back to home.

Lily Anne hit the lock key and slid her phone back in her pocket.

Beside her, Mason stared, his brow furrowed. With a snap of his fingers, he lowered his back foot to the step below them. "Hey, Lil. I just remembered I've got a few more shots to take out at Cut-Through Trails, so I'll meet you at the square. That cool?"

Lily Anne cocked her head to the side, taken aback by the odd tone in Mason's voice. He sounded off, but maybe her mind was playing tricks on her.

"Sure." Lily Anne leaned in and pressed a chaste kiss to his cheek. "Drive safe." Mason tensed on contact, but tried to hide it with a hug. Now, she knew something was wrong. But as she watched his retreating form, she squashed the desire to run after him and ask. With a secret of her own lodged between them, she didn't need to pry.

Chapter Nineteen

cicle lights lit up the town square, making the park shimmer and glisten in the evening shade. Red and pink string hearts hung in the corners of the gazebo and along the rafters. A banner reading "Sweetheart Storytime" stretched between the back two poles where a single microphone stood center stage. Outdoor heaters were staggered about the surrounding shelters and tiny votive candles served as center pieces with chocolate kisses and confetti hearts sprinkled around. The scene, festive and flirty, made the scowl on Mason's face stick out like a sore thumb.

Pastor Clemens dropped on the bench seat beside him. "You better watch out or your face will freeze like that. Out here, it's cold enough to."

"Hey, Pastor." Mason drummed his fingers along the edge of the table, sneaking a glance at his watch. "Lil's on her way."

"Oh, she's got plenty of time." Pastor Clemens waved a hand between them. "You got your letter?"

"I do."

The old preacher hiked a brow. "Does she?"

"Maybe." Mason exhaled loudly and stared at the empty stage, but he didn't see the microphone or the banner. Instead, his eyes focused on a memory from a few nights ago—a spiral notebook left open on the table, his name atop the paper, and a full page of musing following it. *If it looks like a letter, acts like a letter, sounds like a letter? Most likely it's a letter.*

"Doesn't matter." Pastor Clemens stroked his beard, giving the hairs a quick tug before resting his hand on the table. "If she comes with or without it, things will all work

182

out, kind of like money. Whether you've got a lot or a little, either way, you'll survive, and so will she."

"Are you working out some sort of life lesson, sir?" Mason narrowed his eyes a bit before remembering he was talking to a man of God. "No offense, Pastor, but I'm really not feeling it tonight."

Pastor guffawed, loud as his preaching behind the pulpit. "Whew-ee, do I remember those times!"

"What times?" Mason took the bait even though he knew he shouldn't.

"The times I didn't 'feel' it. Marriage is full of those times. Truth be told, it's the times we don't 'feel' it that matter most. When life is easy, love is, too. When life is hard, love follows suit. Hard times are when we need love the most. Does Lily Anne know you're cross with her?"

"Who said I was?" Mason sat up taller. Was he upset? Yes. Did he want to talk about it? Not in the least.

Pastor crossed his arms and stared at him with an I-wasn't-born-yesterday kind of look.

Exasperated, Mason lifted his hands, palms out. "I didn't come right out and say it, if that's what you're asking."

"That's what I figured." Pastor Clemens pinned his gaze directly on Mason. "My best advice to you is to hash it out. Lay all your cards on the table. But wait until after the storytelling. She needs to hear your love letter before you lay into her. You do, too. Love—it's your ace in the hole."

The preacher stood from the table and dusted his hands in front of him like he'd done a hard day's work, then inclined his head to the left.

Lily Anne strolled down the walk toward them, a mass of blonde curls blowing wildly behind her with each step. Mason stared, lost in the way she moved.

Pastor bent at the waist and whispered, "Get ready, son. You're up first."

With that, the preacher was gone.

"Hey." Lily Anne slid on to the seat beside him. "Sorry. There was a train on the tracks."

Mason didn't offer a smile, but gave a slight nod. "No worries, you're right on time."

As if on cue, Mr. Hart, the host for the evening, tapped on the microphone. A couple of thuds boomed through the loudspeaker, garnering the assembly's attention. When all eyes lighted on him, he waved with both hands.

"Good afternoon, I'd like to welcome everyone to the tenth annual Sweetheart Storytime. If you've never been here, you're in for a treat." A trickling of applause waved through the park.

When it had passed, Mr. Hart stepped closer to the mic stand. "Valentine's Day is a celebration of love so during the weeks leading up to the holiday and the weeks that follow, folks in Pine Valley like to swap courting tales and love lessons. The stories bring in the new and preserve the old. The youngins remind everyone how exciting marriage can be while the couples edging toward their golden years set relationship goals for us all. Our first storyteller tonight fits into the youngins' crowd. Mason, come on up and start us off right."

Beside him, Lily Anne went rigid, hand frozen behind her ear, holding a curl. It was less than the inspiring response he'd hoped for, but with Pastor Clemens's words fresh in his memory, he stood and gave a thumbs up. She didn't roll her eyes or tap her fingers or meet him with the smile he adored. Instead, she sat still as stone, with only her lips moving. No, not moving. Counting.

Mason stooped and touched his lips to her temple. She didn't acknowledge him, but when he looked out from the stage, he watched her shoulders relax. The small gesture spoke volumes.

"Hello, friends and neighbors," Mason started, earning a chuckle here and there across the park. "If you'll bear with me, I'm going to try to get through this letter. Don't worry, it's short and sweet." Mason cleared his throat and took hold of the microphone.

"Dear Lily Anne, words aren't really my thing, so I'm going to revert back to what I know: pictures. I've heard a picture is worth a thousand words and I believe that. You are the picture I can't get out of my head. I see my crazy in the kinks of your hair. I see my days in the agendas you love to make. I see my strength in your fears and my redemption in what you think are imperfections. You are the thousand-word shot I don't deserve but promise to cherish for better, for worse, for richer, for poorer, in sickness and in health, as long as we both shall live. Love, Mason."

Claps sounded across the park while Mason made his way back to his seat and relinquished the stage once again into Mr. Hart's capable hands.

Mr. Hart gave an extra clap. "Thank you for sharing, Mason. That was great." He scanned the clipboard in his right hand and leaned into the microphone. "Next up, we've got Lily Anne. Come on up, sweet girl."

Beside Mason, Lily Anne sipped from a water bottle. She twisted the cap back on, stood, and drifted slowly through the park until she made her way to center stage. "That's a t-t-tough act to follow, but I'll give it a go." She opened her notebook, the same one Mason had seen on the kitchen table.

"Mase, growing up, I, uh, I," Lily Anne paused and sucked in a breath. She searched the crowd until her gaze met Mason's. Quickly, she swiped at her cheek.

"Mason, growing up, I never…"

When she stalled a second time, Mason folded his arms on the table and leaned in, beads of sweat dotting his brow. He waited for words of affirmation, a confession of love, a promise for the future. Something—anything—to prove their relationship wasn't one-sided, that she felt for him like he felt for her, but Lily Anne gave him nothing but a sad stare. His shoulders sagged as she choked the mic stand, addressing the crowd a final time. "I'm so sorry. I can't. I just can't do it."

Though she hung her head as she descended the stage, there was no hiding her quickened steps as she sped away. Mason shut his eyes tight, preferring the darkness to her pain. When he opened them again, Pastor Clemens stood on the other side of the table, hands raised as if to ask what happened. Without an answer, he simply shrugged.

The preacher stuck a hand in his pocket and leaned in closer. "You'll figure it out."

"Yes, sir."

With that, the preacher patted Mason on the back and wandered away. As Mr. Hart called the next speaker, Mason snuck back to the inn. On the way to his room, he noticed Lily Anne's door shut tight and the lights flipped off like he'd expected. The taped envelope on his own door, however, caught him off guard. Mason pulled it free and slipped into his room.

He took a seat on the edge of the bed and gently worked a finger along the seam until the flap came free. Realizing the folded journal paper was not the letter from the notebook he'd seen before, Mason sighed, until he read the words Lily Anne had penned:

Here's the picture. A thousand words coming soon.

Realizing a second part of the message awaited him, Mason reopened the envelope. Sure enough, there was more. When he tilted it to the side, an old Polaroid slipped out. On instinct, he shook it a time or two for good measure before flipping it over. Mason stared in amazement at the photo he held in his hand. The scene captured the reunion proposal from a side view. Mason's profile on bended knee, Lily Anne with her fingers skimming her thigh, and the makeshift ring between them. The shot lacked finesse and the angle leaned a bit toward the right, but Mason had never seen a more perfect picture.

It was the last thing he saw before going to sleep, still wondering why she hadn't read her letter.

Chapter Twenty

L ily Anne spent the Sunday following Sweetheart Storytime the same way she had spent every Sunday since
Mason signed the Valentine Agreement, in a church
pew beside her fiancé. Unlike weeks prior, though, Lily Anne
found it impossible to focus on the preaching. Not because
of anxiety over her failure in the square, but because of Mason's snores. Loud, erratic, unable-to-ignore snores. Each
time she swung an elbow into Mason's side, she stifled a
giggle. By the time service had ended, she sincerely worried
about bruising.

As soon as the two of them walked through the door at
The B&B Inn, Mason made a beeline to the coffee pot, started a fresh brew, and plopped down to wait for it. When he
laid his head down on the table, Lily Anne lost it, a chorus of
sniggers breaking free between her lips.

Mason raised slightly, resting his chin on his folded arms.
"What's so funny?"

"Nothing, really." Lily Anne managed to get out between
a laugh and a snort. This time, she didn't bother covering
her face. "Just wondering if you make a habit of napping
during Sunday service or if church this morning was a rarity."

A groan ripped from his chest as his face flushed. "A rarity, Chief. For some reason, I didn't get much rest last night."

Lily Anne clasped her hands in front of her as her laughter subsided, silence filling the space between them. Keeping herself up all night worrying about the letter fiasco was
bad enough, but being the cause of Mason's sleepless night
was worse. She'd never meant to hurt him. "D-d-did you
find my letter?"

Mason smiled, but it didn't brighten his eyes like usual.
"I did."

Lily Anne swallowed hard as she mapped out the best course of action. There was no denying the two of them needed to talk, but with Mr. Rowe already on his way over for their business lunch, Lily Anne thought it best to wait to hash things out. She did have time for an apology, though.

"I'm sorry about last night, Mase." Lily Anne snagged a mug from the drying rack, filled it up, and set it in front of him. "Will this help?"

"A little, I hope. Our lunch guests might not take too kindly to my snoring." Mason chuckled, but Lily Anne knew it was forced. She blinked and when she opened her eyes again, she saw Mason in a different light. Not as a trouble-maker or famous photographer, but as a soul deflecting hurt with humor. How many times had he used that joke-and-de-flect maneuver to hide his pain? Better yet, how many times had she missed it?

Ignoring the question, Lily Anne laughed along, hoping it sounded more genuine than it felt. "No, I don't think Mr. and Mrs. Rowe would be impressed by that. What time are they coming?"

"Soon. Mr. Rowe said to expect him a little past one, so maybe a half hour."

Snapping her fingers, Lily Anne skirted around the table to the cupboard. "Perfect. That's just enough time for me to set the table and change."

Mason tried to offer his assistance, but she shooed him away before he got a word out. She buzzed from one seat to the next until plates, bowls, and utensils were neatly ar-ranged and a vase brimming with flowers stood as a center-piece.

"There." Lily Anne dusted her hands in front of her, sat-isfied with the lunch presentation. "What do you think?"

"It looks beautiful, Chief." Mason draped an arm around her shoulder. "Thank you."

"Of course. Is there anything left to do?"

"The beef stew is warming in the slow cooker and Ma picked up some fresh rolls on her way home, so we're all set. I think she put them in the warming drawer under the stove."

"Good. Um, do we have time to talk?" Lily Anne stood behind the table, gripping the edge for support like Mason's answer might blow her away.

Mikie's voice boomed as he stomped through the foyer and into the kitchen. "Talk about what? The new lawnmower being delivered today?"

Mason side-eyed his brother and blinked slowly. "That's not what I had in mind, Ace, but sure. Tell us all about it." With a sweep of his hand, he gestured to Mikie that the floor was his.

The Montgomery brothers were a sight, loud but loveable and perfect entertainment on a Sunday afternoon. Lily Anne bit her lip to keep from having another gigglefest, but there was no stopping the eye roll. She didn't even try. They had to know how ridiculous they were.

Mikie took a step closer to Mason, lifted his chin, and grinned. "Don't mind if I do. It's green and mean and drives like a dream, or so the salesman said. It's got a hydrostatic transmission, bumper-to-bumper warranty for not one, but two years, and enough horsepower to mulch, mow, and bag without breaking a sweat."

Lily Anne raised her eyebrows. "Wow, Mikie. It sounds like you picked a good one." She rounded the table to join them where they stood.

"Thanks, Lil. I figured with the wedding next week it was best to concede defeat." Mikie turned to face Mason and extended a hand. "Congrats, Deuce. I lost the bet, fair and square. I should have known you were capable of the impossible, especially after that senior prank you pulled off. Glad you finally got the girl."

190

Lily Anne shook her head. Had she forgotten to clean her ears this morning? She hoped so, because Mikie's words sounded an awful lot like a smoking gun, shooting the truth about Lily Anne's broken nose point blank.

"Senior prank?" Lily Anne took a step forward and crossed her arms. "Got the girl?"

She looked from the older Montgomery brother to the younger, the one she'd promised to marry. Mason's eyes had grown from drowsy to wide awake.

A danger sign flashed in her brain, but she stepped forward again, this time toward Mikie. "What are you talking about?"

Mikie chuckled. "Nothing but nonsense."

"Tell me about it then." She clasped her hands in front of her. She needed to stay cool and collected, at least until she got the story out of Mikie. Maybe he didn't mean what she thought he did. Maybe she misunderstood. Or maybe Mason had been lying all this time about the senior prank.

"When Mason told me he proposed, naturally, I was shocked. The idea of Mason marrying was hard to wrap my brain around, but he assured me it was happening. I still didn't believe him, so I wagered him Ma's lawn duty. If he got married, I'd take over the landscaping. If he chickened out, he had to do Ma's *and* mine. See? I told you it was nothing."

"Right, right." Lily Anne grew quiet, but when Mikie started to walk away, she gently pulled him back. "What did you mean about a senior prank, though?"

Mikie clapped Mason on the back loudly "Just that I shouldn't have doubted Mason's ability to work miracles. Pulling the fire alarm in a packed cafeteria and never getting caught? That takes skill."

Lily Anne's heart thundered in her chest as she watched Mason's eyes grow even wider. At the same time, the ground seemed to shift beneath her feet. She didn't move physically, but with that admission, an invisible gulf opened between her and Mason.

Slowly, Mason cupped her elbow and whispered in her ear, unaware of the canyon he needed to cross. "Lily Anne, can we talk?"

His touch lit a torch beneath her skin as her anger boiled hotter. "Uh, sure, yeah." Now more than ever they needed to talk. But not before she had a moment to clear her head. "A-After I change for lunch. Mr. Rowe will be here soon, so if I'm going to change, I have to go now."

Turning to Mikie, Lily Anne pasted a smiled on her face. "Congratulations on your lawnmower. I'm sure you'll get your money's worth out of it."

With that, she squeezed between them and jogged up the stairs. Her steps didn't slow until she shut the door behind her. The heavy wood supported her frame as she slid down it onto the floor, pulling her knees into her chest as the first tear slipped free. Mason, the jokester in high school, had lied to her. The boy with the good heart and sweet smile lied to her about the senior prank that broke her nose. Had Mason 2.0 lied, too? About the proposal? His crush?

Loving her?

Chapter Twenty-One

As soon as Lily Anne was out of earshot, Mason let out a curse he'd need to pray about later.

Mikie laid a hand on his shoulder. "Deuce, I'm sorry. I wasn't thinking. But, seriously, man, why didn't you tell her about the bet?"

"Gee, let's see. Telling your fiancée you bet on your wedding isn't a real great way to get her down the aisle." *Neither is unintentionally breaking her nose in high school and not admitting to it.*

"Normally, no." Mikie moved his hand up and down in front of Mason as if he was on display. "But you're, well, you."

"What's that supposed to mean?"

"It means, you don't have a serious bone in your body, and Lily Anne knows that. If you would have told her, she'd have gotten a kick out of it."

"Probably about the prank, too." Mason mumbled as ran a hand down his face, trying to come up with some way to apologize that would cover all his missteps, past and present. *Why didn't I come clean at the farm? I had the chance to explain and I blew it.*

With a deep breath, Mason turned back to his brother. "Listen, do you still need me? Because Mr. Rowe is going to be here any minute and I'd really like to talk to Lily Anne before he arrives."

"No, but I do need Chase's bookbag." Mikie pointed beneath the check-in counter. "It's under the register."

Mason stomped to the foyer, grabbed the bag, and tossed it to Mikie. He caught it with ease and Mason shot daggers at him, daring him to brag.

"That all?"

Mikie nodded. "Yeah, Deuce. That's all. Listen, I really am sorry. Call me later and let me know you two are good, huh?"

"I'll try."

Leaving his brother to see himself out, Mason went back into the dining room. He grabbed four tall glasses and placed them to the right of the plates. Then he filled a serving tray with an assortment of cheese, crackers, fruit, and nuts to put out as appetizers. A pitcher of sweet tea completed the table.

"Nice touch." Lily Anne leaned against the wall and pointed to the added items just as the front door slammed shut.

"Hello, there, Miss Lily Anne. Mason." Mr. Rowe strolled into the dining room, holding his wife's hand and Mason's future. "How's your Sunday going?"

"Fine, sir." Lily Anne nodded with a tight smile. "Yours?"

"Same, same. Say, have you two met my wife?" Mr. Rowe put a hand on his wife's back as he asked the question.

Mason and Lily Anne both shook their heads.

"Let me introduce you, then. This is my better half, Sylvia. Sylvia, this is the couple I've been telling you about, Lily Anne Dawson and Mason Montgomery. They're interested in buying Mama's old place and the studio."

"Oh, it's so nice to meet you." Sylvia stepped forward and pulled each of them into a hug. "Stan hasn't stopped talking about the two of you for weeks."

Mason tilted his head and smiled. "All good things, I hope?"

"Heavens, yes." She nodded in Lily Anne's direction. "Especially you, young lady."

"Oh." Lily Anne ducked her head but not quick enough to hide the pink of her cheeks. "Thank you. Are you hungry, ma'am?"

"Starving. And call me Sylvia, dear." She tugged at the collar of Mr. Rowe's coat once before proceeding to remove her own. Sylvia held her arm out for her husband's jacket and pointed to the closet in the foyer.

Lily Anne rushed to the closet and opened the door for her. "Yes, ma'am. I mean, Sylvia." Lily Anne blushed again as Sylvia hung up the coats. Mason came up behind her and slipped an arm around her waist. She caught his hand, patted it, and removed it discreetly so that their guests didn't notice. Mason, however, got the message loud and clear.

In buffet style, they all filled their bowls, the rich aroma of roast circling about them every time the lid was lifted. Mason swapped the flowers for a breadbasket and filled their glasses. Together, they sat and Mr. Rowe blessed the meal. From then on, it was a frenzy of grins, good food, and small-town gossip, with the topic eventually turning to the sale of Forget Me Not Photography.

"Mason, I know we've discussed this before, but now that you've seen the house and made an offer, I have to ask again. Are you sure you're ready to take on the studio? It's a big responsibility."

"Mr. Rowe, I assure you I'm ready. The last few years, I've been blessed to photograph things I never imagined in my wildest dreams and I've enjoyed every minute of it. I thank God for the doors He's opened, but it's time to come home. I'm ready." Mason reached across the table and took Lily Anne's hand. This time, thankfully, she let him. "We're ready."

Sylvia smiled at her husband. "Isn't that sweet, Stan?"

"Sure is." Mr. Rowe sipped his tea, raising his glass toward Lily Anne before sitting it back down. "If Mason hadn't been hiding this pretty little thing away, we'd probably be signing titles tonight instead of having a meet-and-greet. But he never said a word about you at the first meeting. Did you drive separately to the reunion?"

"Y-y-yes, I did." Lily Anne studied Mr. Rowe while she answered, but quickly averted her gaze to find Mason's. Wide copper eyes asked questions he wasn't sure how to answer.

Oblivious to the silent conversation going on around him, Mr. Rowe shook his head. "Such a shame. Mason showed me portfolios and sales projections, but a good girl like you would have sealed the deal. Profit isn't the heart of Forget Me Not Photography. Family is, and I wanted a family man to take over. Glad to see I've found one."

"Thank you, sir." Mason drained the rest of his tea to keep his mouth from going dry.

As he did, Lily Anne stood. "Oh, no! The pitcher's empty. Let me go make some more." She slowed as she passed Mason's chair, still clutching the handle. "I think the tea shelf is too high for me to reach. Can you help me in the kitchen, please?"

"Sure, Chief." Mason answered around a mouthful of stew. "Excuse us."

"Take your time." Mr. Rowe winked and Mason wanted to crawl beneath the table. He knew what awaited him in the kitchen was a far cry from the romantic rendezvous the old man insinuated.

As soon he crossed the threshold, Lily Anne lit into him. "Do you even want to marry me? Or am I just a pawn to get your way?"

"Of course, I want to marry you!"

"I'm finding that really hard to believe right now, Mason." She stared for a moment and then started pacing in front of the sink.

Mason held up his hands like a caught criminal. "If this is about the bet, I can explain."

"It's not about the bet." She huffed and crossed her arms over her chest, never breaking stride. "That's just brothers having fun."

The throbbing in Mason's chest rose to his temples until the pounding in both matched. With a deep inhale, he placed himself in front of Lily Anne, gently catching her by the arms.

"You're mad about the prank, then?" Mason paused and searched her face, but her expression gave nothing away. "Chief, I never meant for you to get hurt."

With a shake of her head, Lily Anne took over the conversation. "It's not about the broken nose, not really. It's that you didn't tell me about it. Not in high school, not ever. Mikie had to tell me. I asked you point blank a week after the prank happened and you laughed it off. You made me think I was crazy for suspecting you, just like you let me think you had no ulterior motive in proposing. If you had just told me everything from the start, I would have understood." Lily Anne jerked free from his hold and resumed her pacing in front of him.

"I didn't know how to tell you," Mason snapped, momentarily forgetting about the thin walls and lunch guests in the next room. He licked his lips and tried again, lowering his voice. "But while we're talking about secrets, do you mind telling me about the letter? You let Pastor think it wasn't finished, when I know for a fact it is."

Lily Anne's jaw dropped as she peered up at him. "How do you know that?"

"Because I saw it." Mason pointed at the floor as if the offending letter was at his feet. "You left your notebook lying on the table. I saw my name and a full page after. It was done."

Lily Anne clasped her hands in front of her, giving them a good squeeze. "Yes, Mason. It was done, but I couldn't read it."

"Why not?" Mason cringed at her admission. "Did you realize you didn't mean what you wrote?"

Taking a step forward, Lily Anne's breaths quickened. "No, nothing like that."

With trembling hands, she reached for him. Mason wanted to take what she was offering. Her excuses. Her explanation. Her hand, in the moment and in marriage, but he was tired of being the puppy begging for scraps.

Mason slipped his hands in his pockets to keep from caving. "What, then? I poured my heart and soul out to you on that stage and I got nothing in return. Why didn't you read it?" Pressing a hand to his chest, Mason rubbed at the pressure on his sternum while Lily Anne tapped her fingers against her thigh.

She stopped suddenly and threw her arms out wide. "Because I couldn't! Legally, I couldn't."

"What do you mean?" Mason cocked his head toward her. "*Legally*?"

Laying a hand on the counter, Lily Anne exhaled as she met his gaze. "I wrote the letter *to* you, but *for* a magazine. For *As the Belle Told*."

Mason's jaw dropped. "You're joking, right?"

Lily Anne shook her head, her chest heaving like she'd been running for days. "I'm not. Mrs. Campbell commissioned me to do an essay about our engagement, but I was having trouble finding my angle until Pastor Clemens gave us the assignment. I thought, why not write one letter for both? By the time Sweetheart Storytime rolled around, the magazine already had the draft and first rights. Reading it would have broken the contract. I couldn't. Don't you see?"

Mason averted his eyes from her guilt-stricken stare to the ceiling. "I think I'm beginning to." He blew out a breath toward heaven and walked closer to where Lily Anne stood. "Tell me something, Lil. When did Margie offer you the article? Three weeks ago? Two?"

Mason waited, but she didn't speak. The silence was telling.

He tried again. "When, Lily Anne?"

"The day you gave me my ring."

"Wow, Chief." Mason sharply inhaled, the air movement producing a light whistle. "I knew your writing was important to you, but it takes dedication to marry someone for it."

"You know I wouldn't do that, especially not after what you told me. I'm not like those girls who chased you, hoping to ride your coattails. They make me sick." Lily Anne stomped and Mason resisted the urge to retaliate with one of his own.

He huffed instead. "Those girls make you sick, but Mrs. Campbell doesn't? Her feature ruined my reputation as a Christian man. Doesn't that matter?"

"More than you know." Wide copper eyes pleaded with him as Lily Anne bit down on her lip. "If you'll just give me a little time, I can explain everything."

"Like why you agreed to the story so fast? We'd barely gotten our feet wet as a couple. At that time, there's no way you knew we'd work out."

"You're right, I didn't know." Lily Anne dropped her shoulders. "But I was hoping."

Mason started toward her again, but when he was an arm's length away, he stopped. If he touched her, he'd never get the words out and he needed to hear her answer.

"Hoping for a husband? Or for a break in your career?"

She winced and closed her eyes. When she opened them again, gone was the hurt he'd seen before and in its place, fire glistened back at him.

"Both." Lily Anne took in a breath. "I won't stand here and say I wasn't giddy about the essay and where it might lead. But that night at the reunion, I had no idea how things would play out and I still agreed to marry you."

Finally at his wit's end, Mason threw both hands in the air. "Because of Dr. Branham. You were scared into saying yes because you wanted a baby."

A single tear rolled down Lily Anne's cheek as she gave a light laugh, like his accusation was so ridiculous she couldn't believe it. "That may have been true, at first, but I told you about my medical issues as soon as I caught feelings for you. Feelings that I never thought I'd catch. But then you came along and made me believe I was worthy. You let me believe the proposal was just about us, but you had a business on the line."

Lily Anne took a step forward and rushed on.

"After years of telling myself the storybook kind of love didn't exist, you made me want it. In your eyes, I saw my happily-ever-after being written and I couldn't help but keep reading."

She took another step, leaving them only inches apart. So close and yet so far had never rang truer. Straightening her spine, she gave another laugh.

"And now? Now that I can't imagine what my world would be like without you, I run smack dab into the plot twist I never saw coming and find out I'm playing second fiddle to the most important man in my life once again. I did that with my father. Believe me when I say I have no intention of doing the same with my husband." Lily Anne closed the remaining distance between them as the toe of her boot touched his. Tear-filled eyes stared back at him as she whispered, "Was it all a lie?"

The words, low and heavy, hung between them, stretching the moment into slow motion. Mason shook his head while he unclogged his throat. "None of it was, not a single word. I was going to tell you about the prank. You have to believe me. I've wanted you, *waited for you*, for years."

Lily Anne slapped the back of her hand against her palm. "How do I know that?"

Unable to keep from touching her, Mason cupped Lily Anne's shoulder and squeezed. "Because I've proved it to you every day since I proposed. I should have told you the truth back in high school, but I was young and dumb. I'm not the boy who lied to you about that stupid prank."

"You're exactly right, Mason. You're not that boy any-more." Lily Anne covered his hand on her shoulder with hers. "Now, you're the man who convinced me love was real by breaking my heart."

"Chief, please."

Lily Anne drew in a long breath and held it for a beat. Then, she exhaled through pursed lips before finally meeting his eyes. "I need some time to clear my head."

"*Now?* What about lunch?"

She dropped both arms to her side and shrugged out of his hold. "Yes, the *business* lunch."

Mason cringed. He hadn't meant to insinuate the dinner's importance, but once again he'd stuck his foot in his mouth.

Ever the picture of the perfect hostess, she retreated to the dining room door. "We're going to walk back out there, hand in hand. You're going to tell a joke, I'm going to laugh, and we're all going to have a lovely meal. When Mr. and Mrs. Rowe leave, I will, too."

Lily Anne leaned against the door facing and smiled, the plastic smile she gave to everyone. Mason hated it. He wanted the megawatt grin he'd seen when they played Smack or when she teased him about his feet.

Mason stepped beside her. "Lil, you don't have to go."

"I really do, Mason. I think better when I'm alone." With trembling fingers, Lily Anne grazed his cheek.

The warmth drew Mason further into her hold. He didn't want to let her go, but the tenderness in her caress gave him the hope he needed to agree. "If that's what you need, okay. But I don't like it."

"Me, either." She removed her hand and pushed the door, stopping mid-step. "Mase?"

"Yeah?"

"Please get the tea from the fridge." A corner of her mouth tugged up, but not enough to qualify as a smile. He didn't bother trying for one, just followed her instructions and trailed behind her.

Setting the pitcher down, Mason relayed his eyes around the table, lighting first on Mr. Rowe, then on Lily Anne. He let out a humorless laugh and took his seat. Mason had worked so hard to make sure the Sunday lunch was perfect, convinced his future lay somewhere between the roast and the rolls.

Turns out he'd been right, in more ways than one.

Chapter Twenty-Two

On Monday morning, the text stuck on Lily Anne's phone was bittersweet.

I MISS YOU.

A sigh rushed past her lips. Lily Anne didn't have the heart to send Mason a reply but lacked the strength to close the message. It lay open while she glazed a pan of honey buns. She wanted to believe the text had everything to do with Mason's feelings for her and nothing to do with their upcoming visit to the bank, but a voice in her head whispered the opposite. As the phone vibrated on the table, she held her breath, expecting another text from Mason. When she looked at the screen, though, the display showed a call instead.

Lily Anne set the bowl of glaze aside and answered. "Hello?"

"Good morning. May I speak with Ms. Dawson, please?"

"This is she."

"Hi, Ms. Dawson. This is Bev, one of the nurses from Dr. Branham's office. It looks like you were waiting to get the results of your lab work. Is that right?"

"Yes, ma'am." Lily Anne crossed one leg over the other and tapped her fingertips against her thigh.

"Well, I'm sorry it's taken so long. There was mix-up with the lab and the results went missing. But we've got them now. Since everything looks good, we can go over them if you want."

"Good?" Blinking hard, Lily Anne repeated the word to herself before going on. "But what about the inconsistencies with my cycle?"

"Without knowing your history, it's hard to say for sure. Do you stay stressed a lot?"

"That's an understatement." Lily Anne rolled her eyes. Stressed didn't begin to cover it.

"There you go, then. Stress makes your hormones go haywire. For some women, it can cause you to be late or miss a month altogether. With these numbers, though, I wouldn't worry. Your estrogen is a tad on the low end of normal, but still within limits. My best advice for you is to relax."

"Easier said than done." Lily Anne laughed into the phone and the nurse did, too.

"Well, unless you need us, we won't see you back for another year. But if you start having more trouble, give us a call and we'll schedule you for that ultrasound Dr. Branham mentioned. Right now, though, she doesn't think it's necessary."

"Sounds good. Thank you."

"Thank you, Ms. Dawson. Bye, now."

The line went dead and Lily Anne bowed her head. As praise filled her heart, tears filled her eyes until rivers rolled down her cheeks. With great fear comes great relief and Lily Anne had been petrified by the possibility of infertility. In similar fashion, the comfort that rallied with the resolution was immeasurable.

A jingle from the door interrupted her moment of thanks. Lily Anne swiped her shirt sleeve beneath her cheeks like a mad woman. When it was too soaked to work anymore, she used the tail of her apron to pat her skin dry before scurrying to her position behind the display case.

"Don't be mad." Logan stood in the lobby with hands lifted as a sign of surrender.

"Why would I be mad?" Lily Anne scrunched her face.

Before he had time to answer, another man entered the shop and waved. "Hi, sweet pea."

Dad? Lily Anne shut her eyes, expecting when she opened them her dad would be gone. *Just like growing up*. But when she looked again, her dad and Logan were both watching her. Warmth spread across her cheeks, but not from embarrassment. She counted to three through clenched teeth.

Planting her hands on her hips, Lily Anne worked a stare between the men before letting her eyes land on Logan. "Y-y-you promised not to interfere."

"He didn't." Her dad placed a hand on Logan's shoulder and sidled up beside him. "I saw the engagement announcement in the paper. You looked happy. It's been a long time since I've seen you smile that big."

"You know, that could be because the last time we were face to face I was a kid begging her father to come to graduation." She leaned against the top of the display, hoping he'd be able to see the fire raging in her eyes. Ten years was a long time to go without seeing a parent in person, but she'd done it, making herself too busy to get away whenever he suggested the two of them meet up.

Her dad straightened his stance. "That's not the last time I saw you."

"Oh, no?" Lily Anne huffed. "Wait, you're right. We did Facetime a few years ago on my birthday for maybe five minutes."

He shook his head and Lily Anne turned back toward the kitchen. The point was moot. When he saw her—if he saw her—didn't matter. It was a blip in time, part of the past neither of them was able to change. With quick steps, she headed for the prep table. She was halfway there when her father called out.

"The last time I saw you smile like you did with Mason, you were at the baseball field, *after* graduation."

In seconds, Lily Anne was at the counter, searching her father's face. Brown eyes, deep and true, stared back at her. Dark circles hung beneath them like low-lying crescent moons. Stubble lined his jaw and chin.

Her father went on. "You and Emma walked the bleachers up and down singing the school song at the top of your lungs."

Lily Anne's knees buckled beneath her, making her stumble back. The memory of that night burned bright in her mind. Everyone gathered at the football field for a bonfire, she and Emma included, but they hung back. She was mad at her dad, anxious about college, and not feeling the party. Emma, being the bestie that she was, took one look at her and suggested they take a walk. Within minutes, they'd made their way to the ballfield and were racing around the bases. She'd never told anyone about their private graduation party, which meant only one thing.

Lord, it can't be. It can't be.

Unblinking, Lily Anne stared hard, trying to reconcile the words coming out of her dad's mouth with the man who'd abandoned her. "But that means you were there."

"I was. Barely, but there." Her father squeezed the back of his neck and blew out a breath. "A guy on my crew switched me his night shift for my day. I pulled my double and drove straight over, full of coffee and covered in dust. I earned myself a couple of weird looks when I walked in like that, but at least I made it. Three kids walked the stage and then your name was called. I whistled and clapped, but there were so many people, you never noticed. I tried to call after the ceremony, but ..." He shrugged, "Did you get my voicemail?"

"Sort of." Lily Anne twiddled with her shirt sleeve. "It came through, but I deleted it without listening."

A loud chuckle echoed from the corner of the shop. Lily Anne and her father both turned to find Logan leaned back with his chair on two legs. When he realized they were watching, he threw his head back and laughed harder. The sudden movement shifted more of his weight to the back of the chair and it toppled to the floor.

"Ooof." Logan groaned, but jumped to his feet like a cat. "Sorry. Y'all keep talking. Pretend I'm not here."

Lily Anne blinked feverishly, reminding herself that she loved her brother to keep from tackling him. She turned to face her dad once more, unsure what to make of the sudden revelation. What was there to say?

On the one hand, he was ten years too late. On the other, he wasn't late at all. He came, ran himself ragged to get there, and then watched her from the sidelines without saying a word. *Just like Mason.* He had done the same thing, kept quiet and watched her from afar.

Lily Anne's insides twisted at the similarities. She'd shut her father out for putting work before family, given him zero chance to explain and never looked back. Her unforgiveness had kept them from a conversation that could have changed both their lives for the better. The worst part? She'd been wrong about her father, at least, partially. He loved her, just not how she expected to be loved.

Was she wrong about Mason, too?

If Lily Anne let it, the cycle would keep repeating itself, like an earworm on loop. She didn't want to make the same mistake with Mason that she had with her father. They needed to talk.

But Mason wasn't in front of her. Her father was. Standing there, she took a long look at him. His hair was graying around the ears and new wrinkles winked at her when he smiled. She had wasted so many years being bitter.

Not wanting to waste a second more, Lily Anne swallowed her pride. "Dad, I'm sorry. I should have called you and talked things out. If not that night, then after one of the hundred voicemails you've left me between then and now. It was wrong to ignore you. So was not telling you about the wedding. I'm sorry for that, too."

"No. I'm sorry. Your stubborn streak ain't news to me, Lil. I should have reached out before now. But I was so sure you'd call me after your Lex-Post interview. When you didn't, I thought I'd lost you for good."

Lily Anne untied her apron and stormed into the dining room, pointing at her father. "The Lex-Post interview? You knew about that?"

"Of course, sweet pea." He slipped a thumb through his belt loop with a shy smile. "I arranged it."

Lily Anne studied her father, looking for any sign of deceit. When she saw none, she whipped around to her brother. "No, Logan did."

Logan's brows knit together as he shook his head dramatically. "Lil, I didn't even know about your interview until after it was over."

"Yes, you did." Lily Anne matched Logan's emphasis by nodding furiously. "You went to dinner with that sportswriter's son. What was his name? Tall, broad shoulders, playing ball in Boston, or he was last I heard."

Logan scratched at the scruff on his chin. "You mean, Eddie? Eddie Bowers?"

"Yeah, that's him. The next day, I got called in for the interview. I figured it was your way of saying thanks since you woke me up at midnight to crash on my couch."

"Oh, yeah." He snapped his fingers as recognition dawned on his face. "I did do that, didn't I?"

"Yes, Logan, you did. That's an awfully big coincidence, don't you think?"

"It is." Logan nodded. "But that's all it is. Eddie was a new transfer to my team, so we were celebrating. Hate to break it to you, but we talked ball and girls, no mention of the paper. Sorry, sis." Logan turned his attention back to his phone, passing the conversation back to her dad.

"You thought I forgot about the interview, didn't you?"

Lily Anne nodded. "Since you didn't care enough to come to graduation, I assumed you wouldn't care enough to keep your word about Lex-Post."

"Of course, I cared. It took me a little longer than originally planned, but after your mom told me you'd put in your resume, I reached out to my buddy. By that time, he'd worked himself up the ranks to managing editor. You were—are—so talented. It was the least I could do." Turning the tables, he pointed at her and wagged his finger. "Make no mistake, though. You earned the job. I just got the ball rolling."

"I don't know what to say." Lily Anne tucked a curl behind her ear to have something to do. Something *other* than bear-hug her father like she wanted to. "Thank you?"

Her father looked her directly in the eye and smiled, changing his face from worn to warm. "You're welcome. I know it doesn't make up for all the things I missed or fix what I've broken between us. I've never been the father you deserve and that's on me." He swallowed hard and stepped forward. "But I miss you and I'd sure like to try again, if you'll let me."

Lily Anne almost ran to her father. Almost. But as much as she loved him, the hurt still ran deep. Knowing he'd been working in the background didn't take the pain away. It did prove his love, though, and that was a start. Against her better judgment and every fiber of her that screamed to keep her distance, she hugged him. Immediately she transformed from an almost married woman to a child who loved and missed her daddy.

Lord. I'll try to forgive and forget. I'll try to move on, but you gotta help me.

"Okay, Dad. You're not the only one who made mistakes. I've been wrong, too. I shouldn't have shut you out the way I did. You've tried to reach me numerous times, but I've ignored you every way possible. Call. Text. Heck, I think I may have even deleted your emails a time or two. But that ends today. If you're still willing to put in the time to fix us, I say, let's go for it."

He held her shoulders and pulled away just enough to meet her gaze with his own. "Yeah?"

"Yeah." Lily Anne nodded as tears welled up. "I still love you, Daddy."

"I love you more, Lily Anne."

Her dad tugged her close again and she began to cry. Through her tears, she saw Logan in the corner of the dining room. He was smiling with his fists out in front of him, like a boxer. She didn't understand why until he pumped his arms. Then, she got it. But by that time, he was already charging them.

"Group hug!" Logan's arms snaked around them and tightened. She squealed when he started rocking them all side to side.

Lily Anne wiggled and twisted in her brother's embrace. "Logan, let go before my guts bust out!"

He squeezed again and laughed, before finally freeing them. She smoothed the flyaway hairs knocked loose in the shuffle. Then put a little distance between herself and the men, feeling lighter than she had in years. It was time for a fresh start and what better way to begin anew than a wedding?

Lily Anne glanced at her engagement ring. "Dad, I don't know if you know this or not, but I asked Logan to walk me down the aisle."

"I know, and I respect your decision. He's been there for you. I haven't."

Lily Anne bit her lip. "That's true, but will you come to the wedding? Sit on the front row, maybe dance with me at some point? I promise not to disappear before you get to say hello like at graduation."

Her father opened his mouth, but when he hesitated before speaking, she cut in, afraid of what he had to say. "I mean, you don't have to. I know it's short notice so if you have other plans, I understand."

"Lily Anne." Her father tapped the end of her nose. "If you want me there, I want to be there. It's your day, sweet pea."

"Thanks, Dad." She gave him another long hug, the clock over his shoulder catching her attention. The ticking reminding her she still had a schedule to keep. "I hate to, but I've got to get back to the kitchen. Mom will have a conniption if I leave all the dishes for her tonight and I haven't washed a single one."

With a chuckle, her father released her. "If you must. Call me tonight so we can work out the details for the wedding. I'm so happy for you, Lil. You're going to make a beautiful bride." Her dad kissed her forehead, the way he used to before tucking her in, and waved. Logan ruffled her hair on his way to the door, stepping straight to the street without another look back.

Lily Anne returned to the kitchen and went back to glazing before moving on to the angel food cakes. By the time the case was full, the dirty pans stood about to her chest. Reluctantly, she filled the sink with water, added the dish detergent, and mixed the cleaner around with her hand, making it good and sudsy. The dishwasher took care of almost everything used in the bakery, but the angel food pans required more attention than the machine could give. She managed to get halfway through the pile before the bell on the door jingled. Hustling, she waited on the customer and rushed back. The screen on her phone was lit with another text from Mason.

MR. ROWE MET ME AT THE BANK AND WE MADE A FEW CHANGES. I DIDN'T WANT TO LEAVE YOU OUT, BUT TODAY WAS THE ONLY TIME HE WAS AVAILABLE. PLUS, I THOUGHT YOU MIGHT BE MORE COMFORTABLE SEEING GEORGE WITHOUT ME AT THE SCHEDULED APPOINTMENT TOMORROW. YOU

CAN KEEP IT IF YOU WANT. IF NOT, THAT'S FINE, TOO. DID I SAY I MISS YOU? BECAUSE I DO, CHIEF.

Lily Anne's fingers hovered over the keypad. She knew what she wanted to say but not how to say it, so she texted back a quick reply and got back to work. Between the crusty pans, in-and-out customers, catering orders, and prep for the next morning, the day flew by. The next time her eyes found the clock on the wall, it was time for closing.

When she locked up shop, she was dead on her feet, moving at a snail's pace through the parking lot. Her phone dinged as she unlocked her car. Expecting another text from Mason, Lily Anne hesitated a moment before looking at the screen. Instead of a message from her fiancé, though, her mother's name appeared.

THE BEAST HAS BEEN CAUGHT!!!!

At first, Lily Anne chuckled. Then, realizing she'd be able to sleep in her own bed again, she thanked God for the unexpected turn of events while she slid in the driver's seat and buckled. The cold seeped through her clothes and Lily Anne welcomed it. Exhaustion, physical and emotional, attacked her body, but the chill combined with her nervous energy roused her wide awake.

As she drove home, questions filtered through her mind like a slide show. Did Mason really love her like he said or was it all an act to convince Mr. Rowe to sell? Did she love him, not as a safety net, but as a man to build her future with? Better yet, could the two of them move past their secrets and forgive?

After parking the car, Lily Anne closed her eyes. Leaning her head against the seat, she focused on the question of forgiveness. While it was true Mason had kept his part of the nose-breaking incident a secret, Lily Anne had done the same with the article. Even if it had been for a good reason, she had still made a mess of things.

But maybe they could fix it. Maybe their marriage had a chance to be more than she originally thought. Instead of being the worn-and-torn hoodie kind of comfy, maybe it could be ugly-sweater kind of crazy. Instead of their agreement being a safety net, maybe it could be a sky dive. If only Lily Anne had the courage to let herself fall.

There in the dark with just her and God, Lily Anne decided to believe what the Apostle Paul wrote, that love bears all things, believes all things, endures all things.

Hopes all things.

She prayed that Mason felt the same.

Chapter Twenty-Three

Tuesday greeted Mason with a full schedule and a smiling brother bent on interrupting his morning coffee. While Mikie sauntered into the dining room, Mason drained the rest of the brew he so desperately needed.

"How about a donut to go with that, Deuce?" Mikie dropped into the seat across from Mason and pushed a bag next to his mug. Mason glared, but eagerly unrolled the top of the sack. A Long John stared back at him.

"If you're trying to make up for spilling the beans to Lily Anne, this isn't enough." Mason plopped the donut down on a napkin and motioned to his empty mug. "Unless you get me a refill, too."

Mikie took his cup and filled it nearly full before handing it back to him. "Now, you want to tell me about it?"

"I'd love to, but I don't rightly know myself."

"So why don't you go find Lily Anne and figure it out?" Mikie curled his lips but took a quick sip of coffee to hide the action.

Mason ignored him and went for the Long John. "I can't. I have a big shoot today for Jewels and Jams in Hickory Hills. Janice needs a new catalog and I'm taking pictures of nearly every piece she has on hand. I'm not sure what time I'll be back, so talking today is pretty much out of the question."

Across from him, Mikie held up his phone and punched the screen, no doubt checking on orders for the store. Mason sunk his teeth into the dough, smushing half the thing into his mouth at once. Instead of smiling as he savored the treat, the usual response a Long John incited, he gagged, spitting the half-chewed monstrosity into the napkin while he grabbed his coffee cup. Mason chugged, preferring a burnt tongue to the awful taste coating his mouth. When his mug was empty and he was sure there was nothing left to wash down, Mason faced Mikie, who'd been shockingly quiet through the whole thing, still fiddling with his phone.

"What kind of donut was that?" Mason reached for the bag to inspect it. "Where did you get that thing from?"

"Country Confections. I ordered it especially for you." Mikie looked at his nails and then wiped them on his shirt sleeve, clearly pleased with himself.

Mason stared at the pastry, wiping his mouth with the back of his hand. "What was in it?"

"Mayonnaise." Mikie shrugged and sipped from his cup, like condiments and pastries were the next bread and butter. "Man, your face is priceless! Wanna watch the video before I upload it?"

Mason shook his head wildly trying to understand his brother's odd behavior. "Video? You're not making any sense."

"Oh, but I am." Mikie motioned for him to come closer. When Mason leaned in, Mikie bonked him on his forehead and stage whispered in enunciated syllables, "It's. A. Joke."

Mason blinked at the confession, opened his mouth, and shut it just as quickly. Mikie laughed and rose from the table. He laughed all the way to the front counter and back while Mason sat there, stunned into silence. When another white paper bag identical to the first landed in front of him, a shudder ran through him.

Mason side-eyed the sack like it might reach out and bite him, or gag him, whichever came first. "You don't joke."

"Correction, I didn't joke." Mikie wagged a finger between them. "Thought I'd give it a try."

"Why?" The question flew free before Mason fully decided he wanted to know the answer, but once the word was out, it was too late to take it back.

"Because if you take life too seriously, you'll never get out alive." Mikie attempted a smile again, a little more successful this time around.

"Two jokes in a row? I never thought I'd see the day." Mason shook his head and laughed softly, hoping to lighten the mood. When his eyes met Mikie's suddenly shiny ones, he knew things were about to get heavy. "Why the sudden change of heart?"

"Davey Barnes, that's why." Mikie tipped his head toward Mason as he spoke, solemn but sure, like a man acknowledging night for the first time after a life filled with sunshine.

"You went and saw Davey? Why didn't you tell me? I'd have gone with you, man."

"It was a spur-of-the-moment thing. But seeing him there, like that, put a lot of things into perspective for me. We could have lost him, Mase. He was just changing a tire and the jacks gave way. It made me think, you know?"

"Yeah, I know exactly what you mean. That's how I felt after Dad's stroke." Mason scrubbed a hand down his face, embarrassed to bring up bad memories after the wounds had scabbed over. But the look on Mikie's face urged him to continue.

Mason tried his explanation again. "Not knowing if he'd ever walk again, talk again. That first week at the rehab center was rough. Dad sat and stared out the window for hours while Ma rambled on and on about how good he looked and what a great job he'd done in physical therapy. He never even acknowledged her. We'd been there all day and I begged Ma for a snack until she finally caved. Remember, Ace?"

Shifting in his chair, Mikie nodded. "I remember. I was so mad at you for pestering her, but I was hungry, too, so I went with her to the vending machines."

"Yup." Mason took a quick sip of his coffee, hoping to swallow down the bitterness against his brother as he did. "While I waited for you guys to get back, I showed Dad the joke book I borrowed from the library, not really expecting anything, but I had to at least try. I opened it to the first chapter and started reading. It took me half a page, but I finally got a smile from him and then a page later, another one. The next week, I got a chuckle."

"That's why you were always goofing around?" Mikie broke in with wide eyes.

"Well, yeah." Mason scratched his jaw. *In for a penny, in for a pound.* If they were going to talk things out, they might as well talk it all out. With a sigh, he pushed on. "And I needed something to do since you had the golden-boy spot covered already."

"I did not." Mikie squared his shoulders.

Mason leaned closer to his brother. Of all the times Mason wanted to be taken seriously, this conversation topped the list. He didn't want to take the chance of Mikie not seeing that. "Yes, you did, Ace. You stepped right into Dad's shoes. Taking out the trash, mowing the lawn, washing the dishes, killing your classes. You were quite the impressive son."

Tracing circles on the tablecloth, Mikie sighed. "I was only trying to help. I didn't know what else to do."

"I know that now." Mason crossed his arms. "But I wanted to help, too. Since you had the big stuff covered, I had to get creative. Being the prankster gave me a role to fill. Making Ma laugh, making *you* laugh. It wasn't much, but it made the days go by easier."

Mikie reached up and tousled Mason's hair. "It was everything, Deuce. Do you have any idea how bad I wanted to be you? Carefree and happy and so full of life? I know I rag on you, but you have to know you pulled us through then, man."

Mason pushed back his chair and leaped to his feet. "Come off it, Ace. I know you hated me for it. You remind me how much every time I'm in the same room with Chase."

Meeting him toe to toe, Mikie stood, too. "That's because Chase idolizes you. I need him to understand there's more to life than having fun. He looks at you and sees laughs and good times, but that's it."

"That's all you see, too, right?" Mason gritted his teeth, hating every second of the conversation.

Mikie leaned into Mason's space. "Are you that dense, Deuce?" He knocked Mason lightly across the head with his knuckles, or tried to, but Mason batted his hand away.

"Cut it out, man," Mason warned.

Instead of retreating, Mikie placed a hand on each of Mason's shoulders and looked him dead in the eye. "Of course, that's not all I see. I know how hard you've worked to get to where you are. The long hours, the lonely nights, the sacrifices you've made. You're not that knucklehead kid following me around anymore. You're a man I'm proud to know, as a brother and as a friend."

Mason tilted his head. "If that's true, what was with the bet?"

"I was yanking your chain, man."

Mason blinked three times trying to wrap his head around his brother's admission. Then blinked again. *Who was this guy?*

Slugging Mason in the arm, Mikie laughed. "You're not as cool as you think you are. I watched you follow Lily Anne around all through high school. It was obvious you had it bad for the girl. The minute I heard about the proposal I knew you were still the same lovestruck fool that you'd always been. I was trying to get you to fess up."

"Well, I have no problem admitting it now." Mason threw his arms in the air, desperation fueling his movements. "You want to hear it? Fine, I'll say it. I love Lily Anne. I always have."

Mikie tapped the tabletop once. "I know, Deuce. That's why I think you might want to do something about it while you still you can."

As much as he hated taking Mikie's advice, Mason knew this was one time his big brother really did know best. With a nod, he resolved to make a date with Lily Anne before her nerves got the best of her and she locked herself away from him.

For good, this time.

Chapter Twenty-Four

Lily Anne watched the hands on the clock tick around as she debated her meeting at the bank with George. *To go or not to go.* That was the question. Back and forth she went, eventually deciding to talk to Mason before making up her mind. The loan was in both their names and she needed to know where they stood before signing it. She tossed on her coat and drove toward the inn.

Standing on the porch, Lily Anne paused to collect herself. The place had become her second home and to think it might be the last time she walked through the door was a tough pill to swallow. The mere thought of it sent her into a tizzy, panic shooting through her. She breathed in through her nose and held it. *One-Mississippi. Two-Mississippi. Three-Mississippi. And—*

The door swung open and Chase crashed into her. Lily Anne dug her feet into the wood planks and straightened, trying to stay upright. Instinctively, she grabbed his forearms to help balance.

"Woah! You okay, Lily Anne?" Chase stepped back and looked her over. "I didn't hurt you, did I?"

Lily Anne adjusted the hem of her shirt trying to curl up and smiled. "No, I'm fine. But where are you running off to in such a hurry?"

"The shed. Gramps is finally letting me go through the baseball cards." Chase made a move to scoot past her and she swatted him on the arm.

"Slow down," she called, but it was too late.

"Can't." Chase hollered as he ran down the steps and around to the back of the inn. Lily Anne trudged through the open door, half expecting to see Mason in the dining room, drinking coffee and eating breakfast. Instead, Mr. Montgomery sat alone at the head of the table with a heaping tower of pancakes in front of him. The sweet aroma of hot maple syrup wafted from the miniature pitcher next to it. On the other side, a platter was piled high with bacon and sausage links.

Lily Anne involuntarily licked her lips as her stomach growled. "Hey, Mr. Montgomery. Is Mason around?"

"Nope, he's gone to that jewelry shop over in Hickory Hills to work on some shots for a new catalog." Mr. Montgomery eyed the table, abruptly changing the direction of his glance from the food to her. "Did you eat yet?"

"I haven't, but I can't stay long. I'll just grab a bite on the way to the bank."

"This is better." Mr. Montgomery pointed at a clean plate with his fork. "Sit down, darlin'."

Not wanting to be rude, she dropped into the seat nearest to him. He snatched the plate, shoveled a few pancakes on, and smothered them with syrup, adding two squares of butter on top and a strip of bacon on the side. Then, he shuffled over to the coffee pot and poured two cups. He placed a mug next to each of their plates and sunk back into his seat. "Need anything else?"

Lily Anne shook her head. "I think I'm good. Thank you."

Together, they ate in silence, both too busy chewing to hold a conversation. In the middle of the meal, Chase stomped back in with a stack of cardboard boxes almost as tall as he was.

"Take the cards in through there and I'll come help you in a minute." Mumbling around a mouthful of bacon, Mr. Montgomery waved toward the living room.

"Can do, Gramps." Chase didn't even stop, just hollered over his shoulder on the way through.

Mr. Montgomery stretched in his chair and patted his stomach. "So how are things with the wedding planning? Not much longer now, huh?"

"About a week." Lily Anne studied the tablecloth as if the answers to all her problems were stitched with invisible thread. Maybe if she looked hard enough, she'd see them.

"That's what I thought. I'm sorry I haven't been around much to help. It seems like you and I are always missing each other. By the time I head out to the rehab center, you're already gone and when you get home, I'm usually upstairs tidying the rooms." He blew on his coffee a time or two before taking a small sip, carefully replacing the cup on the table when he was done.

Lily crossed her legs as she leaned back. "I didn't know you worked at the rehab center."

"Oh, I'm not an employee, just a volunteer," he said, cutting his last pancake into pieces. "I play games with the residents in the rec room, take walks with some of the guys, listen when they feel like talking. Nothing major, but I remember what it's like to be in their shoes."

Lily Anne wanted to ask what he meant, but Chase interrupted, plopping a stack of photo albums between them.

Mr. Montgomery swatted at the boy's hand playfully. "Didn't I tell you to take those things in there?"

"Yeah, you did, Gramps. But I'm dying to find the Ken Griffey Jr. card you told me about it."

Tapping the top album, Mr. Montgomery sighed. "Which box did you get those out of?"

"I don't know." Chase blinked at the box for a few seconds before giving up on the answer. He shrugged. "It had Mason's name on it."

"It's not in there, then." Mr. Montgomery took another drink of coffee as he studied the album cover. Without looking up, he pointed toward the front door. "You need to find your dad's old stuff. He was the card collector, not Mase."

"Hmph." Chase wrinkled his nose at the books before spinning on his heels. With heavy steps, he started back the way he'd come. Lily Anne eyed the abandoned albums. Now that she knew the photos were Mason's, they called to her.

"May I?" Lily Anne asked, gesturing to the stack.

Mr. Montgomery nodded and handed her the album. "Sure, sure."

Lily Anne took the book, intending to start with it, but the second one caught her eye. It wasn't plain like the rest of them. The front was decked out with the year of their graduation and commencement symbols.

"What's that one?" Pointing at the pile, Lily Anne stretched closer.

"Lord, I ain't seen that in years." He chuckled and ran a hand over the raised date on the front. "That's Mason's scrapbook. He made it senior year. Did he show it to you yet?"

"No, this is the first time I've seen it."

"Well, then, this should be interesting." Mr. Montgomery leaned across the table. "Open it up and take a look. I've got a feeling you'll get a kick out of it."

Lily Anne lifted the book from the top and set it on the table. When she opened it, scenes from her past jumped off the page: senior breakfast, awards night, homecoming, varsity court.

Amazed, she turned to the next one. It was dedicated to the newspaper staff. Papers littered long white tables and teenage heads hung over them. A few slackers played cards in the back, probably Smack. Lily Anne smiled and kept flipping.

More memories came to life on every page. The decorating committee, prom night, the end-of-the-year picnic, including a shot from after the water fight. It was eye opening to see the year through his lens. He truly had a knack for catching the moment.

On the last page, her car stared up at her. It was the shot he'd managed to sneak in the slide show during graduation. She was leaned over the hood, writing in her notebook. Concentration painted on her face. Lily Anne still had no idea when the picture was taken, but it made her giddy knowing he'd included her in the book. She smiled and gently returned the album to the pile.

Mr. Montgomery watched her with a smirk, the same one Mason used on her. "You see yourself?"

"Yeah, on the last page." She blushed and lowered her gaze to the half-eaten pancake left on her plate.

"The last page, huh? Lily Anne, take another look." Mr. Montgomery reached her the book again.

With shaky hands, she opened the album, studying the pages more intently this time. She found her face in the background, then toward the right, again on the left. Once, twice, three times, then four. So many times she lost count.

"Oh my gosh," Lily Anne whispered, more to herself than anyone else, as she snapped her head up.

Mr. Montgomery lifted an eyebrow. "Go, on. Keep looking."

Frantic, Lily Anne searched the open book, scanning for her image again. She touched each and every photograph. More nervous than before, she flipped the page and repeated the process, again and again, until she shut the book and hugged it to her chest. She didn't know what to make of it.

Mr. Montgomery propped his elbow on the table, cradling his chin in his hand. "How about this time?"

"I'm in every photo." She managed to choke out.

"Yes, you are. Funny, huh?" His smug expression said he knew exactly what she'd find in the scrapbook, so there was no need for her to answer. After neither of them spoke for several moments, he frowned. "You okay, darlin'?"

Lily Anne peeled the book from her chest and returned it to the table. "Y-y-yeah, fine. I hate to eat and run, but I've got an appointment to get to. See you soon, Mr. Montgomery." She stood, pushed her chair under the table, and started walking toward the door. She'd made it halfway when he called after her.

"Please, call me Blake."

Lily Anne turned around and waved. "Thank you, Blake."

"Anytime."

With that, Lily Anne yanked the door open and sped down the steps. By the time she started her car and pulled out onto the highway, she was more confused than when she'd left the house. Mason had confessed to crushing on her, but seeing his scrapbook took his admission from theoretical to factual, proving he'd been serious about his feelings for her. That knowledge gave Lily Anne hope that the same affection that created the scrapbook had prompted his reunion proposal as well.

Lily Anne parked in front of the bank, still unsure if she wanted to go in. She'd never been the type to seek forgiveness instead of permission. Likewise, she didn't like to renege on an obligation after she'd committed. As a loan newbie, the process was lost on her, so it was possible she was making a big deal over nothing. After mulling over the options, she decided the best thing to do was to speak with George about the process. That way she'd be able to make an informed decision.

Patrons weaved around her as Lily Anne crossed the lobby, hightailing to George's office. The door was open, so she knocked on the facing lightly to alert him of her arrival. He stopped clicking his mouse.

"Hello, Miss Dawson." With a smile, he motioned her in and pointed to the chair. "You ready to sign the last of the paperwork?"

"I think so." Lily Anne sat down. "But what happens if I change my mind after I sign?"

"Let's see if I can explain this." George rested his forearms on his desk and steepled his fingers, tapping the tips together a few times as he mulled over the question. "The long and the short of it is, nothing. Either party has until the final signing to back out. So, if you or Mason change your minds about the house, or the studio, we can call off the sale. The same goes for Mr. Rowe, who won't be able to sign until a survey of the land is turned in. He's expecting to have that around the first of March. Even though you're signing today, you've still got some wiggle room. Are you having second thoughts?"

"You might say that." Lily Anne smiled softly, hoping to placate George. "I simply wanted to check about the legalities of the situation. You never know what can happen."

"How right you are!" George tapped the top of the desk with his fingertips. "I've seen some crazy things happen to couples."

Lily Anne swallowed. "I believe it."

George chuckled lightly as he rummaged through his desk, eventually coming away with a manila folder and an ink pen. "We'll start with the house. I need you to sign here, here, and here." He pointed and Lily Anne scrawled her name on the indicated lines, praying she'd be able to make a home out of the house in question. When that was done, he pulled another folder out of a drawer. "Now, this one is for the studio. Did Mason tell you there'd been a couple of changes made concerning it?"

"Yes, he mentioned it, but didn't go into detail." Lily Anne squirmed in her seat. No need to explain she hadn't spoken to Mason in days.

"Let me go over it, then. The first thing I want to point out is that while your name is on the title, it is not on the lease. You are an owner in the business, same as Mason, but the debt is his alone. The only time you'd be held responsible is in the event of Mason's passing. Then, the loan would fall to you as his living spouse. Make sense?"

Lily Anne folded her hands in her lap. "The logistics, yes, but why would he do that?"

"It's my understanding he wanted you to reap the rewards without any of the risks." George smiled and quickly averted his eyes, making Lily Anne think he knew more than what he was saying.

"R-r-right. Uh, what else was changed, George?"

"The name. Once the sale takes place, Forget Me Not Photography will be no more, at least not while it's in Mason's hands. Should he ever sell, Mr. Rowe requires the company to revert to the original name. Until that happens, the studio will be known as Thousand-to-One Photography. Catchy, huh?"

"It is." Lily Anne nodded, an attempt to hide her astonishment, but tears pooled in her eyes regardless. "Entirely unforgettable."

Lord, this man.

Once again, Mason had resorted to his wheelhouse— photography—to prove himself. He was a man of action and the changes he'd made to the contract demonstrated his love for Lily Anne as loudly as the letter he'd read in the square. Without reservation, she reached for the pen and poked it toward the paper.

"Oh, right." George pointed at several blank lines. "Here. Here. And here." With blurry vision, she signed and pushed the document toward him. He stood and extended his hand. "That's it, Lily Anne. You're all done."

Sniffling slightly, she accepted and shook. "Thank you, George."

"My pleasure. You have a nice day."

Fighting to keep her composure, Lily Anne waved and rushed to her car. As soon as the door was shut, the crying commenced. Never had Lily Anne felt more loved, more adored, more cherished than in that moment with the assurance of Mason's love pouring over her. He had proved himself in a big way, the biggest as far as she was concerned. Now, she needed to do the same.

Lily Anne reached for her notebook in the passenger seat and began jotting down ideas through her tears. As she sobbed, a plan began to take shape. It wasn't going to be easy, but with a little help, it was doable, if she started the process immediately. Sensing the urgency, she unlocked her phone and dialed the number to *As the Belle Told*.

It was time to set the record straight, once and for all.

Chapter Twenty-Five

Mason stared at the manila envelope in front of him, pretending to have x-ray vision as the front door shut. Part of him wanted to shred the letter open and put himself out of the misery of not knowing, but the bigger part liked playing detective. It kept his mind off a certain blonde with his ring on her left hand. A blonde he'd not been able to pin down for nearly a week.

But today was Saturday and Mason knew for a fact she had the day off. Today, he'd lay his heart on the line and tell her the truth. Right after he solved the riddle of the mystery mail. With no clue as to who sent the envelope, Mason exhaled and worked the back free.

As he pulled out a familiar set of stapled papers— the official Valentine Proposal—his fingers began to shake. The document was different this time, though, with one new, life-changing alteration: the word *VOID* stamped in red. A plain white index card with Lily Anne's handwriting was paper clipped to it, a place and time her only instructions. *The square. 3:00 PM.*

Not the square, again.

Snippets of last weekend sifted through Mason's memory like coins in a change machine, clinking as each tumbled and settled. His letter, Lily Anne's tears, the look on her face as she fled the stage. If they were meeting at Sweetheart Storytime, the odds were already stacked against him. Mason shot a look at the clock, the face showing half past two. He'd slept later than normal and then wasted hours playing with some editing software before finally making his way down to the dining room. It was a long shot, but maybe there was still time to catch Lily Anne before she left.

Mason finger-combed his hair and pulled the collar of his t-shirt up for a quick sniff. Smelling nothing, he called it clean and moved on. Mason shoved the papers back into the envelope, grabbed his Long John—a mayonnaise-free one—and clicked the start button on his key fob as he rushed out. In no time flat, he was weaving his way through the desks at *The Valley Vine*, scoping the terrain for a mess of yellow curls or bouncy topknot.

"She's not here."

Mason spun toward the voice behind him, locking eyes with Howard when he'd finished a quarter turn. The editor stood in the door of his office, leaning his shoulder against the frame looking more like a protective father than the un-affected employer.

"Do you know where I can find her, sir?"

Howard crossed his arms and tapped his fingers against his bicep. "Not here and not at Country Confections."

"Thank you. That's a start, at least." Mason rocked back on his heels, expecting to be dismissed with nothing more than a wave. But instead of a wave and push out the door, Howard clapped Mason on the back.

"You might try her apartment. Danny Jo finally got rid of that crazy opossum, so Lily Anne's been back home since then."

Mason knew that already but didn't bother mentioning that to Howard. "Right. Thanks." Grateful for the help, Mason nodded. He didn't deserve it, but he'd sure take it. "If you see her, will you tell her I dropped by?"

"Sure thing." Howard snapped his fingers, pointing at Mason before dipping into his office. In seconds, he was standing in front of him, holding a magazine. "Say, you wanna check out this month's *As the Belle Told* before you leave? I just happen to have an advance copy and there's a heartwarming piece on page twenty-two I think you might like."

"That's very nice of you, but I'll pass." Mason didn't want to be rude, but the thought of reading Lily Anne's words about him—about *them*—tied his stomach in knots, especially since he didn't know if *them* still existed.

"You know what? I've got an extra copy. Take it in case you change your mind." Howard tilted the issue toward Mason. When he didn't reach out for it immediately, the old man waved it in front of him a time or two. Mason shook his head, but the old man repeated the process, narrowing his eyes and moving a step closer to him. When he cleared his throat, Mason grabbed the magazine as all the fight flew out of him.

"Thanks. Have a good one, Howard."

"You, too. And Mason?"

"Yeah?"

"I hope you change your mind about page twenty-two." With that, Howard tapped the door jamb and disappeared into his office.

Mason fanned the magazine but didn't dare open the cover. To keep from it, he rolled it up and tucked it under his arm as he made his way back to his jeep. The clock at the bank flashed 2:42 as he pushed the key into the ignition. There was no way to get to Lily Anne's house and back without being late for Sweetheart Storytime. Mason tapped his forefinger on the steering wheel, prayed for guidance, and then backed out. The motor hummed beneath the hood as Mason headed toward the square.

The decorations were the same as last time. Same banner. Same lights. Same confetti hearts. The déjà vu made Mason's head reel, especially with most of the same people staring at him as he settled at a table.

When he caught a glimpse of blonde hair in the far corner of the park, Mason let out a sigh. The need to hold her tugged at his heart, so much so he was halfway out of his seat before he noticed her pacing and her company. If the look on her face was any indication, Lily Anne wasn't happy. Far from it.

Chapter Twenty-Six

"I can't do this." Lily Anne toggled her gaze between Emma Lou and Eliza Lee, her reinforcements for the afternoon. The pair had been loitering around the square when Lily Anne ran into them, literally, while trying to find Mr. Hart before the festivities began. Then, she'd been fairly calm as she shared her plan to win Mason back, but now her nerves were jumping like a jackrabbit. She forced her feet to still and grabbed Eliza Lee by the shoulders, needing something, or someone, to hold on to before she spun out of control.

"You. Can. Do. This." Eliza Lee punctuated each word to make her point, her steady green gaze exuding a confidence Lily Anne wished she could borrow, if only for a few hours.

Lily Anne swallowed and dropped her arms to her side as she restarted her pacing. Emma Lou stepped in front of her, grabbing her by the arms.

"Lil, you wanted to make a grand gesture. You wanted to show Mason what he means to you. This is your chance. If you don't do this, you'll regret it. You love him too much not to."

With a loud exhale, Lily Anne nodded. Emma Lou was right. Lily Anne would regret it, more than any failed story or career misstep or family feud she'd ever been in the middle of. After seeing the scrapbook and the name change at the bank, there was no doubt Mason loved her. More so, there was no doubt Lily Anne loved him.

"Thanks, girls." Lily Anne gave each of her friends a quick hug just as Mr. Hart appeared in her peripheral vision. With slow, steady steps, he made his way to the microphone exactly as he'd done the previous week. This time he gestured to where Lily Anne stood. With a wink, he called her up to the stage after welcoming the crowd.

"Let's give it up for Lily Anne." Then Mr. Hart stepped into the shadows and clapped softly.

Lily Anne felt all eyes on her as she walked to center stage. Their stares were hot against her back and even though she looked straight ahead instead of at the crowd, she couldn't keep her thoughts from racing. *Get it together, girl.* Lily Anne licked her lips and smoothed her dress, the same one she'd worn to the reunion. In fact, she'd recreated the entire outfit, right down to the red blazer, pearl earrings, and the soda-bottle ring Mason proposed with.

With slightly sweaty hands, she grabbed the mic. *I can do this. I can do this.* Lily Anne looked out into the crowd and her vision began to blur along the edges. Still, she repeated the mantra. *I can do this.* As she did, she surveyed the audience, her gaze catching on Pastor Clemens. He waved, and the sight jarred the key verse from Sunday's message loose in her mind. 1 John 4:18. *There is no fear in love; but perfect love casteth out fear.*

For years, she'd tried to be perfect, hoping to gain the attention and affection from her father, only to be left with empty arms and a lonely heart. But on that stage, Lily Anne accepted herself for who she was, flaws and all. She was far from perfect, but that didn't matter, because the love that had bloomed between her and Mason felt perfectly imperfect, strong enough to offer forgiveness and bold enough to overcome fear.

Lily Anne took a breath and counted herself down. *One-Mississippi. Two-Mississippi. Three-Mississippi. Go.* "Hey, guys. Thanks for giving me another go at this, especially considering what happened last time." Lily Anne smiled as the crowd laughed.

"I'd say I'm out of my comfort zone up here, but the truth is, I've been out my comfort zone since a certain photographer came back to town." Lily Anne found Mason and their eyes locked. A smile shot across his face, wider and brighter than she'd ever seen, while another round of laughter ripped through the crowd. She waited a beat for the noise to die down and continued.

"Last week, I skipped out on y'all and let you down. To make things worse, I walked out on my sweetheart. I'm sorry. *So, so, sorry* about that. I tend to let my nerves get the best of me sometimes."

At that, Mason clapped, loud enough that people turned to watch him. Lily Anne waited for her anxiety to rush in, for the finger tapping and the hand wringing and the shallow breathing to start. But it didn't. Relieved, she rushed on.

"So, if you'll bear with me, I'm gonna try to make it up to all of you with the letter I should have read last week."

Lily Anne shuffled her weight from one foot to the other as she grabbed the microphone stand and began reading.

"Dear Mason, growing up, I never read you as a love story. You were comedy and satire, with a little suspense mixed in. You and I weren't even in the same genre. You were the loud to the quiet I craved, stormy to the calm I chased, and chaos to the control I created. The funny thing is, not much has changed. You are still all those things. Yet, in your eyes I read the most riveting romance ever penned. Ours.

"I didn't expect you, but all of a sudden, you were standing right in front of me, and I fell in love. I fell like rain falls in the hot July evening, a sudden downpour from a cloudburst of fury. From the first hello to now, you had me. I didn't know it, but you did, and you held on tight when I let go." .

Lily Anne paused and twisted the plastic ring on her left hand. What patience Mason had! Anyone else would have given up, but not him. Invigorated by his devotion, she stood up straighter and went back to the letter.

"I said yes to the boy called Deuce, to the memory of who you used to be. But now that I've seen you—the heart you have, the love you give, the man you are—I can say with all certainty, you are no deuce. You're everything. My three wishes come to life, a four-leaf clover in a field of weeds, a sleeper five-star review, and straight sixes in a game of Yahtzee. You're a row of sevens in Vegas at the end of the night, an eight ball with perfect predictions, the ninth inning walk-off homer, and a ten out of ten across the boards.

"You are the joker when I take life too seriously, a jack of all trades, and the ace of spades to my single life. More than any of that, you're my forever valentine, Mason. The king of my heart, and I am honored to be your queen. With love, Chief."

Lily Anne resisted the urge to cover her face as blood filled her cheeks. Whistles flew around the square while applause echoed off the pavement beneath the tables. Lily Anne watched as someone from behind Mason slapped his back while the crowd rose to its feet, leaving him as the only person still sitting. *That won't do.* Lily Anne ran straight to him and tugged him to his feet. After another round of thunderous clapping, the park grew quiet and Mr. Hart returned to the mic.

Finally out of the limelight, Lily Anne guided Mason to an unoccupied shelter in the back of the square far away from prying eyes and listening ears. She took a seat and pulled two manila envelopes from a tote bag under the table. They were identical to the one she'd left at the inn for Mason.

Mason dropped in a chair beside her and she held the first envelope out to him. "Before you say anything, open this. Please."

Mason's eyes narrowed, but he didn't say a word as he took the envelope, gingerly broke the seal, and removed the contents. He huffed as the cover of *As the Belle Told* came into view and tried to set it aside. Before he could, she grabbed his wrist, stilling the motion.

"Look right here." She slapped the issue open and pointed.

Mason followed her finger to the name under the article and Lily Anne watched as he read silently. Just to make sure it registered, Lily Anne read aloud.

"*Howard Ousley.*"

When Mason's head snapped up, he was blinking hard, as if coming out of a daze. Lily Anne held back a giggle as he did a double take, like maybe his eyes were playing tricks on him. Trying to assure him they weren't, she smiled.

Mason shut the magazine. "Lily Anne, this isn't your story."

She ignored Mason's declaration and dived deeper into her explanation.

"I know, but those are your pictures from Davey's homecoming. I got signed waivers from Jim and Davey. I probably needed you to sign one, too, but I was pressed for time and we weren't really on speaking terms. Your name is listed under each image as the photographer, though, and there's a check in the mail for your work."

Mason opened his mouth, most likely to tell her where Mrs. Campbell could send the check, but she held up a hand, stopping the slew of comments she probably deserved from tumbling out.

"Before you tell me to have her cancel it or stop the printing, let me read from page six." Lily Anne pulled the magazine in front of her and cleared her throat. "We at *As the Belle Told* would like to offer our most sincere apology to our readers and to widely respected photographer, Mason Montgomery, for the use of an unvetted quote given by one Rachel Duncan, which may have insinuated promiscuity on the part of Mr. Montgomery. Furthermore, we at *The Belle* commend Mason on his dedication to the Christian faith. He is a rarity, one of the last of a dying breed of southern gentleman, and we are honored to work with him."

When finished reading, Lily Anne laid the periodical on the table. "Look, Mase. Right there."

She pointed to Margie Campbell's electronic signature and another verbatim quote. This time, though, her name was attached to the excerpt that read, "I am grateful that my fiancé, like myself, believes in the sanctity and holiness of 'marriage things' and that he continues to prove those beliefs with his actions. It makes me love him even more."

Mason jerked his eyes from the magazine to Lily Anne, mouth agape. "How did you pull this off?"

Lily Anne shrugged, her shoulders nearly touching her ears. "Margie agreed to give my feature to Howard. As it turns out, he's been vying for a page in *As the Belle Told* for years and when I pitched the idea, he jumped at the chance. Margie's got a soft spot for soldiers, so she agreed. But what really made it possible was the printer snafu. I shouldn't have had time to make the switch, but the printing company the *Belle* uses ended up being shut down for a week because of a carbon monoxide scare. It gave me time to configure Howard's article structure to my old one to keep the magazine layout intact."

With his jaw still dropped, Mason shook his head. "That's not what I meant. How did you get Margie to run the retraction?"

A gust of wind blew between them and Lily Anne shivered. She popped the collar of her coat and tugged it as high as possible. Her lips trembled as she answered. "I made it part of the contract agreement for the feature. When I heard about Rachel's comment and how much it hurt you, I wanted to help."

Mason opened his hand at his side and stretched his fingers out wide. Lily Anne caught sight of the motion and started to reach for him, but before she worked up the nerve, he stuck his hand in his pocket and sighed. "Lil, you didn't have to do that."

Lily Anne followed suit with a loud exhale. "As much as I'd like to say I did it all for you, I didn't. When Mrs. Campbell offered me the story, I jumped at the chance. My career has been abysmal, one failed attempt after another to break into the publishing world. I was selfish and agreed before even asking you how you felt about it.

"I shouldn't have done that. I didn't have any idea about the bad blood between you and the magazine, but when I found out, I should have called the whole thing off. Instead, I hatched this crazy scheme trying to get both of us what we wanted—a retraction for you and a byline for me. I'm glad it *half* worked."

"I don't know what to say." Mason shook his head and stared. "You gave up your byline? For me? Lil, I didn't want to keep you from your dream."

Lily Anne held up a hand in protest, her heart pounding inside her chest. She shut her eyes tight and focused on the dark, wondering if the adrenaline rushing through her was what made people go skydiving. She'd thought before that marrying Mason could be like that, but her fear had held her back. Now, she was ready to find out.

As she opened her eyes, Lily Anne let her heart fall. "I know you didn't, Mase, but I couldn't let you think I used you for my career. Trust me, I'll keep working toward a by-line. Now, though, I've got a bigger dream to reach for, one that revolves around you and me and that little house by the lake."

Mason tilted his head in her direction, studying her. "Do you mean that?"

Lily Anne drew a cross on her chest. "Cross my heart. I'm sorry I ran off. I should have stayed and talked things out."

"And I should have told you about Mr. Rowe from the start." Mason kicked his toe at the ground, reminding Lily Anne of the last kid picked on the playground for dodgeball.

She laughed a little, partly because of how cute he looked and partly to work up the courage to ask the one question still hanging between them. When the humor died, she blurted it out before she lost her nerve. "Did you honestly propose to get Mr. Rowe to sell?"

Chapter Twenty-Seven

Mason swallowed hard and ran a hand through his hair while Lily Anne straightened her back. The sudden shift of posture made Mason flinch as he recognized the defense mechanism. She was bracing for bad news, expecting the low blow answer of a resounding yes. The worst part was she was right. *Partly, anyway.*

"Yes and no." Mason winced at both the tremble of his voice and Lily Anne's fallen face. He made a sort-of-kind-of motion with his hand, tilting it up and down at an angle, and rushed on. "Mr. Rowe wanted a family man and when the pact was read, I saw a way to be that man. I really owe him, too, because his rejection gave me the shove I needed to make a move. But if it hadn't been you, I never in a million years would have gone through with it. Since it was you, I took the chance God gave me, for the business and for love."

"How's that working out for you, Mase?" Lily Anne drummed her fingertips along her thigh as she waited for an answer, her lips drawn into a thin line. It wasn't a frown, but it was a long way off from the smile he wanted to see there.

"Depends. I already told Mr. Rowe I won't buy the studio without you. You mean the world to me, Lily Anne, way more than the best business money can buy." Mason laid his hand on the table, hoping Lily Anne would take it. She had to initiate contact. When she didn't reach out, his hope faltered.

Until her lips drew into a grin.

Lily Anne reached across and laced her fingers with his. "I figured that out when George showed me the new studio name. I signed, Mason. Thousand-to-One Photography now belongs to you—I mean us—if you want it."

Mason covered the joined hands with his free one and squeezed. "You signed?"

"I did," said Lily Anne. "Right after I saw your scrapbook. Chase accidentally uncovered it when he was looking through baseball cards. You, sir, were sneaky."

"I kind of was." Mason offered his best lopsided grin, hoping to direct attention away from his pinkening cheeks. When hers took on the same blooming shade, he knew she had seen them anyway.

"I'm flattered, Mase. I may have been oblivious to the crush you had back then, but I'm not now. I saw your love for me in those pictures. It jumped off each page, and then, again, when I read the new name at the bank." Lily Anne slipped her hand free and pushed a curl behind her ear while the breeze kicked up around them again. The strand immediately flew back and Mason re-tucked it, resting his hand against her cheek.

"Yeah?" Mason asked, leaning in close.

Lily Anne nodded and time slowed down as Mason processed their conversation. She'd signed. Forget Me Not Photography was his. Scratch that. Thousand-to-One Photography was *theirs*, and that was even better.

Mason's shoulders relaxed. "Well, in your defense, when a guy likes a girl he usually doesn't break her nose."

They both laughed, but when Lily Anne opened the second envelope and presented him with a copy of their official Valentine Proposal, voided just like the one left for him at the inn, all joking went out the window.

His seat creaked as Mason straightened. "Lily Anne, before you say or do whatever you have planned, answer me one question?"

Folding her hands in front of her, Lily Anne stared at the stapled papers. "What?"

"Why did you say yes?" he asked, tapping the agreement in front of him.

"Because you asked."

Lily Anne stood from her chair and took a few paces. Mason left the table and joined her where she stood, reaching out to weave his fingers with hers. Before he could, though, she folded her hands out in front of her.

"That day in marriage counseling, you hit the nail on the head. You were my safety net. I'd already failed in my career and with the medical issues I was facing, I thought I had to act fast or I'd become a failure in my family life, too. So I said yes." She shrugged and planted her hands by her sides. Mason ghosted his palms on top of her hands, refusing to let her anxiety rear its ugly head. She stilled at once and took a deep breath before continuing.

"I should have told you then, but you'd just dropped a bomb on me, telling me you'd cared for me since high school. I didn't want to ruin the moment, not when I knew I was falling for you. That's why this doesn't work for me anymore." Lily Anne grabbed the Valentine Proposal and waved in front of him a time or two before ripping it to shreds.

"When I signed this, you were a safe option, but that changed. You're not safe anymore, Mason. You're the farthest thing from it, and knowing that terrifies me." Lily Anne took in another mouthful of air at the same time Mason dropped his head. He didn't want to show how bad her words hurt, but it was impossible not to.

Lily Anne wasn't having it, though. With a hand to each cheek, she forced him to look up. Her eyes were rust pools speckled with glittering golds, bright and shiny, but filled with the same regret holding him hostage.

"Losing you terrifies me more."

Before he could blink, Lily Anne's lips found his, sweet and gentle. Instinctively, he wrapped both arms around her waist, bent on deepening the kiss, but she leaned back before he could and placed a hand to his chest.

"Mason Montgomery, you were never my first choice and you're no longer my safe choice, but you are my only choice. I love you and I promise to choose you over and over again, for better or worse, in sickness and in health, for richer or poorer as long as I live, even if you break my nose again." Lily Anne angled her body to face him. When she kissed his cheek and held up a ring made of film strip, he shook his head and chuckled.

"Will you still meet me at center court on Valentine's Day, not because of a stupid bet you made with your brother, not because of a business deal, and not because of a promise you made ten years ago? Will you meet me because of what you feel right here, right now?" She licked her lips and lifted the ring to the end of his finger. "Will you meet me because I love you?"

"Yes, Lily Anne Dawson." Smiling so wide it hurt, Mason refocused his gaze from the ring to her watery eyes. "Because I love you, too."

Lily Anne pushed the ring on his finger and he thanked God it fit. Mason dipped his head, keeping his eyes wide open. He needed to see Lily Anne's love shining back at him, he needed to show her that same love, to assure her she was all he'd ever wanted. Ever so slightly, Lily Anne slid into him, and when her crooked nose brushed his, she sighed. Her breath hummed across his lips, her mouth hovering so close not even a news page could slip between them. With a slight tilt of her chin, their lips greeted one another. Gently, he moved his mouth over hers and she softened like butter in the sun. If this was his reward for leaping without looking, he'd gladly do it every day for eternity. Lily Anne was the best leap of faith he'd ever taken.

Long before he wanted the kiss to end, Lily Anne pulled away, giggling, softly at first. The laugh quickly escalated to a full-on snigger fest that ended in a snort.

Mason kissed the tip of her nose. "What's so funny?"

"Nothing, really." Lily Anne shrugged as she caught her breath. "I was just wondering. What did the bride-to-be say to her groom a week before their wedding?"

Tightening his hold on her, Mason shook his head. "I have no idea, Chief. What?"

"Nothing. He kissed her speechless."

She grinned and Mason smiled before proceeding to make her awful attempt at a joke a reality. In a heartbeat, her arms looped around his neck as he fused his mouth with hers. He tasted and teased as long as she let him. When they finally separated, copper eyes full of love shone up at him, a red-tipped nose from the chilly air glowed, and swollen lips plumped from his kisses smiled wide. She was breathtaking. Standing there, staring at her like a loon, he swore he'd never see anything more perfect if he searched the world over.

***

A week later, Mason ate his words while the wedding march played. At the sight of his bride, he nearly swallowed his tongue. Lily Anne was a vision in white as Logan guided her across the gym floor. He was so mesmerized by her, he never registered her father walking toward them until he kissed Lily Anne on the cheek. After Logan placed her hand in Mason's, he did the same and took the seat next to Mark. Then, Mason and his bride stood by themselves before Pastor Clemens, with the exception of Ol' Man Rowe running circles around the three of them, snapping picture after picture.

The ceremony went by in a blur. Rings were exchanged and traditional vows repeated. When the command was given to kiss his bride, Mason lifted the veil with shaky hands and Lily Anne lit up. Curls fell over her bare shoulders, pink lips smiled wide, and when her eyes met his, warm copper shone up at him. Just before his lips touched hers, Mason detected the soft click of a shutter.

In that moment, he knew he'd captured the prettiest picture of his life.

THE END

If you enjoyed this book, will you consider sharing the message with others?

Let us know your thoughts. You can let the author know by visiting or sharing a photo of the cover on our social media pages or leaving a review at a retailer's site. All of it helps us get the message out!

Email: info@ironstreammedia.com

 @ironstreammedia

Brookstone Publishing Group, Harambee Press, Iron Stream, Iron Stream Fiction, Iron Stream Kids, and Life Bible Study are imprints of Iron Stream Media, which derives its name from Proverbs 27:17, "As iron sharpens iron, so one person sharpens another." This sharpening describes the process of discipleship, one to another. With this in mind, Iron Stream Media provides a variety of solutions for churches, ministry leaders, and nonprofits ranging from in-depth Bible study curriculum and Christian book publishing to custom publishing and consultative services.

For more information on ISM and its imprints, please visit
IronStreamMedia.com